'In your present situation, Mistress Philippa, I would consider that my coming is an answer to your prayers in the cathedral. You have need of a man's guidance and aid.'

Could she detect a note of mockery in his tones?

'Then you would be wrong. The only thoughts in my mind concerned my father's soul.' She swallowed. 'You do realise that—that . . .'

He nodded, and gave a grimace. 'That was what all that talk about murder was about, then . . . I'm sorry, Mistress Philippa. But I wish you could have told me last night who you were. It would have saved us both a lot of time and trouble.' He blew out a weary breath and got to his feet. 'I suppose I shall have to take you to London with me.'

'London?' She lifted her chin, not liking the way he had spoken. 'You don't have to do anything of the sort! You might not have noticed,' she continued in a determined voice, 'but I have no baggage with me. I have no other clothes, and barely any money. My home is burnt to the ground. I am filthy, hungry, weary to the bone . . . my serfs have revolted . . .'

'It seems that I came just in time then.'

June Francis was born in Blackpool during the war, but bred in Liverpool. Her father taught her the alphabet from a signwriters' book of lettering, and told her stories from memory; so passing on a love of storytelling. Although she always wanted to write she did not begin until her youngest son started school—greatly encouraged by her husband. She has had many articles published, as well as short stories broadcast, but her first love has always been the historical novel. History has always been a passion with her—due, she says, to an incurable curiosity about the past. Her other interests are walking, cycling and swimming. She has been happily married for over twenty years, and has three sons. The eldest, who is at Oxford studying Classics, also wants to be a writer.

June Francis has written two other Masquerade Historical Romances, *The Bride Price* and *Beloved Abductor*.

MY LADY DECEIVER

June Francis

MILLS & BOON LIMITED
ETON HOUSE   18-24 PARADISE ROAD
RICHMOND   SURREY   TW9 1SR

*First published in Great Britain 1988
by Mills & Boon Limited*

© June Francis 1988

*Australian copyright 1988
Philippine copyright 1988
This edition 1988*

ISBN 0 263 76180 0

*Set in Times Roman 10 on 11 pt.
04-8809-79017 C*

Made and printed in Great Britain

HISTORICAL NOTE

In 1381, the peasants in England revolted, mainly because of their grievances against their lords. Most peasants were villeins, who belonged to masters and were obliged to give service, and dues on special occasions such as the harvest. They were not free to marry, and could be sold. Some lords did free their tenants and paid them wages, taking money for rent of houses and land. Naturally arguments arose over wages, so these freemen were dissatisfied also.

The revolt was triggered by the imposition of a poll-tax, the third and heaviest set in five years. It was a groat (five pence) per head, and was to be paid by all those over fifteen years old, except widows and genuine beggars.

The main focus of the revolt was Kent and Essex, where during the spring, men hid their womenfolk and lied about their children's ages when the tax collectors came round. The deception was soon realised, and royal officials went out again to collect the withheld taxes. Some men refused to pay, and the collectors were stoned. The rebellion grew when the council of King Richard II dithered about taking action against the first rebels.

The peasants' main aim was to destroy proof of their bondage and dues, so lawyers were attacked and property destroyed. Prisoners were also freed.

In Kent they were led by Wat Tyler, who probably came from Maidstone and could have been a soldier returned from the French wars, who knew how to command men. The man who put all their hopes into words was John Ball, a priest from York, who had tramped England for twenty years, preaching against greed and pride in high places.

The Lollards followed the teachings of John Wycliffe, also from Yorkshire, who had translated the scriptures into English. He also laid down the need for changes in doctrine in the church, and challenged the authority of the priests. The Lollards also preached the equality of men, as did John Ball. Some believed the Lollards to be the instigators of the revolt.

Richard's government was extremely unpopular. The chancellor was the Archbishop of Canterbury, a good and honest man, but inexperienced in finance. Financial matters were so bad that the king's jewels had been pawned.

John of Gaunt, Duke of Lancaster, the king's uncle, was hated by many of the common people. Rumours that he had freed his bondsmen in the north reached Kent via the pilgrims in Canterbury, and caused his villeins in the south to decide to declare him king if this were true, and to swear loyalty to him over and against that to Richard.

Probably the words taken from one of John Ball's sermons puts in a nutshell the peasants' belief in equality: 'When Adam delved and Eve span, who was then the gentleman?'

CHAPTER ONE

SOMEONE WAS COMING! Philippa Cobtree let the lid of the chest slip from her fingers, sending a crash reverberating against the wooden walls of the deserted hall. Swiftly she stuffed the leather package down the front of her gown until it stuck. As the front door burst open she turned, her hands gripping the chest behind her.

'I thought you would still be here,' gasped the maid who had entered at a run. 'They are coming, and you must flee!'

'Where's my father, Rose?' she asked in a trembling voice, moving forward with haste, her blue linen skirts brushing the rush-strewn floor. 'I will not go without him!'

The two girls faced each other. Both were fair-haired, of a similar height, and had been born in the same month of the same year. After a momentary hesitation Rose spoke huskily: 'There is nothing you can do for him. You must go now!' She seized Philippa's arm, and began to pull her towards the back of the hall. 'I fear for you, the mood they are in!'

Philippa shook off the maid's hand, and halted. Her face was pale and her heart beat with thick, heavy strokes. 'Tell me, what have they done to him?'

Rose cast a glance over her shoulder before answering, a shadow darkening her pretty features. 'He is dead.' Her voice shook. 'He—is—dead!'

'I don't believe you!' Philippa stared at her, the green eyes dilated. 'It can't be true.' Her voice broke on a sob.

'Whether you believe me or not, now is not the time to delay. You must go!' insisted Rose roughly, pushing her out of the doorway with frantic hands.

Instantly the clamour of men's voices sounded on the evening air. It was all too real, thought Philippa, her legs feeling as if they could not support her. 'How did he die?' She choked on the words.

Rose made no answer; she did not know how. So she forced her mistress on, past the bakehouse, the storeroom, the stables, until they reached the wicket gate set in the wall at the furthest end of the herb garden.

'I shall leave you here. Go swiftly!'

'Rose, tell me, did he have a priest?' Philippa's face was taut with anguish, her fingers curled tightly on the gate.

Only for an instant did the maid's hand tighten over hers. 'It happened so quickly.'

'I see.' Tears filled her eyes. 'Do you come with me or stay with them?'

'It would be best if you went alone. Tom...' Rose's expression revealed her anguish. 'I shall tell them you weren't here.'

'Tom!' Philippa's voice was bitter. 'If it weren't for your brother, Rose Carter, the others wouldn't have listened!'

'Maybe, but you don't know what it's like to be a serf!' she cried. 'Best you go to London, and now! If you get there, I shall try to find you.' She turned and raced back to the house.

Just for a second Philippa stared after her, then turned, opened the gate and ran. Within moments the long grass of the waste was whipping her legs as she sprinted towards the forest looking dark and massive ahead. The breath rasped in her aching lungs and throat as she reached the trees, but still she ran on, with pain spreading in her side. There was a place she was heading for, and she was nearly there. The hollow tree was in sight. Years ago it had been struck by lightning, and her brothers had told her it was haunted, the home of a wood-spirit.

From the front of her gown she pulled the leather package and hid it in the hole in the tree. Then she slid to the ground, resting her back against the trunk, her legs, aching and trembling, stretched out in front of her. The agony of not knowing what the rebellious serfs had done to her father was a nagging thought that would not be still. Tears slid down her cheeks, and she rolled over, burying her face in her hands, and cried.

Eventually the tears ceased and she turned on her back, staring up at the golden-green leaves that laced overhead. A slight breeze set the branches moaning, and at any other time being alone in the forest at nightfall would have terrified her. But now it was a haven. Trees and plants did not turn on their masters, refusing to work or to obey, nor did they demand higher wages and the right to be free. Within hours on this day Philippa's safe world, bound by her father's command and his manor limits, had collapsed.

Would that her father had heeded the rumours about the serfs roaming the Kentish countryside, gathering in great numbers, destroying the rolls that contained their names and the records of their dues towards their lords. Houses had been pillaged, sometimes destroyed, and many landowners had fled to London in terror. Her father had refused to go, not believing that his villeins would revolt. If only the hedge-priests had not come, spreading dissatisfaction and rebellion among the men! She could picture them now in their ragged russet habits, their eyes fiercely fanatical with the strength of their cause. Freedom for all men, they had preached, saying that God had not ordained that some men should lord it over others. Already their brothers in Kent and Essex were throwing off the bonds of serfdom, and marching. Tom, Rose's brother, ambitious and disgruntled, had helped the priests.

Philippa's fists curled tightly so that the nails dug into her flesh. Her father had not been cruel or harsh, but a man conscious of what was his due as lord of the manor. She had begged him not to go and talk with them, but he had refused to listen, ordering her to stop fussing and to take the roll and betrothal agreement from the chest and hide them. She doubted he had meant her to put them where she had, but there was nowhere else she could think of on the spur of the moment. What had they done to his body? Did it lie—unshriven, unburied— for the crows to find?

Movement! She could hear movement! She lifted her head in fear, and immediately a cony darted away, its white tail bobbing. Beneath the hollow trees the dusk was gathering, and although she no longer gave credence to the tales of spirits, she had no great desire to stay in the forest all alone.

Alone! Her brothers and mother had died in an outbreak of the plague years before, and now her father was gone. She pushed back a handful of ash-blond hair that had worked loose, and as she did so, her eyes fastened on the green gemstone on her middle finger. Touching it pensively, she recalled how Sir Hugo Milburn had placed it there—not that he had been a knight then!

The betrothal had taken place nine years earlier, when she had been ten. He had been twice her age; an enormous young man towering over her. The ring had been much too big, the weight of the stone causing it to slip round on her finger. When they had stood her on a stool so that her head was level with his shoulder, how she had wished they had not. With his head so close to hers, he had appeared even more frightening, although her mother reckoned him handsome. Flaxen-haired, ruddy-complexioned, his pale grey eyes had gazed into her face—not unkindly, but with a definite critical appraisal—and she had been convinced that he found her wanting. So nervous had he made her that she had slipped from the stool and his brother Guy, standing just behind, had caught her. Shorter and more slender than his elder brother, he had surveyed her with kindly, but teasing, brilliant blue eyes, before setting her back on the stool. She had stammered an apology, aware of her mother's disapproving gaze. She had wanted to die! Especially when he kept his arm about her waist, and she had seen the two brothers exchange dancing mischievous looks.

As the words binding her to the giant of a man at her side droned on, she had wished herself beautiful and composed, like the women in the courtly romances. Then suddenly the ceremony was over. Hugo had kissed her on one cheek, and a moment later his brother had kissed her on the other. Her betrothed had turned away in response to her father's call, and it had been Guy who had helped her down from the stool, enquiring whether she still felt faint. What she had replied had passed from her memory, but he had kept hold of her hand until his brother turned back to them. Then he had given her hand into his, saying lazily, 'Yours, I believe, brother. Take good care of her.'

Her betrothed had attempted to make conversation, but her mother had strictly impressed on her that men expected women to listen to them and not babble out their own opinions. So she had answered in monosyllabic tones, and in the end Hugo had gone off to talk to her brothers. Afterwards there had been a feast, and she had disgraced herself by being sick halfway through the evening. She had been sent to bed, where she could still remember the relief at escaping from a world that made her fearful of failing.

Two more days the brothers had stayed, but she saw little of them. Once Hugo had sat beside her while she sewed and she had tried hard to converse sensibly—but nerves made her tongue the more tied the longer he sat there. It had not been so arduous with his brother, who had just talked, not seeming to demand any response, telling her about his home in Yorkshire and how he would miss it. They were leaving for France in the train of John of Gaunt, Duke of Lancaster—in the hope of making their fortunes. This had been said with a twinkle, and had brought a responding smile to her face. He had said she should smile more often.

At their going, she had been able to summon up enough courage to wish her betrothed 'God speed' and to offer her face to him for a kiss. He had laughed and lifted her off her feet, giving her a great bear hug. Even so, despite the warmth of that embrace, she had sensed he wanted to be off. Her farewell to his brother had been more circumspect: a kiss on the forehead and a 'God keep you', before they had ridden off. That had been the last she had seen of either of them.

There had been talk of a marriage taking place when she was fifteen, but instead Sir Hugo had gone abroad. Several times she had asked her father when she was to wed, but he had brushed aside her questions, saying he was in no haste to be rid of her. She had been content, in a way, with Rose for a companion. They had comforted each other after their mothers' deaths, for Rose had also lost her mother in the plague.

What had she said? Go to London. But how—and to whom? If only her own father had not been killed! She sniffed and wiped her eyes. Her father! What had they done to his body? Unable to stay still any longer, she scrambled to her feet, retracing her steps until she came to the edge of the forest.

There was a fire burning...a great fire! Such a rage seized her that without pausing to think of the danger she began to run in its direction. Vaguely she was aware of singing, then she saw the line of torches bobbing a serpentine path towards the village. They had believed Rose after all, it seemed, and were not going to search for her.

As Philippa walked through the garden, the heat of the flames caused her to recoil. What had she thought she could do? Her laugh was a travesty. She stood transfixed by the flames, watching until they died, and walls collapsed, sending sparks flying. The taste of smoke was in her mouth, and her eyes watered with more than the physical effects of the fire. It was as another wall collapsed in a shower of sparks that she saw it hanging from a beam, like a figure that danced in paintings of hellfire; some remnant of clothing still clung to the blackened form. The scream had barely left her throat before she slid to the ground.

At first when Philippa regained her senses, she thought it had all been a nightmare, until the hardness of the ground made itself felt and she rolled over, to see once more the dangling figure. Her limbs trembled, but she forced herself to stand. Then the rope suddenly snapped, and the body fell into the ashes. She would have run away in terror, only her legs refused to move. A long time she stood there, her eyes shut, forcing steel into her heart and limbs.

On opening her eyes, her glance fell upon the spade leaning against the storeroom wall. Bury him! She must bury him! No sacred ground was available, but did not all the earth belong to God? Unsure about that, she knew she had to believe it, as she would have to believe that God, and the mother of Christ, and the saints would have mercy on her father's unshriven soul. Somehow she managed the task, although it was as though someone else, at her mind's dictate, did it for her. Someone else recognised the silver buttons as they parted from the charred fabric. She had given them to him for a New Year's gift. They were placed in her purse. The tears rolling down, that other person automatically said the prayers for the dead while replanting a thyme-bush. Then that same person sat back on her heels, staring down at

the newly-turned earth, her whole body aching with an
unaccustomed painful lethargy. One more thing was
necessary. Philippa walked across the hot ground,
heedless of the pain that seared the soles of her shoes,
and dragged a charred crossbeam from the ruins with
the dirty spade. So intent was she on her task that she
did not hear the sound of hooves.

'What has happened here?'

The wood fell from her fingers with a dull thud, and
she stared up at the dark outline of horse and rider
dominating the night sky.

'Answer me! Or have your wits gone begging?' She
looked like a wild creature of the night, he thought, dismounting. Her hair was light coloured, but tangled in
an unruly fashion about her dirty face, and on her
shoulders.

'You are a stranger, sir?' Somehow Philippa forced
the words out slowly. Her fingers tightened on the handle
of the spade, since she had no cause to trust strangers.

'A stranger to Kent? Ay. What has happened here?'

'A fire! A—burning!' She gasped out the words.

He was silent, his eyes darting from the upturned face
to the ruins of the still smouldering building. He stood,
his hands on his hips, his shoulders flung back, wearing
some dark garment. His hair was also dark, and his
profile showed the etched outline of a jutting straight
nose and square chin.

'This is peasants' work! What has happened to the
folk who live here?' He stared down at her, and she
lowered her eyes.

Was this some trick intended to make her give herself
away? Had someone seen her running back to the house?
He could be one of the men who had come with the
hedge-priests, clever men, who could twist an argument.
Stumbling back on her heels, she clutched the spade
tightly. 'I don't know where they are, sir,' she replied in
a dull monotone.

'What are you doing here? Are you one of the peasants come to gloat over this night's work?' He was growing impatient. She gave no answer. Was she half-witted? 'Come, think, where have they gone?'

Philippa got to her feet, still holding the spade. 'They have both left this place,' she answered dully. 'You will have to search elsewhere for the Cobtrees.'

'But where have they gone?' he demanded with asperity, rubbing a hand across his chin. Something his brother had told him flickered in his mind. 'Canterbury! Could they have gone to Canterbury?' His insistent voice rose.

Startled, Philippa dropped the spade. Her hands were shaking, and she felt cold. Why could he not go away and leave her alone in her grief?

He seized her shoulder suddenly, and shook her. 'Did they go to Canterbury?'

'How should I know?' she cried frantically, and tore herself from his grasp. Before he could prevent her, she was out of the garden and running like a hunted hare across the waste.

He let her go, seeing no advantage in chasing her. There were more important matters on his mind than hunting half-witted peasant girls. Perhaps he would find them in Canterbury? Best go and see.

Philippa gazed after him from her hiding-place in the rank grass. Her head was muzzy, and no longer did she feel safe anywhere near her own house, or on her land. What could she do? Rose had told her to go to London, but it was so far! Who could help her? Forcing back a tumble of hair she rubbed her forehead, and the faintest gleam from her ring reminded her again of her betrothed. She had long tired of waiting for him, and part of her mind was convinced that he would never come to claim her. Although he had lands in Yorkshire, he was often elsewhere about the business of his lord, John of Gaunt, Duke of Lancaster. If he could be found, she would be able to leave everything in his hands, but who could help her to find him? She sighed, trying to think, then remembered her uncle William, who was a lawyer, the widower of her dead mother's sister. He was just the man. She must force herself on and visit him.

Pain was something she knew on rising. It burned in her arms and shoulders, her back, and on the soles of her feet. Tears took her unawares, and she dabbled at them, trying to wipe them away as she walked. Lifting a fold of the now filthy blue linen, she scrubbed at her face, determined not to give in to the wave of misery and fear that threatened to swamp her. Squaring her shoulders, she lengthened her stride. Fortunately the nights were short at this time of year, and the gates of the city would be open at dawn.

From dazed eyes Philippa cast a swift glance at the knots of men gathering on the corners of the crowded lanes. She had rested briefly in a field, but fear had prevented her from sleeping. Mercery Lane was in view, and for a moment, when she came to the booths and stalls set at its corner, she paused. The customary souvenirs were on display to entice the pilgrims visiting the shrine of Saint Thomas à Becket: the ampoules said to contain some of his blood; the Canterbury bells that pilgrims hung on their mounts' bridles; badges to prove that one had visited the holy place. Maybe after she had found her uncle, and rested, she would go inside the cathedral church of Christ and pray for her father's soul.

She forced herself on, up one lane, down another, until she came to where her uncle's house had stood. The buildings on each side were there still, but uncle William's house had gone! A wave of disbelief and desolation poured over her, drenching her in misery as she stared at the heap of rubble, dirty straw and broken beams occupying the place where it had stood. A door opened in the next house, and a woman came out. Philippa looked wearily into the plump, disapproving face.

'Good wife, prithee tell me where Master Elston has gone?' There was hope in her voice. 'I have come a great distance, only to find this.' She waved an arm wildly to encompass the ruin. 'Please tell me where I can find him?'

'And why should I tell the likes of you?' The woman shifted the basket on her arm. Philippa made to speak, but she rushed into further speech. 'Besides, you are too late. Some apprentices and unruly elements from the fields pillaged his house. A fire they made of all his scrolls. He has most likely fled to London.' She sniffed as her gaze ruthlessly took in the state of Philippa's person and clothing. 'Off with you! We want none of your sort. Be gone, or I'll have my husband out to you!'

'You are mistaken! I am Master Elston's niece,' protested Philippa. This could not be happening!

'A likely tale! Now be on your way.' The woman advanced on her, swinging her basket.

Philippa backed away and blundered up the lane, pushing her way through the crowds. With part of her mind she realised that the crowds were greater than usual for June. In July, the time when the feast of the Translation of Saint Thomas took place, the place swarmed with pilgrims.

Suddenly two boys, running, dodging and weaving, brushed past her and sent her tumbling backwards as her heel caught in the torn hem of her skirt. She would have hit the ground had two hands not grasped her firmly about the waist. Her feet sought a hold, and she trod on a foot; instantly she caught the sound of a swiftly bitten back oath.

'If this is what happens to knights bent on rescuing damsels, it is no wonder it is going out of fashion!' The biting humour in his voice did not conceal his northern accent.

'I beg…your pardon!' Philippa's heart began to thud as he set her on her feet, facing him. Attempting to quash her inner trembling, she took in his appearance by daylight. The dark hair grew thick and smooth, and was bobbed just beneath his ears. There was a faint hollow under the cheekbones, and the curve of his mouth was cut with some beauty for a man.

'You are unhurt?' Long-lashed blue eyes regarded her with some exasperation.

'If you would let go of my arm, sir!' She struggled to free herself.

He frowned. 'Do I not know you?'

'No!' The colour drained from her face as his eyes held hers, and she felt like a cony trapped by the hypnotic stare of a stoat.

'I *have* seen you before,' he said softly.

'You are mistaken.'

Again Philippa attempted to free herself, but it would have been in vain if several men had not erupted out of an alley and forced them apart. Immediately she was away, squeezing between people, heading up the same alley. At its end, she spared a second to glance back, only to see him standing there, so turning left she ran round a corner, only to discover she had gone full circle. A swift look over her shoulder, and she was off again. A group of pilgrims were queuing to go inside the cathedral, and without hesitating, she dived in among them and wormed her way forward, inside the building. Her heart lifted when she could see no sign of the stranger.

She moved along with the pilgrims, thinking to hide in the cathedral for a while in order to allow the man time to give up his chase. She came to a spot where many had prostrated themselves full length on the floor in front of the richly decorated shrine of Saint Thomas. Kneeling, she had no mind for confession or reflection, although she did attempt to pray for her father's soul, despite her agitation. She glanced about her, before moving on, noticing that the nave was still under construction. Her heart jumped into her throat as she caught sight of the man. Hurriedly she paced over to the tomb of Edward of Woodstock, father of the young king Richard II now on the throne of England. Black and gold, in full armour, the prince's effigy had always roused her admiration, but now she could only think of hiding behind it. Her ears pricked, her head bowed and her heart beat wildly at the sound of approaching footsteps. They stilled, and after a few moments moved away again. Stealthily she peered round the corner of the tomb and saw a broad back clad in blue. The dark head was turned away.

Out of the corner of her eye she saw another group of pilgrims wending their way in her direction, and, lost in their midst, she went with them to the altar bearing fragments of the broken sword of one of Becket's murderers . . . watching, listening. Some of the people cried out and wept bitter tears at the sight of the gold-mounted portion of the saint's skull that also lay there, but there were no tears left inside Philippa. Only an icy blackness clutched her heart as she stared at the relic. Once she had wondered and wept, but today the skull was just a skull, and the saint was as dead as her father. No miracle had saved either of them from their murderers.

Glancing over her shoulder she saw no sign of her pursuer, and quickly left the group to make her way to the door. She was almost there, when a hand reached out and seized her sleeve.

'Unhand me!' she cried, struggling to pull her arm free.

'I'll be damned if I will!' he said in a terse voice. 'I haven't hunted in every nook and cranny of this place to let you go so easily.' His blue eyes studied her intently. 'I'm certain you were there last night!'

'I don't know what you are talking about,' she insisted, lowering her face swiftly. 'If you do not let me go, I shall scream!'

His dark brows drew together, and his mouth thinned.
'I shall not stop you.' The hand on her arm tightened
so that it hurt, and she opened her mouth, gazing frantically about her, wondering why nobody took notice of
her plight, then realised that the Mass was about to begin.
Years of training reasserted themselves, and she knew
that creating such a disturbance would not be welcome.

'Had second thoughts? Good!' He smiled sardonically. 'If you had screamed, I would have told them that
you picked my pocket.'

Philippa gasped angrily. 'I would deny it! Why don't
you let me go? I have done you no harm!'

'I didn't say you had. Neither have I done you any
harm—so why run away?' he said softly. 'I saved you
from falling, and all the thanks I received were several
squashed toes.'

'I begged your pardon for the toes. And I don't converse with men I do not know, so release me, if you
please,' she demanded in a low voice.

'You know my answer to that, little maid.' His eyes
narrowed. 'What are you frightened of? I want only to
ask you a few questions.'

'Why should I answer your questions? You are a
stranger to me, and there are many strangers in Kent at
this time who are not welcome.' Even as she spoke,
Philippa was aware that there was something familiar
about his face, and this made her even more convinced
that he was someone she had seen on her manor recently.

'What harm would there be in answering a few questions?' He frowned down at her, and his scrutiny of her
features was just as keen as hers had earlier been of his.
'There's something about you. You're hiding something. Perhaps you are a thief?'

'Why should I hide anything from you? I don't know
you,' she replied desperately, struggling again. 'And I
am no thief. How dare you say that!'

'Why should I take your word?' He grabbed her other arm, forcing her to be still. His face was grim.

Philippa stared up at him, still angry. 'Why should I listen to you? Why should I even speak to you? You dare to touch me!' Her green eyes flashed fire. 'More likely it is you who are the thief—perhaps even a murderer. You are dressed finely, but one can never tell who is who these days.'

'What are you babbling about, wench?' he demanded in exasperated tones. 'You're talking nonsense. What's this about murder? I am no murderer.' The blue eyes were hard.

'You mightn't call it murder,' she retorted in a quivering voice. 'Perhaps you think you were justified? That your cause is the right one? But who are you to decide whether a life is worth ending or not?'

He stared at her incredulously. 'I do not understand what you are talking about. But let us have a quiet conversation—elsewhere.'

'I don't want to talk to you, or to go with you.' She had begun to tremble, her nerves stretched to breaking-point, then realised that he was listening not to her, but to a noise coming from outside.

The deep-toned babble grew in intensity, and suddenly men, ragged, thin and hungry-looking, came pouring through the doorway so that they were both forced backwards. He spun her round so that she was shielded from that flood of humanity by his body, but still they were pushed back and back until the pair of them were wedged against a pillar. Her nose was squashed against his padded doublet, and for a moment she felt as if she could not breathe and had to force her head up, gasping. Immediately the stench of unwashed bodies mingling with incense and burning candles was repugnant to her. Men like these had killed her father! The filthy scum had destroyed her home, had driven her uncle from Canterbury and made her a refugee in her own land! She trembled with the intensity of her emotions.

'Don't worry. I'll get us out of here,' rasped a voice in her ear.

Philippa was suddenly aware of the stranger's breath on her cheek and his eyes on her face. How close he held her, one arm wrapped about her waist, the other about her shoulders. The beating of her blood was loud in her ears, and his thigh was pressed against hers. Never had any man held her so closely, and had she been able, she would have wrenched herself out of his arms, because the experience was singularly disturbing.

The peasants surged past them and on into the cathedral's vastness. Shouts filled the air, disrupting the Mass and causing the monks to turn in fright.

'Come on!' His hold slackened, and taking Philippa's hand, he pulled her towards the doorway. Once there, he stilled as a name was roared from thousands of throats, and as one, they turned and gazed at the motley crowd. Some had fallen on their knees, apparently overawed by the soaring magnificence of the building. Still the shouts rang out, but no longer did the stranger delay. He pulled her out into a sunlight that beat down from a clear blue sky and on to face a crowd that was almost as great outside as inside the cathedral.

Again Philippa tried to free herself, but he kept hold of her wrist and plunged into the mass of people. Blindly she was forced to go with him, unable to see anything because she was not tall enough. Within that crowd she sensed the same tension, the breathless, excited waiting, and the uncertainty she had felt the day her father died. Now the mob wanted the archbishop's head, it seemed. Chancellor of all England, him they blamed for the ills that plagued the country. She wanted to be out of Canterbury, somewhere safe, away from the peasants and from this man who forced her through the people with a ruthless determination that paid no heed to curses or toes trodden on. At last he reached a lane that was almost empty of people, and there he halted, steadying her as she swayed with weariness.

She shrugged his hand off her shoulder. 'Can you not leave me alone? Have I not suffered enough from your kind this last night?' she cried in a seething voice.

'My kind? What do you mean by that, I wonder? You called me a murderer before.' His eyes narrowed. 'I am no murderer—nor am I a lord who would beat you for any jewels you might have purloined last night.'

'I never thought you a lord! A Lollard, sir, is what I deem you. One of those men who roam the country stirring up trouble and unrest in this realm.' She turned from him and would have walked away if he had not forced her to a standstill.

'A Lollard! You thought...' He rubbed his chin with his free hand, staring down at her intently. 'Last night you were there on Cobtree manor—what were you doing?'

Philippa twisted in his grip. 'What were *you* doing there, gone midnight?' she countered, puzzled by his reaction to her words.

'That's my affair. A personal matter,' he replied shortly. 'Do you know where Master Elston is?' His grip slackened.

'Who?' She attempted to conceal her shocked dismay.

'You know whom I'm talking about!' he snapped. 'Was it because of Master Elston that you came here? Do you know where the Cobtrees are?' There was a pucker between his sable brows. 'Are you Mistress Cobtree's maid? Did you come here seeking her, or the peasant army?'

'I? Seek the peasant army?' Suddenly her laugh rang out. 'I hate the peasant army—I hate them!' Her voice shook uncontrollably.

'If that is so, then you seek your mistress. Or...' His eyes studied her intently.

Philippa's mouth was suddenly dry, and she felt sick. 'Master Elston's gone to London, most likely,' she said swiftly. 'That ... is where everyone seems to be fleeing to these days.' She began to walk on, her mind in a turmoil.

'What about Master Cobtree? Perhaps you seek him here? Maybe you were his whore?' He forced her to a halt by stopping straight in her path. 'You wouldn't be the first serf to lie with her master. Keep still a moment! You have a habit of not answering questions openly, so that I can learn little.' He stared at her. 'What is it?' How pale she was—as if she might swoon, and she was trembling! 'Listen—I don't intend you any harm. I need to find your master and mistress.'

She stared at him from furious, glistening green eyes. His words had shocked her, and yet at the same time she realised that if he were seeking her father, he could not know that he was dead, and that meant he could not be involved in his murder. But who was he?

'Pardon my bluntness,' he said quietly, touching her arm, 'but I have little time to waste, to consider your sensibilities.'

'Do you?' Her voice trembled. 'That is apparent, sir, but I am no thief or whore.' She stepped back and round him.

'No?' He allowed her to walk on, and fell in by her side. 'Then who are you? You were there last night. I remember...' his face creased in concentration, 'you had a spade in your hand.'

'I did?' Philippa slowed as she came to a corner. Her throat was tight, and so was her chest. She did not want to think of last night. A smell of burning teased her nostrils, and the crackle of flames was unexpectedly loud. For a moment she thought it was her imagination, that her senses were deceiving her, then she rounded the corner. A mass of men cavorted round a fire, throwing rolls and parchments into its heart, chanting and cheering as they did so. Fear gripped her, and she drew back hurriedly, bumping into the stranger.

'What is it? You're frightened!' He grabbed her arm.

He seems concerned, thought Philippa in surprise. The ground was going up and down, and the buildings and his face were beginning to blur. 'You—You want to know what I—I was doing last night?' Her tongue ran over dry lips. 'I—I was burying him. They burnt his body... and I was burying... him.' Her legs gave way beneath her.

Hands lifted her, and he spoke, but she could not make out the words, only that they seemed to be curses. Then her head drooped on his arm and she lost consciousness.

CHAPTER TWO

FOR A MOMENT Philippa lay still, gazing up with unfocused vision at the face so close to hers, then she struggled to sit up.

'Easy now!' He pulled a face as he forced her down on the mound of straw. Then he moved away to lean against a wooden partition, behind which a horse stirred. 'Do you feel like telling me who you are?'

'Telling you?' She drew a shaky breath, studying his face.

He nodded, his attention firmly fixed on her, the narrow-cheeked face serious. 'Either you are a thief, or...'

'I am no thief,' she declared vehemently. 'I wish you would stop saying I was. Who are you that you take such an interest in me? Who are you to accuse me all the time?'

'I know who I am—it is you that I wish to learn more about.' He folded his arms. 'If you are not a thief, then...' sighing, 'you must be—incredible as I find it— Mistress Philippa Cobtree.'

'Why should you find it so incredible?' she demanded, her cheeks flushing.

He came closer, and sat back on his haunches. 'Because you don't look in the least as I remember you, except...' he gazed at her, 'your eyes are still cat's eyes.'

'Cat's eyes?' she exclaimed indignantly, blushing deeper for some inexplicable reason. 'I don't have cat's eyes!' She clenched her fingers, for he was uncomfortably close, and she was unable to back away as she would have liked to.

'I hazard you have claws, too!' His face showed the slightest of smiles.

Her green eyes flashed, but she made no answer to his comment, merely saying, 'You have the advantage of me, sir. You seem to know me, but...'

'I am Guy Milburn. It's not the least bit flattering that you don't recognise me, Mistress Philippa,' he said dolefully. '*I* have an excuse, since you were only a child when last I saw you, and you have changed much.' A whey-faced girl with no breasts or hips—that was how his brother had referred to her before he had left Yorkshire.

'Sir Hugo? Is he here too?' She sat up hurriedly, dismayed, realising that it was not only because she had been a child when last he saw her that he had not recognised her.

'No,' he replied shortly. There was a flicker of some emotion deep in his eyes.

'No! Then where is Sir Hugo?' Philippa hunched her knees and pillowed her chin on them, annoyed.

'My brother is in Yorkshire,' replied Guy, attempting to see beyond the dirt of her face. Her nose was small, but slightly freckled still across the bridge. He remembered the freckles, and the green eyes, which were really too large for cat's eyes, although they slanted slightly upward at the outer edge. Her mouth was a little large for her small face, and she had a dimple in her chin. No beauty, but definitely more comely than he had remembered.

'Would you like to see my teeth?' She had begun to feel uncomfortable under his scrutiny.

He grinned. 'That's not necessary,' he said smoothly, surprised that she had a sense of humour. Strictly serious and very religious, he remembered her being in the past. 'My brother, having intended to go to Berwick with the Duke of Lancaster, was gored by a boar when hunting. He has been forced to curtail all activities, so he has

decided to wed you, now that he has time on his hands.'
His voice was dry, and he cocked a dark brow.

Philippa let out a tiny gasp. 'His words, or yours,
Master Guy?'

'I beg your pardon—I spoke without thinking.' He
inclined his dark head slightly. 'In your present situation, Mistress Philippa, I would consider that my
coming is an answer to your prayers in the cathedral.
You have need of a man's guidance and aid.'

Could she detect a note of mockery in his tones? 'Then
you would be wrong. The only thoughts in my mind
concerned my father's soul.' She swallowed. 'You do realise that—that . . .'

He nodded, and gave a grimace. 'That was what all
that talk about murder was about, then . . . I'm sorry,
Mistress Philippa. But I wish you could have told me
last night who you were. It would have saved us both a
lot of time and trouble.' He blew out a weary breath
and got to his feet. 'I suppose I shall have to take you
to London with me.'

'London?' She lifted her chin, not liking the way Guy
had spoken. 'You don't have to do anything of the sort!
You might not have noticed,' she continued in a determined voice, 'but I have no baggage with me. I have no
other clothes, and barely any money. My home is burnt
to the ground. I am filthy, hungry, weary to the
bone . . . my serfs have revolted . . .'

'It seems that I came just in time, then.' His gaze
ruthlessly surveyed her appearance in the torn and dirty
blue linen gown. Her hand went to her bosom, where
there was a rent. He raised both eyebrows this time.
'Somewhere we'll find something else for you to wear.
You can *wash*—and when we've put some distance between Canterbury and ourselves, we can rest and eat.
Now, up with you!' Before she could prevent him, his
hand was on her arm and he was pulling her to her feet.

'I must go back to my manor. I have left the rolls hidden there with all the names of the serfs, and the betrothal agreement. Could we not . . .'

'No!' he said firmly. Then, hesitatingly, 'You have more wit than I realised. Where have you hidden them?'

Philippa frowned, annoyed that he would not go back with her, and also reluctant to tell him.

'Well?' he demanded. 'You still don't think I am one of them, do you? I might believe in some of Master Wycliffe's teachings, and have some sympathy with the serfs' cause, but not to the extent of joining a revolt.'

'I hid them in the hole of the wood-spirit's tree. It was the only place I could think of,' she stressed quickly, flushing. 'I escaped to the forest before they burnt the house down.'

'The wood-spirit's tree?' He smiled lazily. 'And there was I thinking you a strict daughter of holy church! You still believe that tale your brother told you?'

'Of course not,' she replied indignantly. 'It was the only place. I know it's superstitious nonsense that trees have voices and souls. Besides, that tree was struck by lightning, so it's dead.' Her cheeks were extremely warm. His smile had grown. 'Do we go back and get them?'

'I think not. There are only the two of us, and if there are still rebels about, I don't mind a fight. But I think you've been through enough for one day.' His voice was sympathetic and caused tears to well in her eyes. She blinked them away, not looking at him. 'Are they wrapped up to keep them intact and secure from damp and insects?'

'In leather,' she said unsteadily. 'It will not last for ever.'

'Nothing lasts for ever.' He rubbed his unshaven chin, wishing he could bring her comfort somehow, but knew that there was no way. Only time would heal her grief. He had not wanted to come on this journey, but his brother had been insistent, making all sorts of promises, and he had agreed, hoping that, by doing so, the rift between them could be healed. Now it seemed that there would be just the two of them for the road, and his brother would not like that! Perhaps they might find the uncle in London. He would be the man to advise Philippa what action to take about the revolt on her manor. His own task was to get her to Yorkshire—and to his brother.

'We are going to London, then?' Philippa had managed to swallow her tears. She rubbed at the dirt on her cheek before smoothing back her hair.

Guy nodded. 'We could seek out your uncle.' He put a hand on her shoulder. 'He will need to know about your father.'

'I—I still find it hard to believe,' she muttered. 'He did not treat them harshly. I suppose it is the spirit of the times: the war with France and Castile; so few victories now. Even our holy church is threatened from within and without and does not provide guidance on what is right and wrong.'

'Ay! Having two popes isn't the best way of leading a church that is already weakened by dispute,' commented Guy soberly, moving over to his horse.

She nodded. Some of what he had said was an echo of what the Lollards preached. Too many bishops and clergy chasing after power, pandering to the wealthy, reaping earthly rewards, instead of tending the poor of their flocks—and preaching about the kingdom of Heaven. She watched him saddle up his horse. Guy Milburn! He had changed from what she remembered of him. Not his features, or the colour of his eyes—but he was not so slim, and muscle showed where his hose hugged his calves and thighs. He wore the more fashionable shorter doublet, and it suited him. His shoulders had broadened also, and the expression on his face was not so youthful or carefree. What had been happening to him since last she had seen him? Little news had reached her about her betrothed's family.

'Are you ready?' Guy led his horse over.

'I'm not dressed for riding,' she declared in embarrassed tones.

'No.' He smiled. 'But you'll have to manage as best you can.' Putting his hands about her waist, he lifted her, then went over and flung wide the door. Instantly, shouts and screams were loud in their ears.

'It looks as though we are going to have a rough ride. You'd better hold tight.' His expression had darkened, but his blue eyes were bright with determination as he pulled himself up in front of her.

Philippa was nervous as the horse clip-clopped out into the lane. People were running towards them, pursued by a gang of ruffians. Across from the stable, shutters were being flung down and a man was climbing through the window of the house. Guy dug in his heels, and her nose collided with his spine so that tears came to her eyes. She clutched at the back of his doublet and let out a yell as a man ran up and sought to drag her from the horse. Guy twisted and kicked out at him, and the man fell back as the horse increased speed.

'How well do you know Canterbury?' Guy asked roughly, slowing, and gazing about him.

Philippa lifted her eyes and peered over his shoulder with some difficulty. 'If you cross the Stour, we can skirt the city wall and come to the Westgate.'

'So, left it is.' Guy gave the horse its head, making Philippa cling more tightly. She closed her eyes, unaccustomed to such an undignified mode of travel, and prayed that she would not fall off.

'Nearly there! You were right, good lass!'

There was warmth in Guy's voice, which caused her spirits to rise. Relief soared within her as she caught sight of the Westgate's immense twin towers soaring to the sky, peasants barred their path and she expected Guy to slow down, but instead he urged the horse on and like an arrow they shot towards the gateway. For a moment she thought the men would not give way, then they were scattering. They were through, and under the archway, over another branch of the river, and then cantering up the road to Whitstable. They passed Saint Dunstan's church, and took the road to London.

'I never thought we would get this far.' Philippa's voice broke the long silence. 'Back there, I thought you would have to stop.'

'For the sake of a handful of men? No one in their right senses stands in the way of a galloping horse! I knew they would fall back. You weren't hurt at the stables, were you?'

'No.' Philippa yawned, and her fingernails scraped the fine blue wool of his doublet. 'I think they were after my girdle.' She hesitated. 'Was that why you thought I was a thief?'

'In part, but I also recognised the betrothal ring on your finger. My mother had it from my father—and she died before your betrothal, so the ring was given to my brother,' he replied in a conversational tone. 'It was one of the prizes gained when my father fought in France with the old king.' He eased weary shoulders.

'I remember my father telling me.' Her voice was uneven, and her fingers moved restlessly on his back. Suddenly everything seemed unreal, as though she existed in a bubble and was looking out on the passing scene. Was it really true that her father was dead? It seemed unbelievable, yet here she was with Guy Milburn going to London, so it could not be a dream! His back was warm beneath her fingers, and she was aware of the slightest smell of sweat and lemon. Life truly did have to go on, even if one wanted to catch time back and re-run it, hoping and praying that the ugly and terrifying had not been true. She glanced down at herself. What a fright she must look! She gripped the horse more firmly with her thighs, despite her discomfort. Her skirts were all pulled askew, revealing her calves; there were no bags in which to put her legs for modesty's sake.

'I wish I were on my manor,' she whispered, half to herself; thoughts of the future were unexpectedly frightening. 'Could you not take me back? I would see it once more to convince myself that it all really happened.'

'What are you saying?' Guy sounded weary. 'It seems to be like nonsense. If it had not happened, would we be here on our way to London?' He glanced over his shoulder at her. 'I'll get you there as quickly as I can. And then to Yorkshire.'

'Yorkshire? It is so far away. Why has your brother waited so long before wedding me? It is not very flattering!' She swayed with weariness; her hands went round his waist, and she rested her head against his back. 'My father kept saying that he was in no haste to be rid of me, but I knew he, too, wondered why Sir Hugo did not come to claim me.' She yawned sleepily. 'I fear my father tired of keeping a watch on me. Perhaps it was that your brother did not consider me? I do not think he regarded me highly when we were betrothed.'

'It would be diplomatic of me not to answer that, Philippa.'

She caught the smile in his voice, and sat up straighter. 'Why? If it were true, say so! I was not blind all those years ago. I knew he did not find me attractive, but I was only ten years old. What did he expect?' she asked indignantly.

'Not what he is getting now, I shouldn't wonder,' he replied blandly.

'What does that mean?' Was he laughing at her? 'I know I am filthy, but I don't always look like this.'

'I never doubted that for a minute—once I realised who you were. I meant that you have altered. You have more to say for yourself, for a start, and have more spirit.'

'It was hard for me to utter a word among you four men all those years ago! Besides, my mother did not encourage me to be anything other than meek and mild. I suppose she thought that was how men liked women, but after she and my brothers died, I discovered that my father enjoyed talking to me. He encouraged me to do so many things. But perhaps your brother is as my mother thought him, and he would prefer me to be a wife who is docile. And, besides, marriage is a business— not a union of souls and lovers,' she said dispassionately.

'You are speaking like a woman of good sense. So many women have their heads stuffed with romantic dreams! It is good that you don't expect my brother to be like a knight in a tale, who would woo you with words and stay constantly at your side. He will expect you to provide him with several lusty sons, to control his household for him, to be obedient in all that he asks of you. There you have your future in a nutshell.'

'It sounds just as I expected, and just as unexciting.' She sighed, and they both fell silent, too exhausted for further conversation.

The sun was almost touching the horizon, its rays sending shining swaths of gold across the gentle, undulating countryside, when at last Guy halted by a stream. A wild cherry stood like a sentinel on the bank, its browning blown petals a carpet for the horse's hooves.

'Why are we stopping here?' Philippa's weariness was apparent in her voice, as she lifted her head and stared about her.

'I thought you might like to tidy yourself,' said Guy, dismounting. 'You surely don't want to go inside the inn looking like that?' He held up a hand to help her down, but her green eyes had darkened, and ignoring his hand she clambered from the horse.

'I suppose you are ashamed to be seen with me.' She folded her arms across her breast, not looking at him.

'It's nothing of the sort,' he responded with a barely controlled impatience. 'But if you want to go inside looking like a slattern, I am too tired to argue.'

'Where is this inn you speak of?' she asked.

'It's beyond the trees, up that slope on the other side of the stream.' He pointed. 'I'll go and see if they have room. And whether I can find you something else to wear.'

'You would leave me here alone?' Her eyes widened, and she clutched at his sleeve.

'It won't be for long, and, besides I thought you might be glad of a few moments on your own,' he replied in a gentler tone.

'Of course! I am being foolish. It's just that...' She took her hand from his arm.

'I do understand—and I shall return as swiftly as possible.' He mounted again, and the horse splashed through the stream.

She did not watch him go, but tossing her hair back, leaned over the water and placed her palms on the stony bottom. The water ran over her wrists, cooling them, and she stared into its shallow depths in an attempt to see her reflection—but the stream ran too swiftly. Swishing the water, she brought her hands up to her face and began to rub at the dirt. There was a lump in her throat as she thought of the last twenty-four hours.

By the time she had finished, the tingling effects of the water had revitalised her. A slattern! Was that how she appeared to him? She tried to smooth her hair, combing it with her fingers, but it was impossible to untangle the knots. Her gown would never be clean again. What would her father have thought of her in this state? The aching void that the lack of his presence caused was a pain so deep that tears caught her throat and made her eyes smart. She took the silver buttons from her fitchet and stared at them, remembering...

'I've brought you a clean gown. That is, if you don't mind plain brown homespun?' Guy's voice so startled her that she would have fallen into the water had he not leapt the stream and pushed her back on the bank. His hand was still warm on her shoulder as he knelt on one knee in the grass. 'Were you falling asleep?'

She gazed up at him and shook her head wordlessly. When he saw the tears glistening on her lashes, he thought it wiser to say no more, and dropped the gown in her lap. 'It was the innkeeper's daughter's.' He lowered himself on the bank next to her.

Philippa's hands folded about the gown; the fabric felt rough. She cast him a glance, which he caught. 'Best to change here,' he said quietly. 'There is no privacy at the inn.' She did not move. 'You are perfectly safe with me,' he added irascibly, running a hand over his chin, and turning his face away. 'Hurry up, for I wish to make an early start in the morning.'

'But...' began Philippa nervously, turning the gown over between her fingers.

'But what...?' His voice rose as he turned and looked at her. 'You didn't want me to leave earlier. If you wish me to leave you here—in a state of undress—when it's almost dark...' He made to rise.

'No—No,' she stammered, glancing over her shoulder. 'I did not think...' She pressed her lips firmly together as he averted his gaze and sat down again. With her eyes firmly on him, she rid herself of her old gown and pulled the new one over her head. Not without some difficulty could she ease it over her breasts and hips, wondering, as she did so, how old the innkeeper's daughter was. Her fingers scrabbled for the fastenings at the back, but she could manage only a few. Perhaps they could be left undone? But on feeling the gap with her trembling fingers, she knew it would not do. She cleared her throat.

At the sound, Guy looked round. 'You are ready?' he drawled sleepily.

'Not—Not quite. I can't reach all the fastenings.'

'Here, I'll do them.' He rose and came close to her. It was almost dark, and they could barely see each other's faces.

'Thank you.' Philippa felt him part her hair, pushing it forward over her shoulders in an untidy mass. His fingers were cool and seemed to caress her skin, and she was suddenly aware of him, just as it had been in the cathedral. The thought caused her to fidget, and to wish he would hurry. When at last he finished and twirled her to face him, her thanks were flurried. His eyes gleamed, but he did not speak, only smoothing back her hair from her face. The back of his hand brushed her cheek, and she jumped.

'You're not frightened of me, surely, Philippa?' There was a derisive note in his voice.

'No, of course not! It is getting dark, so surely we should be going?' As she backed away, he grasped her arm and pulled her towards him. 'No! Don't, please! Let me go,' she squeaked, pushing a hand against his chest.

'You would rather fall in the stream?' he demanded as he let go of her.

She clutched at his sleeve as she teetered on the edge, and he snatched her back. 'I'm sorry! I thought...'

'What did you think? That I would dally with my brother's betrothed?' he said in mock horror. 'Do you always suspect any man who touches you to indulge in a flirtation?' Taking her hand, he said, 'Jump!'

Philippa jumped, for she had no choice as he leaped the stream on the word. As soon as they were on the other side, she pulled her hand from his. In a voice that quivered, she said, 'You are the first man who has ever laid a finger on me, and if you...'

'The very first? I am overcome by such a singular honour. My brother will be pleased by such faithfulness—after all these years.'

Philippa could not fail to hear the mockery in his taunting voice, and vexed, wishing she had a string of lovers who had adored her and about whom she could boast, she turned and ran up the slope.

Guy caught up with her as she reached the trees. 'That was a stupid thing to do!' he snapped. 'You could have tripped in the dark. What did you think I was going to do?' He took her arm. 'Now stay with me.'

'Don't touch me!' Philippa struck at his hand. 'For some reason you are deliberately trying to embarrass me. First you say I look like a slattern, then you mock me because I am chaste and have kept myself for your brother,' she panted. 'Would you have me be a harlot?'

Guy stared at her through the shadowy darkness beneath the trees. 'You misunderstand me. I admire such purity in a woman, and I am surprised, that is all.'

'Surprised at what?' She was still, wanting to know, and prepared to listen.

He caught her chin with gentle fingers, and tilted it. 'I am surprised that no one has ever flirted with you. Has no lover truly ever written verse in praise of your eyes? Would they say, I wonder, that they sometimes sparkle like iridescent raindrops when the sun shines through leafy boughs in a forest?'

Her heart was racing, and it was infuriating that his touch and words should have such an effect on her. 'Very pretty,' she said in a humorous voice. 'I don't see how you can see all that! And when you could see my eyes— you compared them to a cat's. You are a liar, Master Milburn—and an accomplished flirt!'

'You don't believe me?' he murmured dolefully. 'Or is it that you are not used to having pretty words spoken to you—about yourself?' His fingers caressed the curve of her jaw.

'I—I know I am not pretty—or beautiful, so let us have an end to this nonsense!' Her voice quivered slightly.

Guy released her. 'Of course. It *is* nonsense—but pretty nonsense. And you are mistaken, Philippa. Whoever told you that you were without attraction...' He left the sentence unfinished with an abruptness that teased her thoughts all the way to the inn.

So many pairs of eyes turned towards them that Philippa was immediately conscious of the tightness of the brown gown, its shortness, and the tangles in her hair. Her first instinct was to turn and go out again, but Guy took her elbow and urged her to the end of a table. They sat on stools, and she stared down at the trestle top, reluctant to speak or to look at him.

A platter was put before her, on it a fowl steaming in a shining red-brown sauce. She realised how hungry she was, and fell upon the food. It tasted of garlic and honey and red wine, and was delicious. The wine set at her elbow was also surprisingly good. She had rarely stayed at an inn, but realised, gazing about her, that the host would have to cater for the wealthy as well as the poorer pilgrims who frequented the road to Canterbury. At last she could eat no more and leaned back against the whitewashed wall, sipping her wine, her eyes closed.

'You feel better now?'

Philippa forced her eyelids wide. Guy had one elbow on the table, his chin cupped in his palm, while he swilled the wine round in his cup. She nodded, in no mood for dispute.

'Now are you able to answer a few questions?' He was gazing at her from drowsy blue eyes.

'What questions?' She rested both elbows on the table. A yawn escaped her, despite her efforts to prevent it.

'Not many. I won't keep you from your pallet. Were any of the peasants loyal to your father? Did he have a bailiff who could take charge of manorial matters in his absence?' Guy took a gulp of wine.

'Some would be, but the majority were swayed by the words of the hedge-priests. Rose told me that was how it was.'

'Rose?'

'She was my maid. We had known each other all our lives. Tom, her brother, led the revolt. It was she who told me about my father and warned me to flee.' A tremor shook her voice.

'I'm sorry if this is painful for you,' Guy said gruffly. 'But what of the bailiff?'

'Walter? I think he would have remained loyal to my father. He went with him when he left the hall to go and speak with the villeins. Perhaps they allowed him to escape. He was once one of them, but he bought his freedom.'

'There's a possibility that he might return when the danger is past, and maybe carry on until he hears from you? He will know you are alive if the maid tells him.'

She nodded. A wave of sadness and longing for the old days engulfed her. 'Is that all?' She stood up. 'I would sleep.'

'I'll come with you.' He picked the saddle-bags from the floor and led the way to the stairs up to the sleeping chamber.

The room did not appeal to Philippa at all. Its roof was low-pitched, and the one window opening was too small to let in much air. It was stuffy, and already she could smell sweat, and hear people snoring and turning in their sleep. There would be lice, she was convinced!

Guy searched for a space on the floor and beckoned to her. Near the window she lay down, pulling the blanket he had given her about her shoulders. Weariness flowed through her, seeming to tingle in her feet. Within moments she was asleep.

Guy woke suddenly, his hand going instinctively for the knife at his girdle. People were grumbling and a voice called for a light. The sound of muttering interspersed with moans was near at hand. He rolled over, blinking, and realised that it was Philippa. Leaning over, he touched her shoulder. 'Hush, now,' he hissed, 'you'll have everyone awake.'

She stared up at him from dazed eyes, and then her fingers clutched his doublet. 'You—will—not—let—them—burn me?' she whispered. 'You will not...'

'No!' With an abrupt movement he covered her hand with his own. She must have been having a dream.

'They were coming to fetch me. You won't...' She kneaded the front of his doublet with a restless hand.

'No!' repeated Guy, remembering the first night he had seen her, and thought her witless. What had she said? She had been burying her father! 'Never!' he added, for good measure.

'Never?' she echoed, giving a tiny sigh. 'You will not leave me?'

'My word on it.' Easy to say, he thought. It was only a dream that gripped her, after all. The horrors! What horrors had she seen? Considering the past twenty-four hours, he realised that she must have walked to Canterbury. There was more to Mistress Philippa Cobtree than a first look revealed.

'You'll stay with me?' she pleaded fretfully, her fingers twitching beneath his.

'Ay.' Guy sighed, realising that the dream still gripped her and she was only half awake. He had to quieten her somehow, and he lay close to her, stroking her hair with his free hand. Eventually her eyes closed and her breathing became steady and quiet. Staring up into the darkness, he wondered about the rest of this journey. Damn Hugo! Her head shifted on his chest, and her soft body was warm against his. Damn Hugo! His eyes closed. It was still some distance to London. It was even further to Yorkshire, if they had only each other for company. After some time, he slept.

When Philippa woke in the light-filled sleeping chamber, she felt as though in a cocoon of softness and warmth. Someone had wrapped her in two blankets, but the room was devoid of folk. Quickly she scrambled to her feet, bundling the blankets in her arms as the sound of voices beneath the window drew her. One of them was Guy's. Had he wrapped her up so snugly? She warmed to the thought, and leaning on the sill, looked out. It was a bright morning, although mist still curled over the fields, shrouding the grass and the far distance.

'I tell you, the peasants are already marching,' insisted an elderly voice from beneath the window.

'You are certain that their destination is London?' demanded Guy tersely.

'I heard them, with my own ears, talking! The gates will be closed when the news reaches the city—if they can't be turned back. I'm off now.' Bells tinkled.

'God go with you.'

'And you, lad.' There was the clatter of hooves, and then the soft tread of feet before a door was closed.

Philippa turned from the window, her face anxious, and swiftly paced the room. She met Guy on the stairs, and for a second they paused. She could see where the dark hair swirled in a damp wave on the top of his head, and she felt his attraction. 'You should have woken me earlier,' she remarked in a stiff voice.

His eyes perused her face, and she felt herself flushing. 'I thought you needed the rest. But now that you are up, let's be on our way.' He led the way down swiftly.

'It is because of the peasants?' Her expression was serious, the skimpy brown skirts billowing about her bare ankles as he opened the outside door.

'You heard?' He spun swiftly, and she saw that his horse was already saddled up, waiting.

She nodded, concealing her trepidation, but her hands trembled as she gave him the blankets to put in the saddle-bags.

'We'll get to London before them,' he said confidently. 'Now, up with you.' She stared at him, not as sure as he, then put her foot in his looped hands and dragged herself up. Within seconds, they were on their way.

CHAPTER THREE

'THE PILGRIM I had speech with was saying that the peasants have a new leader—one Wat Tyler,' Guy informed her. 'It seems he has had experience of fighting in France and has organised them. They are marching to London to see the king, in whom they have a touching faith, thinking he can right all their wrongs.'

'And when he can't, what do you think they will do?' Philippa moistened her lips. 'Perhaps they'll chop off a few heads?' Her hand went to her throat. 'Maybe they'll even kill Richard?' Her voice rose.

'You're letting your own experience colour your thinking,' he said in an emotionless voice. 'By the time they reach London, the gates will be closed against them. Do not worry until the need arises.'

'You think we shall get there well before them?' Philippa pushed back a handful of hair. It was still in a tangle.

'There is no reason why we should not. The journey might be arduous because there will be little time to rest, but we'll do it.'

'When we reach London, what then? Where do we start looking for my uncle?'

'The Temple is the headquarters of the lawyers. But I have business in the city of my own, as well, that I have to attend to.'

'What is your business, Master Guy?'

'Sheep—wool—cloth, in that order. My brother allows me to graze sheep on the manor, of which I am his steward.'

'You have no land of your own?' The surprise in her voice caused a flush to darken the back of his neck.

'None.'

'Your father made no provision for you?'

'My father deemed it wiser to pass all his holdings to Hugo.' There was a note of bitterness in his tones.

'Most fathers make provision for their younger sons. I do not consider that just,' she remarked frankly.

'No more do I, Mistress Philippa. But why should you be concerned? It is your children that will be the richer because of my father's action,' he muttered vehemently. 'One day I shall have all the land I need.'

Philippa was silenced. Obviously Sir Ralph's not making provision for his younger son had hurt deeply, and she was reluctant to ask any more questions. She knew little of her betrothed's family, only that a bond had been forged on the battlefield at Poitiers in France between her father and Sir Ralph.

The silence between them stretched. There were few workers to be seen in the fields, and the road was not as busy as she had expected. That could have been because of the news of the peasants' army and its advance. The sun was already warm on her head, and the clear skies meant that the day would get even hotter as it progressed. A sudden violent jerk catapulted her forward, and if she had not had her arms firmly about Guy's waist, she might have fallen from the horse. Her nose did indeed collide with his spine, bringing tears to her eyes. As for Guy, it was perhaps Philippa's hold that saved him from being flung over the horse's head. He slid sideways, one hand having clutched at the horse's mane as the beast stumbled and slipped before it fell.

Philippa closed her ears to the oaths Guy uttered as they climbed down. She watched him as he ran a hand over its neck, murmuring soothing words, his face drawn with concern. Thrice he checked each leg, but she did not need him to tell her that the front right one was broken. He stood silently staring down at his horse, his hands on his hips. He knew what had to be done, but did not want to do it. This journey seemed to have been ill fated from its beginning, but perhaps they would still see a satisfactory end to it. He gave a heavy sigh, and moved forward.

'What are we going to do?' She twisted a lock of her hair, her eyes on his face.

'What do you think we're going to do?' His expression was stern as he began to unbuckle the saddle-bags. 'We'll have to walk.'

'Walk! How far?' She did not want to take him seriously.

'All the way to London, if need be.'

'You're jesting,' she exclaimed in dismay. 'I—I couldn't!'

'Damn it, woman, do you think I would make jests about such a thing?' He dropped the saddle-bags on the ground and pulled a knife from his girdle. 'Start walking... I'll catch you up.'

They exchanged glances. 'Cursed hole!' she muttered in a shaky voice. 'Do you...?'

'It's kinder,' Guy's voice rasped. 'You go on.'

Philippa turned and walked away, not looking back. He caught up with her a few moments later, the saddle-bags slung over his shoulder. His face was set with a fierce sadness.

'I'm sorry about your horse.' She touched his arm. 'He was a fine beast.'

He nodded, and attempted a smile. 'I had him since he was a foal.' The blue eyes were bright, and he had to clear his throat. 'I am sorry you have to walk... Perhaps we'll be able to get another horse along the way.'

'You aren't to blame, and if the peasants can march, so can I.' She knew it was unlikely that there would be another horse available.

'Good girl.' Briefly he touched her arm. 'It's not impossible; the only matter is that it will take longer.'

He did not need to say any more, thought Philippa, trying to match her stride to his as they began to walk. If it were going to take longer, that meant they might not reach London before the peasants. She supposed it all depended on her.

After a while, her feet began to drag, and annoyance clouded her face. She could not manage to keep up with Guy any longer. Lifting a hand, she shielded her eyes from the sun. It would take her at least ten minutes to catch up with him, if he would even wait. Sweat beaded her forehead and her throat was dry with dust. She saw him raise a hand and began to walk again, but before she had covered half the distance, he was on the move and she could have wept with sheer frustration. Leaving the road, she walked on the grass verge, pausing only to take off her shoes. When the road veered slightly and took him altogether from her sight, suddenly she was aware of the emptiness of the landscape. The whisper of the wind in the grass and trees was an eerie voice crying to the sky. She shook her head and gave a low laugh. Was she getting fanciful now? Perhaps that was the effect of tiredness. When at last she rounded the bend, Guy was sitting beneath the shade of an oak, drinking from a flask. She flung down her shoes.

'Why did you not wait for me?' she demanded angrily. Her face was red from the sun and damp with perspiration. The brown gown stuck to her, and she itched. Her feet had several blisters, which had burst, and she was annoyed to see him looking so cool and comfortable.

'If I had set my pace to yours, we would still be three miles back. I discovered in France that when the need arises one can walk miles with bleeding feet and half asleep, rather than be left to die by the wayside.' There was an expression of cool satisfaction on his face. 'I was right! You carried on walking because you had to.'

'No thanks to you!' she exclaimed in a seething voice. 'I suppose, if I had not caught up with you, you would have presumed I was dead and left me where I had fallen?' She dropped on the grass, stretching herself flat on her stomach, and buried her burning cheeks beneath her arms. The ache over her eyes eased.

'I knew there was still plenty of walking in you,' he said softly, the barest hint of a quiver in his voice.

'And how did you know that?' she asked sarcastically, lifting her head slightly. 'You were too far ahead to have seen me drop down dead.'

'You didn't drop down dead,' he murmured, 'unless you're a ghost?' He poked her with his toe, and she wriggled away from him. 'No ghost. Would you like a drink? Or aren't you thirsty?'

Philippa sat up, giving him a furious glance as she took the leather flask from him. The first mouthful of ale was so refreshing—exquisitely so—that she held it in her mouth for a moment before allowing it to trickle down her throat.

'Hungry?'

She nodded, and he tossed a napkin with some bread and cheese on her lap before stretching himself out on the grass and closing his eyes. 'Don't drink all the ale,' he said in dulcet tones. 'It has to last us all day.'

Guiltily Philippa stopped gulping, and wiped the top of the flask before replacing the stopper. She began to eat. Even the food last night had not tasted so good, but never had her body been worked so physically hard as during the last two days. When the last crumb had vanished, she sat gazing at her bare feet. She sighed. 'How long do you think it will take us to reach London?'

'It depends on you.' Guy sat up and rested an elbow on his humped knee. 'How much further do you think you can go today?'

'I don't know. But I have no intentions of moving yet,' she declared hotly. She wriggled, itching still. It would be fleas!

'I haven't asked you to. You need a rest.' He snapped off a stem of grass and put it in his mouth.

'I'm glad you realise that!' She scratched her ankle vigorously.

'You'll only make it worse, you know,' he murmured, his eyes on her bare legs, having been unable not to notice their shapeliness the evening before. 'The only way to be rid of lice is to drown them.'

Philippa darted him an irritated glance, and was instantly aware of the amount of leg she was revealing. Flushing, she tried to pull down her skirts.

'What small feet you have!' Guy stretched out on his stomach and his fingers touched her toes. Instantly she drew her legs up, attempting to curl them beneath her skirts. 'No, don't. Wait!' There was an intensity about his voice that caused her to still. His fingers curled about her ankle, and she made to withdraw, but he pinched her ankle so unexpectedly that she let out a scream.

'That hurt!' Her face was mutinous. 'Did you have to pinch me so hard? I consider that you find pleasure in seeing me suffer.' She struggled to pull her foot out of his grasp.

'Then you are labouring under a misapprehension.' His blue eyes teased as he licked his finger deliberately, and then rubbed the spot where the flea had bitten her ankle. 'It's not in making women suffer that I find pleasure in their company.'

'Isn't it?' She frowned down at him. A lock of raven hair fell forward on his forehead, and her senses were unexpectedly stirred. 'Then what do you find pleasurable!' Immediately she was conscious of her words sinking into a well of silence that contained an untangible something she did not quite understand.

'Do you really need me to tell you?' he murmured, releasing her ankle, and sitting up. 'Did your mother—or father—tell you so little about men?' His blue eyes were quizzical.

'No!' she blurted out. 'I know all I need to know.' Suddenly she could not bear to stay any longer, with him so close to her, and laughing at her lack of knowledge where men were concerned. She stood up abruptly, and he looked up at her from lazy blue eyes.

'I think I'll just go for a walk—in that orchard over there. You—you don't have to come with me. I want to be on my own.'

'A walk?' Guy smiled and shut his eyes, knowing he should not tease her, but she rose so beautifully. 'Don't be long,' he murmured, not opening his eyes to watch her go.

Without pausing to put on her shoes or to look back at him, Philippa almost ran to the orchard. Once within its shade, she slowed and let her gaze roam, and noticed some berries near the ground just ahead. They were strawberries, small and sweet, and she picked several, popping them in her mouth, enjoying their flavour. Then she saw the wall not far away. Perhaps there would be people, she thought, and they might have a horse that they would exchange for... for her silver buttons? What had Master Guy said... It all depended on her. She walked unhurriedly towards the wall. It was quiet among the trees but for the birdsong and the whispering of leaves. Through some open gates she went and up a rutted path, eventually coming into a courtyard.

Flies buzzed about a pile of maturing dung. There was a well, and a man winding up a bucket. With a heavily beating heart, she halted abruptly. He saw her the moment she began to back away.

'Come a-calling, have you? Come to see if some-body's at home? Well, they ain't. All gone to London.' His smile showed broken, rotting teeth, and a scrawny elbow poked through a hole in the sleeve of a filthy grey tunic.

Philippa turned to run, but he covered the space between them more quickly than she would have thought possible. She tried to pull away as he seized her in a painful grip. He fastened a wiry arm about her waist, lifting her off her feet as she struggled to free herself.

'You filth! Let me go!' she cried in a panic-stricken voice, kicking at his legs.

'Don't call me filth!' he rasped, seizing a handful of hair and dragging her head back. 'You don't dress like a lady, but you speak like one. But John Ball, the preacher, says we are all equals now.' His breath was rank, and caused her to cough. Forcing her head painfully back, he stretched her throat so that she found it difficult to draw breath. She tried to scream, but could not. His eyes were as dark as charcoal in a face the colour of pale yellow cheese. This was no serf, she found herself thinking. Gaol pallor! The serfs had been freeing the prisoners! The blood seemed to turn to ice in her veins.

'We wants to be alone, don't we, lovey?' he whispered against her cheek. 'There's more of us *filth* in the house—but they be drinking best wine—later they'll want some sport with you. But I'm going to have you first!' His hold tightened, and still grasping her hair, so that tears glistened in her eyes, he dragged her back in the direction of the open doorway of a barn.

The dread and loathing evoked by his words had paralysed Philippa's limbs, but as they reached the doorway, a cat shot out, and the man swerved, his grip loosening a fraction. Fear gave way to action as her eyes swept the dark interior of the barn, and she rammed her feet against the door-jamb. Then began a struggle in which she fought like one demented, and he was unable to get a good grip while attempting to knock her off her feet.

How she managed to release herself Philippa never fully comprehended, but suddenly she was free, and running across the courtyard. Halfway she managed to reach, before realising that he was behind, and whirling, she faced him, her breasts heaving, determined that he would not touch her again, but he seized her and catapulted her forward, her head caught him in the stomach and they both toppled over. Panting with fright, she managed to disentangle herself and scramble away, but did not get far before his outstretched hand clawed at her foot. She collapsed face down in the dust with a sobbing cry. Then she saw the feet.

Hoisting her up and out of the man's hold was the work of seconds. Philippa stared into Guy's furious face, and knew a different kind of fear. He set her on one side, and there was the gleam of a knife in his other hand.

The man gave a snarl, but before he was fully upright, Guy flung himself on him. They rolled over and over in the dust, grappling, and she had a job to see who had the upper hand. Then Guy's knife was against the man's throat, and he was pulling him up by the neck of his tunic. The man was forced back and back, then Guy kicked his legs from under him, causing him to collapse with a shriek into the heap of dung. The sound was quickly cut off as the hilt of the knife caught him hard under the chin. Guy turned and covered the distance between them in a couple of strides. He grabbed her by the wrist, and shouted, 'This stupid episode has cost us time!'

Philippa shot one swift glance at his face. The sound of singing was suddenly loud, and the man on the dung-heap was stirring. Guy put a hand to her shoulder and pushed her from the yard, then he hurried her along the path and out of the gateway. He did not allow her to catch her breath, but forced her on until they reached the road. There they paused. Bending, he picked her shoes up and flung them at her. 'Put them on!'

Philippa winced. 'You—you don't have to shout. How was I to know those men were there?' Her teeth caught at her bottom lip to stop it trembling.

'Of course you didn't, but what made you wander off like that when you know the peasants have been roaming the countryside?' Guy dragged the saddle-bags from the depths of a hawthorn bush. 'It was a stupid thing to do!'

'You didn't stop me!' she countered, her green eyes sparking.

'You said you wanted to be alone—I didn't think you would wander so far.' His fingers ploughed through his thick dark hair. 'It was a damned senseless thing to do!'

'Do you have to swear at me?' There were red spots of colour high on her cheekbones. 'I'm tired of listening to you.' She picked up her shoes.

'I beg your pardon, Mistress Cobtree,' he retorted ironically, bowing slightly. 'Perhaps you would rather I showed no concern?'

'Is that what it is? I thought it was just sheer bad temper because I have wasted your time!' She tossed her hair back, and swung her shoes angrily from the tips of her fingers.

'Bad tempered?' Guy drew a controlled breath. 'You are enough to try the patience of a saint. And I'm no saint!'

'I couldn't fail to notice that,' she snapped, letting the shoes drop to the ground.

'What does that mean?' Guy said in a dangerously low voice, dumping the saddle-bags and coming over to her.

Philippa moistened her mouth, suddenly nervous. 'I— I was merely agreeing with you, that's all!'

There was a silence while he studied her. 'You had better turn round.'

'Turn round?' She stared at him with puzzled eyes.

Guy seized her shoulder and whirled her round so that she gasped. 'No good,' he remarked, and twisted her round again. 'Perhaps you'll agree with me that it was a damned foolish thing to do?'

'What *are* you ... What do you mean by twisting me round like that?' Her expression spoke of her impatience. 'I am not a maypole! If you are talking about that man, I still say that I could not have known he was there.' She scowled at him, wishing he would not stand so close. He made her feel... She could not describe the sensation, because she had never felt this mingling excitement and nervousness before.

'You do realise what would have happened if I hadn't found you?' Guy enquired softly. 'A touch of gratitude would not go amiss, Philippa. Half the fastenings on your gown are torn.'

She lowered her head. 'Of course I know.' Her voice was barely audible. 'There's nothing I can do now!'

'I just wondered, after the way you spoke earlier,' he said drily.

Her head shot up, and she flushed. 'I did not consider what I was saying. My mother told me...what to expect, shortly after my betrothal.' She took a deep breath. 'You could not have been too concerned, or you would have come earlier and saved me from being manhandled by that filth,' she added calmly.

His eyebrows shot up. 'Damn it, woman, you're enough to try the patience of any man!' He pulled her towards him. The blue eyes smouldered. 'Perhaps this will teach you to be more careful in future.' His mouth sought hers and found it, claiming it in a brutal kiss that crushed her lips.

Philippa struggled furiously. There was a peculiar panic inside her, then unexpectedly the pressure of his mouth eased. She thought he would free her, but instead he gathered her closer and continued to kiss her with an amazing gentleness; his mouth moved over hers in a way that was extraordinarily persuasive. Suddenly she knew that if he did not stop, she might easily succumb and respond to his kiss. Her limbs began to quake...then he released her, and she was aware of a vague disappointment.

'Let that be a lesson to you!' His breathing was a little hurried, as he bent to pick up the saddle-bags.

She scowled at him. 'I don't need to be taught what beasts men are!' She pushed her foot inside a shoe.

'I've been gentle with you,' he murmured, frowning down at her.

'Gentle? Humph!' She pushed her other foot in her other shoe, wincing. 'You had no right to touch me.'

'No right at all,' he responded promptly, swinging the saddle-bags over his shoulder, and beginning to walk away.

Exasperated, she stared after him. She had known he would cause trouble as soon as she had set eyes on him. Was it only two nights ago? In such a short space of time he had made her wonder how she would have felt if it was him she was going to wed, and not Sir Hugo. The thought left her strangely unsettled.

'I can't go any further,' Philippa complained, swaying with exhaustion.

'Just a little further. There's an inn beyond the dip in the road,' insisted Guy, easing the saddle-bags on his aching shoulder.

'It is always a little further.' She eyed him mutinously. 'I can't go on.'

'If that is so, I'll go on and come back for you in the morning.' He showed no sign of the anxiety he felt about her ability to carry on to London on the morrow, and started to walk wearily.

She stared after him, filled with a sense of frustration. He had made no allowances for her since the episode with the peasant. Surely he must be as tired as she? She began to limp after him, and surprisingly it did not take her long to catch up. She wondered if he had deliberately slowed his pace.

Guy glanced down at her, and there was a softening in his expression. 'You've changed your mind?' She made no answer. 'If you consider this walk arduous, you should have been on the great march in 1373.' She pretended not to hear, but her curiosity was roused. 'I lost a horse then, also,' he continued, despite her apparent lack of interest. 'So did Hugo. When we set out from Calais in August there were fifteen thousand of us, but by the time we crossed the Auvergne in winter and reached our destination, only eight thousand were left.'

'Why was that?' She noticed the lines of weariness grooving his face, which was engrimed with dust. What a pair they must look! 'Was there a battle?'

Guy shook his head. 'That wily devil, Charles, who sat the throne of France then, would not come out from behind his castle walls to face our archers. He had learnt from past mistakes, perhaps. Most of the men died from cold and lack of food—and the illnesses caused by the conditions.'

'But you and Sir Hugo survived. I remember your talking about what a great adventure it was going to be— and how rich you would be when you returned.'

He grimaced. 'We did not realise, when we left, that the days of capturing French noblemen and ransoming them for a small fortune were over.' He shrugged. 'But we learnt to survive, and when in Calais, I discovered that there were other ways of setting out to make a fortune.'

'Wool?' She halted, and he nodded. They stood on the crown of the hill.

'It would be easier to make that fortune if the war ended.' He gazed down at the sweep of open rolling countryside and the inn below by the wayside. 'It's time the Plantagenets gave up their dream of regaining the throne of Valois. The rebellion of the serfs is the direct result of levying poll-taxes to raise money to pay for such a senseless dream, which in the end will prove unattainable.' He took her arm and led her to the inn.

It was as they were drinking their ale that the man came in. Finely robed in a surcote of scarlet cloth over a blue tunic, he was of ample girth. They exchanged glances as he looked at them. He first surveyed a huddle of men, then made his way down the table to approach Philippa and Guy.

'You have no objection to my joining you good folk?' He pulled out a stool and sat before they could answer. 'What a day it has been!' He rubbed his hands together and his round dark eyes shone. 'Profitable, though, profitable!' He smiled expansively, his double chin wobbling. 'You are on your way to London, good folk?'

Guy nodded morosely. Philippa yawned, and took another drink of ale. She would be glad to get to bed. The man was not put off.

'You know the peasants are marching this way?' He picked up his spoon as a bowl was set before him. 'I have been in their company. Some are feeling the weight of their sins after all this pillaging and burning. I have made a small fortune, I tell you, selling them absolution.' His voice had sunk to a whisper, and he winked.

Guy was suddenly alert and leaned forward. 'How far are they from here? We left them at Canterbury.'

'Travelling by way of Maidstone I have come.' The pardoner picked up a hunk of bread and began to chew noisily. 'They have freed that unrepentant sinner John Ball from prison, and he has convinced them that they have a chance of achieving all their aims. Their leaders plan to make them march through the night, hoping, I suppose, to surprise the city.'

Philippa stared at him aghast, and Guy stiffened, his hand tightening about his cup.

'You are sure of this?' He took a deep draught of the ale, his eyes intent on the man's face.

'They are in good heart, and I doubt not they could do it,' replied the pardoner, nodding vigorously as he chewed. 'John Ball and this Tyler would have all the king's council's heads sliced from their shoulders, as well as Lancaster's.'

'I can believe it! Would you like to drink with us?' Guy smiled.

'That's handsome of you, my good man. Thank you, thank you.'

Guy signalled to a serving-man. 'You have had a good day, you say. Travelled far?'

'Came on horseback from Dover this last week. But a good day? Ay! Managed to part with a piece of Peter the apostle's sail. Over a thousand years old, with not a single hole in it!' His whole body shook as he laughed inwardly.

'A good day indeed,' murmured Guy, not allowing his distaste to show. 'What else did you manage to get rid of?'

Philippa only half listened, wondering why Guy passed the time of day with him, encouraging him to talk and plying him with drink. Since she had come to know him a little, she had thought Guy Milburn would not have crossed the street to pass the time of day with this type. Pardoners gave the church a bad name. Having licences to sell pardons up and down the country, they often tricked the gullible into buying all sorts of so-called relics. Once she had come across one who swore that the blue cloth he was prepared to part with, at a small cost, was part of the Virgin Mother's veil—and that it would bring healing and great blessing to all who touched it. He had been sent on his way speedily!

Moodily Philippa gazed at the two men. She was so tired that her whole body seemed to feel one big ache. When would Guy stop listening and drinking and suggest it was time to retire? The thought of going upstairs alone in this inn was abhorrent, for its occupants seemed an unsavoury lot. What they would do in the morning she was past caring. The news of the peasants depressed her, but she could do nothing about it. Sleep was her main thought.

At last Guy rose, giving a helping arm to the other man, who was much the worse for drink. Stumbling and swaying, they climbed the stairs in front of Philippa, singing a bawdy song. Guy even saw the pardoner to a spot at the far end of the room before moving away to a place not far from the door. Philippa felt vexed with him, and taking the blanket without a word, settled herself on the none too clean straw. More fleas! was her last thought before sleep took her. Guy lay beside her, his hands behind his head, his eyes half-closed, the smallest of smiles lifting his mouth.

Why were they tying her wrists? Ever since she had been a child, she had avoided Tom, Rose's brother. He liked his own way too much, and whenever he had discovered her alone, in the stables, the hall or the garden, he treated her with a scornful disrespect. She had never told her father, because Rose might have suffered. But why did he have to be so rough with her now? She was grown, and he had no right! Where was her father? An icy hand clutched her stomach. There was a man standing in the shadows of the storeroom, watching her. She felt she should know him, but could not see his face. Why did he not come to help her? A rope was being flung over a beam, which burned, even as the cord tightened about her wrists. They began to drag her along the ground towards the burning house. She screamed silently, and struggled, trying to dig in her toes so that it would slow her down, but it did not stop the fire from looming closer. It was raging, and now she saw the men, their faces distorted and made horrible by their hatred. Then she gazed at the man, and she did know him, but however hard he ran towards her, he seemed to be going further away. Now the men had their hands on her feet and shoulders, and she was being swung back and forth, back and forth. They were chanting her name, whispering it over and over, and their fingers were hurting her shoulder. She gasped and whimpered, clawing her way up through the darkness, and suddenly she was awake. Someone *was* holding her!

Philippa opened her mouth to scream, but a hand was swiftly placed over it. An arm about her waist lifted her to her feet. The nightmare still gripped her and she was unable to see in the darkened room. Her teeth fastened on a finger. She heard clearly the hiss of indrawn breath, but the hold on her did not slacken, and she was hurriedly bundled out of the chamber, her heart beating so loudly that she thought she would suffocate.

CHAPTER FOUR

ONCE THE door had closed behind them, the hand was taken from Philippa's mouth.

'Don't say a word,' hissed Guy, keeping hold of her arm.

'Why didn't you say it was you?' Philippa came fully awake. He made no answer, only hushing her, and pulling her down the stairs with some haste. 'Guy?' she whispered.

He pulled open the door that led to the stableyard, before facing her. 'Can't you ever do as you are told?' he muttered. 'Who did you think it was? Your teeth nearly went through to the bone!' He sucked his finger.

'I was having a dream,' she murmured, shivering as her bare feet touched the cobbles. 'How could I tell it was you!' She ached all over, and was in no mood for such a conversation. 'What are we doing here?'

'No questions.' His tone was a little gentler. 'Put your shoes on,' he handed them to her.

'Guy, I'm too stiff to walk today. I'm sorry.'

'Nobody's asking you to,' he surprised her by saying. 'Just put them on, and be quiet.'

'What is this all about?' Philippa asked in a low voice.

'Why do women always want to know everything? Just do as you're told. I won't be long.' Guy disappeared into the stables, reappearing only a few moments later, leading a horse.

'Who does...' she began.

'Don't ask! Just get up!' Guy commanded impatiently. 'You'll have the whole inn awake! Do we have to have a conversation at this time of morning, and in this way?' His hands were on her waist, and before she could speak another word she was sitting sideways, clutching at the saddle, while with some stealth Guy led the horse out on to the road. He shot the upstairs window a glance before climbing up before her. 'You had better make yourself more comfortable, as we are going to ride fast, I hope!'

Philippa clutched the back of his doublet as the horse's pace increased, and for at least half an hour she did not speak, all her attention on not relaxing her hold on Guy. Eventually they slackened speed and she loosened her grip, realising as she did so how tense she had held herself since they left the inn, expecting at every moment a shout of 'Thief!'

'Whose horse is this?' she asked, although she had already guessed.

'Does it matter?' There was amusement in his tone.

'The pardoner's?'

'Why ask, if you know?' He began to sing softly.

'You didn't like the man?' she insisted, realising that he had deliberately made him drunk.

'What do you think? I considered our need greater than his.' He eased his shoulders and rubbed his neck. He had slept little, and was as stiff as Philippa claimed to be.

'So you stole his horse. How will he get away?' She did not really care.

'He'll walk. His trade can wait. And I didn't steal it. We struck a bargain when he was in his cups. Not that I think he will remember when he wakes with a splitting head. Perhaps he will think it a miracle that his horse has been replaced by a silver ring studded with garnets red as any blood spilt by the saints,' said Guy in an uneven voice.

'And I thought . . .'

'Thought what?' He twisted his neck and glanced at her. 'That I wasted my time talking to his kind? I hate his sort: selling forgiveness; tricking the poor. Perhaps he'll think it's retribution catching up with him, and change his ways. I had to do it. I knew you couldn't walk to London.'

'No,' she said quietly, experiencing an unexpected glow. 'Thank you.'

There was a hint of warmth in his blue eyes before the long dark lashes swept down, masking his expression. When he spoke, his voice was toneless. 'Taking care of you is my business, and we must get to London before the peasants.'

Philippa felt suddenly depressed. To Guy Milburn, she was only a piece of baggage that he wished to dispose of as soon as possible. How she wanted the journey to be over! Nervously she glanced behind her, for her fear of the peasants was very real. Fear bred hatred, without needing a just cause for such strong emotion... although she did have enough cause!

'Do you think there is a chance of the peasants entering London?' she asked abruptly, pushing back a dangling braid that tickled her cheek.

Guy hesitated before answering; he had been wondering the same thing himself. 'I hope not. It will surely be known in the city that they are marching this way and they will be making preparations. When I was there last week, the unrest in Kent and Essex was the main topic of conversation in my friend's home, although James seemed to think that there are those in the city who would welcome the rebels. It is not only the serfs who resent the poll-tax and those who lord it over them. Apprentices and journeymen are dissatisfied with their present lives.'

'I—I did not think of you having friends in London. Are you in the city often?' If he could be in London often, what about Hugo?

'At least twice a year on business. I come with the wool—for it to be inspected and taxed, and to go with it to Calais,' Guy explained. 'I have been doing so only since 1377, when it became worth my while to bring the packhorses south.'

'Were you in London during the coronation, then? I looked for Sir Hugo among those about the Duke of Lancaster, but I could not see him.' She remembered her disappointment. A young squire in the livery of Lancaster had smiled at her, but that was all, and she had gone home dejected.

'We were both there. My wife was one of the ladies in the Castilian Duchess Constancia's train,' he added after only a momentary hesitation. 'Hugo did not go to Westminster with the procession.'

'Your wife? I did not think...do not remember your being betrothed.' Philippa suffered a peculiar sinking feeling in her stomach.

'We weren't betrothed,' he said in a noncommittal tone. 'I remember that even Lancaster was cheered in London then. It was a happy occasion. Wine flowed from fountains, and the houses were decked with cloth of gold and silver.' There was a pause.

'Did you see the ceremony?' Her voice bridged the awkward silence. Or was it only she who noted the unexpected tension in the air? A wife! Why had he not mentioned a wife before?

Guy nodded. 'He looked so young, yet beautiful in his white robes, swearing to preserve and maintain the laws of the realm...to do justice and show mercy. All those that had disagreed laid down their quarrels that day. But...' He shrugged.

'Richard is only fourteen now, so one cannot expect... Given time, though, he could be as great a soldier as his father,' she insisted.

Guy shook his head. 'The king is more like his mother—Joan, the fair maid of Kent. The days when his father and grandfather won victory after victory in France are over. He will not bring them back.'

'You sound very sure,' said Philippa stiffly, easing herself into a more comfortable position and a little away from his back.

'Warfare has changed, but the council don't seem to understand that. How long is it since foreign ships sailed up the Thames and sacked Gravesend?' He twisted in the saddle and looked at her. 'You live in the south and surely know of the events that have occurred? We have the Scots in the north—you have the Spanish and French.' His mouth twisted and his eyes were slightly apologetic. 'But this isn't talk for women. Do you not wish to speak of something else?'

'Just because I am a woman, I don't shut my eyes to such matters,' she protested, her face serious. 'Besides, the danger was averted. My father told me how our sea-faring men from the coast fought off the enemy... Even John Philipot, a London grocer and a member of parliament, fitted out a squadron at his own expense and captured fifteen Spanish ships—and their Scottish commander—recovering many lost prizes!'

'I swear you would have liked to have been there,' murmured Guy, amused. 'James is a grocer, and a member of the victuallers' guild. Some of his property was involved, and he and I went with John Philipot. It wasn't really exciting. I've had better fights against pirates in the Channel!'

'You make being a wool merchant appear almost as hazardous as being a knight. Is it so dangerous?' She wondered if his wife worried about him when he was not at home. Did he have children? A son, perhaps?

'It can be risky, and if the pirates win the day and carry off our wool—costly.' He shrugged. 'So far I've been fortunate in that it has not happened to me. But I am thinking, because of the risk and having to pay taxes every time I export, of having my wool woven in England. Already there are a number of Flemings in this country who weave in their own special way, and soon our own folk will learn that craft.'

'Flemings in Kent grow hops, to make beer,' said Philippa. 'It might be worth your while to visit them.'

'I have.' He fell silent, and so did she, and they both became wrapped up in their own thoughts.

It was getting on towards late evening when at last they stood on the south bank of the Thames amid the houses and gardens of Southwark. Across the river they could make out the walls of London, the houses packed tightly inside. To the right, on the far bank, was the Tower. It did not look so far away.

'The cattle are only now being driven in from the fields,' said Guy, urging the horse in the direction of the bridge.

'Thank the saints, we have come in time,' murmured Philippa, easing herself awkwardly on the horse, almost light-headed with the alleviation of her anxiety.

On the other side of the Thames, Guy dismounted and turned to stare back across the water. His hand rested on the horse's mane, and for a short while they stayed there, watching the drawbridge being pulled up.

'I never thought we would arrive! Well, yesterday I didn't,' said Philippa in a dreamy voice. 'Even though you walked the feet off me. You were a bully—but it worked! I never thought I had such strength.'

Guy smiled up at her. 'As a woman, you truly amazed me. And whenever I thought you were bound to pause, you put on a spurt. My brother is a fortunate man.' His fingers curled about her hand and he lifted it to his lips. 'I salute you, Philippa.' His mouth brushed the palm of her hand before he dropped it. Seizing the horse's bridle, he led her away from the river.

Philippa could not understand her overwhelming desire to burst into tears, but she did not give way to her emotions while she gazed about her. The shadows were deepening beneath the solars that projected on wooden pillars above them. Women with handcarts still cried their wares, offering eels, pewter pots and meat pies. A tipler stood at a corner trying to sell drinks from tiny flasks to passers-by. Guy did not pause, but turned right at a corner, and instantly Philippa was confused.

'This is not the way to the Temple,' she declared involuntarily.

He looked up. 'No, but we can't spend the night in the streets, and it is too late to search for your uncle now. Tomorrow will be soon enough. I am taking you to the home of my friend James Wantsum. It's not far.'

It was still warm between the houses—stifling, in truth. Town life had never appealed to Guy, and the year he had spent in London with Catalina several years earlier had made him vow never to do so again. He felt a yearning, almost painful, for the fells of his northern country, although he did not relish the idea of taking Philippa with him. If he could find the uncle, maybe he could accompany them so that they would not be alone together so much.

'This friend—does he have a wife?' asked Philippa, staring down at his dark head coated with dust. She was a little anxious about meeting Master Wantsum.

'James is wed to my cousin Beatrice, and they will both make you welcome.' He glanced up at her. 'She will provide you with a change of clothing—probably a gown she has grown out of. You won't go hungry under Beatrice's roof!'

He made her sound a woman of ample proportions, and he had already said that his friend was a grocer. Philippa remembered her father telling her about the corruption that was prevalent in London. Many of the aldermen used bribes to gain power for themselves and their guilds. The victuallers was one of the most power-ful, and included vintners, fishmongers and the grocers. Because they had the sole right to sell foodstuffs, they

were often known to inflate prices when certain goods
were scarce, thus making huge profits.

'Here we are.'

Guy's voice roused her, and she glanced at the high
walls, then towards the gatehouse. A guard, dressed in
livery, nodded at Guy.

'Master's out, sir, at a council meeting. It's rumoured
that the peasants will be at the gates of London any day
now. Never thought I'd live to see such a happening!'
He shook his head dolefully.

'The bridge is closed to them, so you should be safe
here,' responded Guy.

The guard nodded, but a crease worried his pleasant,
blunt face. 'There's still ways and means, sir. A few boats
could bring them over here. There's many inside these
walls who would welcome them.'

'They would need more than a few boats!' Guy lifted
Philippa from the horse, and she leaned against him.
His arm stayed about her waist, and she was glad of its
support.

'A lot of them, are there?' The man scratched his nose,
gazing openly at Philippa. He had not seen Master Guy
with a woman since his wife died. 'Well, even if they
manage to get inside London town, and I doubt they
will, they won't get inside these walls. Shall I see to your
horse, sir?'

Guy nodded, and then led Philippa through the gates
and across the courtyard towards a building standing four
square at the far end. A light shone from a window on
the ground floor.

Guy knocked before entering, ushering Philippa before
him into the hall. Blinking in the light of so many
candles, her eyes focused on a woman seated on a settle,
busy with sewing.

Mistress Wantsum rose swiftly, her hand going to her
well-formed bosom. Then she smiled and came forward,
both hands outstretched. 'You have arrived safely, Guy!

James will be so relieved. All the talk is of the peasants in Kent and Essex. He is at the council now, arguing the matter, I shouldn't wonder. He says too many of the council members are for caution, for not provoking the peasants, since the king's uncles are out of the city.' Her voice was warm and low, with the slightest Lancashire accent.

Taking both her hands in his, Guy kissed her rosy plump cheek. 'I beg pardon for arriving at such an hour, Beatrice. Also, I have brought you a visitor.' He brought Philippa forward. 'This is Mistress Philippa Cobtree... Philippa, my cousin, Mistress Beatrice Wantsum.'

Mistress Wantsum took her hand and pressed it warmly. 'You are welcome, my dear, but you look very tired. Was the journey arduous?'

'Arduous!' Philippa flashed a smile at Guy.

'Arduous is not the word!' he said, and proceeded to tell Beatrice what had happened. 'But we made the journey to seek Philippa's uncle William in London.' He yawned.

'What am I thinking of!' Beatrice clapped a hand to her head. 'You must sit down—and I shall get you something to eat and drink. Mistress Cobtree, please, do sit down.'

Murmuring her thanks, Philippa sat gingerly on the edge of a settle, watching her hostess as she bustled over to the table. Smaller but plumper than herself, she had dark brown hair, braided and contained in openwork casing each side of her pretty round face. Her scarlet silk gown was cut low at the neck, and a gem brooch sparkled on her bosom. She poured wine and brought it over to them. Guy took the cup and sat down beside Philippa.

'I shall leave you a few moments to go and tell the maids to bring some food. I shall not delay.' Beatrice bustled out of the hall, leaving the two travellers wearily contemplating their surroundings.

Philippa scrubbed at her face with her sleeve, feeling strangely shy, now that she was alone with Guy again. What did Mistress Wantsum think of her? Although she had shown sympathy and kindness, she would be extremely practical, and not one given to dreams, she thought, trying to keep her mind from dwelling on how close Guy was sitting. His thigh was warm against hers, and she was very conscious of it, but she could not have moved away even if her life had depended on it. How weary she was—unbelievably so! Yet she had continued to walk while convinced that she could not put one foot in front of the other. Gazing down at her feet, she noticed a hole in the toe of her shoe.

'You've nearly worn them out.' It was as though Guy had read her thoughts.

'Ay! You got me here, though. I don't think I could travel another step, I am so tired.'

'You think not? If you had to, you would.' He put his arm along the back of the settle just behind her, and stretched his legs out.

'I don't think . . .' She broke off, and yawned, then took a sip of wine, and closed her eyes, leaning back.

'What do you think? That you couldn't?' His fingers moved slightly to rest on the curve of her neck. He felt lazily content just to sit and gaze at her profile. Her downswept lashes brushed the sunburnt curve of her cheek, and he noted that freckles crowded the bridge of her nose and her upper cheeks.

'Hmmm!' Philippa nodded after several silent stretching seconds, and then took another drink of wine. Her body was already responding to its soothing properties, and because she was at rest after so many tense hours. She should really move away from beneath the caressing touch of his fingers, but that was also soothing, and she was so comfortable; even the silence between them was companionable. Yet she should not be thinking, or feeling, like this! He had a wife—and she herself was betrothed to his brother. Still she did not move.

'What do you know about love, Philippa?'

The question took her completely by surprise, so that her eyes flew open and she stared straight into his face. 'Love? I don't understand?' Her cheeks were warming, and her fingers trembled about the stem of the silver goblet.

'Has no man ever spoken words of love to you, truly?' The blue eyes drowsily studied her. 'I still find that incredible. You have not even had a courtly lover?'

'No—and—no! Why do you ask? Did your brother ask you to find out such things of me? I told you I am chaste. My father had me watched carefully.' She could not disguise her irritation on remembering how strictly he had guarded her. 'I have read of such practices, of course,' she added in an uneven voice, 'and consider that it might be quite delightful to have a man prostrate at one's feet enslaved by one's beauty and virtues!'

Guy's mouth eased into a smile. 'Speaking as a man, I find such practices over-rated. To worship—to look upon, but not to touch. I think my desire would soon pall.'

'Perhaps.' Her nose crinkled. 'I am not a goddess, after all, and I suspect I have more faults than virtues. My mother was wont to say that I was too thin, too freckled, and too much of a dreamer.'

'A dreamer?' His fingers stilled. 'What do you dream? Do you remember your dreams?' His face was suddenly serious.

Philippa frowned. 'Sometimes I have dark dreams.' A shudder rippled through her, remembering just a part of the dream that had kept recurring lately. 'But,' not wanting to think about that, 'my mother did not refer to sleeping dreams, but to my habit of what my brothers called painting pictures in my head. I used to make up tales—as well as listen to them.' She flushed and fell silent. He might think her strange, just as her mother had.

'What do you listen to? Psalters and books of hours...or romances?' She had been hurt, he thought, having watched the expressions flit across her face.

'What if I replied that I know of Dante and Boccaccio?' Her eyes challenged him. 'Also the Arthurian tales of chivalry, and Geoffrey Chaucer's "Troilus and Criseyde".' There was triumph in her voice.

'I would say that for a woman you have much talent.'

'Do you know of Master Wycliffe's heretical works?' she asked.

He nodded. 'I have also heard with great interest his translation of the scriptures into English. One tale appeals to me especially, about a son who leaves home and wastes his inheritance, but is welcomed with much love when he comes home seeking forgiveness from his father. I understand it to be a story about God and his forgiveness. Indeed it is about love.'

'About God's love—not about retribution?' She laughed mirthlessly, touching her blistered toe with careful fingers.

'You don't believe in love?' he asked, leaning forward and resting his elbows on his knees. His face was parallel with hers.

Philippa knew then that they were not talking about God. 'Oh, I believe in love,' she declared recklessly. 'But I don't ever intend falling in love. Love means suffering, and I have suffered enough... To languish because some man will not smile on me is too foolish to contemplate!'

'What of Hugo?' he persevered, smiling slightly, interested in her views, thinking her a woman of many surprises.

Philippa took a deep draught of the wine before answering. 'Now that is foolishness you speak! What has love to do with marriage?' she mocked. 'Real love is ill-fated and is never reciprocated. Should one indeed marry, love would die because of the commonplace task of everyday living. One would see that the other was not perfect, after all, but possessed many a human fault,' she finished unsteadily.

'I never thought to come upon a woman of such good sense. We think alike, Philippa, and I did not realise it. My experience taught me that is so, but as for you...?' Slowly his long-lashed gaze scrutinised her features. 'You know then what marriage is about?'

'Of course!' She sat up, resting her back against the wooden upright of the settle. 'It is about duty and doing what one's parents dictate. About protection, rearing children, and about what one can bring to one's spouse in the way of possessions.'

'How dull it sounds!' He leaned back, his elbow on the top of the settle. 'To worship at the shrine of another's wife, to flirt, to languish...is that not how the troubadours see love? It is a courtly love. Look, but don't touch! Do you know the poem Chaucer wrote? His White Lady is said to be Blanche of Lancaster, John of Gaunt's first wife. He wrote it for the duke after she had died of plague.'

Philippa nodded. She felt as if they were treading on dangerous ground. Was he flirting with her? Had he tired of his own wife, and sought a little excitement elsewhere? She was furiously indignant. 'Chaucer might have felt love for the duchess, but as for the duke... Does he not have another wife now? He also has a mistress whom he has forced to live in open adultery with him—and their children. I count his actions as cold and calculated!' She flung the words at him.

Guy's brow had creased. 'Why so angry, Philippa? Can you blame a man in such a situation for trying to have it so—to live with his love? See! I disagree with you. I think he loves his mistress and would marry her if he could, but would it make any difference to how they feel for each other? Having consummated that love, will it still burn itself out in the everyday task of living? Or, if it is kindled the more often, will it not flare and burn steadily?' Guy pressed in a low voice, watching the conflicting emotions flicker in her green eyes.

Unsettled by his argument, Philippa did not know how to answer, but eventually replied. 'For most, love is a dream, and just as unlikely to come true—in the way one would wish.'

'Is it? I wonder. I know some whose relationship I envy.'

There was a silence, and into it broke a voice. 'What were you two talking about when I came in? You sounded so intent.' Beatrice set down the tray she was carrying. A man-servant followed, carrying another.

'We did not hear you coming, Beatrice.' Guy stood and walked stiffly to the table. He sat on a bench, looking up at his cousin, but he addressed Philippa. 'Do you remember, Philippa, that Dante's ill-fated love was named Beatrice? He was only nine years old when they met, and he never forgot her.'

She got up and came towards him. 'But they did not marry, I think. I doubt they even knew each other when he wrote about her. He made her out to be so perfect a maid that, eventually, she was made a saint.' She yawned, and took a seat opposite him.

'By Saint Beatrice herself, Guy, what a subject for conversation at this time of night! No wonder Mistress Cobtree is ready to fall asleep,' exclaimed Beatrice, amusement in her voice. 'Eat, and then sleep,' she commanded, sinking to the bench next to Philippa. 'Guy and my husband often discuss Dante, and it sends me to my bed. Myself, I am more concerned with this life, and what we are to have for dinner on the morrow!'

Philippa's expression lightened. 'You have set before us a feast, Mistress Wantsum. Thank you,' she said quietly.

'It is my pleasure.' Beatrice beamed. 'Help yourselves to what you want.'

Philippa forgot the unease she had felt over the conversation between Guy and herself, but the sudden exhilaration she had experienced was harder to dismiss. Sitting so close to him, talking about love, was something she could never forget, she was certain. She began to eat.

Beatrice smiled with delight, watching them enjoy their food. The tarts were delicious; the dried fruit in the egg custard tangy and sweet. When they were both replete, they sat back, sipping another goblet of exceedingly good Malmsey wine.

Guy had been right, thought Philippa, her eyes closed: she had eaten and drunk well beneath the Wantsums' roof. The conversation between her hostess and Guy passed over her head, for she was almost asleep.

Then Beatrice was at her elbow, shaking her. 'Come, my dear, you would be better in your bed. And Guy tells me that your feet are sore, and some salve would not come amiss. I shall show you to your chamber.'

Philippa rubbed her eyes. 'I have need to wash, Mistress Wantsum. I am so dirty!'

'There is water in your chamber. Come. Guy is waiting to see James, so we shall go up together.' She put an arm about her waist and helped her up.

For only a second did Philippa's sleepy gaze hold Guy's, then she was going with Beatrice through a door at the side of the high table, and up the stairs. They passed through several rooms, but she was too drowsy to notice anything but that they were dimly lit, and that in one the bed was extremely large and covered with an embroidered coverlet, with a canopy above it, with silk hangings on each side.

The room they stopped in was smaller, but warm. The bed was narrow. On a stand, a metal bowl steamed gently. A young maid, yawning, was placing a towel on a stool. She bobbed a curtsy.

'You will help Mistress Cobtree to undress and wash, Marjorie. She has lost all, because of the peasants.' Beatrice bustled forward, having relinquished her hold on Philippa's arm. 'You have the soap?' She turned to Philippa. 'It is new and from Castile. The finest!'

'We have talked of Castile,' muttered Philippa, walking unsteadily towards the stand. 'His wife is from Castile, isn't she?' She stifled a yawn.

'If you refer to Catalina, my dear,' murmured Beatrice, placing a small jar on a stool, 'she died three years ago, in giving birth to a stillborn son. He has a daughter, Constance, but she often stays with my brother's young family in Liverpool. A woman called Ann lives in, and keeps house for him...' She shook her head. 'But there—Guy is in no haste to wed again, and is busy trying to make his fortune.'

Philippa stared at her, her eyelids drooping. 'I did not know she was dead. He never told me.'

'He doesn't talk about it. To Guy, the past is the past. There is only one hurt he finds difficult to forget.' Beatrice sighed, automatically smoothing the coverlet, her face absorbed. Then she shook herself. 'Now you get into bed, my dear, and I'll see you in the morning. Then I shall bring you some gowns to choose from.' She smiled and left the room.

Philippa stared after her, a lightness in her heart—the meaning of which she did not intend to think deeply about. Then she turned and submitted herself to the maid's ministrations.

CHAPTER FIVE

PHILIPPA WOKE to the sun squinting through the edges of the shutters. The knock came again, and sleepily she called, 'Come in!'

Beatrice entered, carrying some garments over her arm. 'I have brought you the gowns I promised.' Her expression was serious. 'Guy thought you might rather stay in bed this morning than go with him to the Temple.'

'Stay in bed? But he doesn't know my uncle, and it would be much better if I went with him.' She would have scrambled out of bed, except that she had no clothes on.

'Now you are not to excite yourself. He is going with James, and they know your uncle's name. They are bound to find him. Besides, it would be safer if you stayed here.' Beatrice set the gowns down on the foot of the bed. 'You should dress and then come down, and the maids shall prepare us some collops to break our fast.'

Philippa frowned. 'What is it? What has happened?' She would have risen, but Beatrice pushed her back against the pillows.

'You must not worry, Mistress... Oh, this is silly. You must call me Beatrice, and I shall call you Philippa. It is likely that you will be in London for some days.'

'What do you mean? Tell me, Mis— Beatrice, please!' She gripped the coverlet tightly.

After the barest of hesitations, Beatrice spoke. 'The peasants are on the other side of the Thames at Blackheath, and are demanding to see the king. Apparently last night they set the prisoners free at the Marshalsea and set fire to several buildings.'

Philippa's face paled. 'Oh no!'

'You are not to be downcast.' The older woman's expression was uneasy. 'We have my husband's men on watch at the gates, and they are locked. And, besides, they might never set foot this side of the Thames.'

'Your guard said that there were men on this side who would be willing to let them in. There are ways and means, he said,' murmured Philippa soberly.

'He was probably exaggerating.' Beatrice took her hand. 'You must not worry. The council will have to do something now that the peasants are here!' She forced a smile.

Philippa was not reassured. 'They should have acted before now, and not allowed matters to go so far! The danger is real.' She removed Beatrice's hand, swung her legs out of the bed, and grabbed one of the gowns at its foot. 'I must find out what is happening.' Her voice was emotionless, her expression impassive.

'Philippa! You cannot go outside the gates. Guy said . . .'

'Guy said! Guy said!' Her fear erupted into a tirade. 'He forced me to walk and walk, with my feet bleeding, telling me all the time that we must get to London before the peasants, and then we would be safe! But it seems to me that I have escaped one horror only to face a more terrible one. I should not have come with him! I should not have come!' She drew a shaky breath. 'But I will go to seek my uncle, whatever he says.' She inched the green gown towards her.

Beatrice placed a hand over it. 'If that is how you feel, then I shall go with you,' said she in resigned tones. 'But there is no need for such haste.' Sitting on the edge of the bed, she looked at Philippa's rebellious expression. 'It is much too late to catch up with them. You must let Marjorie braid your hair, and I shall give you a head-dress. Do not be angry with Guy; he is doing what he thinks is best for you,' she pleaded. 'Really, you should rest those feet of yours, and I must find you some shoes. The only thing is that my feet are smaller than yours,' she said, with a pucker of her smooth white brow.

Philippa's anger partially dissolved and she experienced a stab of mortification. 'I'm sorry. You must think me ungrateful, but truly I'm not. It is just that the last few days...' A tremor quivered in her voice. 'Everything changed so suddenly. Still I find it hard to realise that it is all true. That my father is dead, and I have no roof over my head. I know Guy meant well...but I must find my uncle.'

'Guy will do his best to find him, my dear. But even if he doesn't, he will take you to Yorkshire.'

Philippa nodded slowly, her expression not showing the disquiet she felt. To go to Yorkshire alone with Guy Milburn would certainly be unwise. *She* had to find her uncle, despite all Beatrice's remarks about Guy and her husband doing so! If matters were as serious as they sounded, they might not have time to search for him properly. As for staying here meekly and resting her feet! She had been able to walk to London, so to search its streets should not be beyond her capabilities. Besides, she had a mind to see herself how matters were. She bit her lip and regarded Beatrice seriously. 'Do not be angry with me,' she pleaded, 'but I must go. My father told me to stay and wait, and he never returned. I cannot remain here just waiting and waiting. You have shown much patience and kindness to me, so please understand? And there is no need for you to come with me. I know London well enough not to lose myself.'

Beatrice's expression showed shock. 'But you cannot go alone! What will Guy say? You are a lady! If they do get into London, God only knows what might happen to you.'

'I'll risk it,' declared Philippa in a determined tone. If you are worried about my looking like a lady, there is no need. Pass me that brown homespun in the corner, and my own shoes. My hair can stay as it is.'

'Oh, my dear, should you be doing this?' wailed Beatrice, sinking on to the bed.

'What else is there for me to do? There was rioting and pillaging in Canterbury, but I survived.' For a moment she quailed, remembering it might have been different if Guy had not been with her. 'Everything will be all right this time, unless they get inside the walls, of course.' She scrambled out of the bed naked, and swiftly snatched up the gown from the corner, not looking at the older woman. It was the work of minutes to dress and pull on her shoes, not without some difficulty or pain.

'Please think again!' Beatrice jumped up and clutched her arm. 'Or at least ask one of the guards to go with you.'

'I'll think about it,' said Philippa in a soft voice, prying her fingers loose.

Beatrice nodded. 'Do be careful.'

'I shall.' Impulsively she kissed her cheek and then left the chamber swiftly.

The guard stared at her in amazement. 'Let you out, mistress? Is this some kind of jape? The master said we were not to open the gates for nobody but himself and Master Guy.'

'He meant not to let anybody *in*, fool!' she snapped, impatient to be on her way. 'Now open up and let me through. I have urgent business to attend to at the Temple.'

The man still looked doubtful. 'I'm not too sure about that.'

'Of course that is what he meant! You are not to let any peasants or unruly elements through the gates. That is if they do get into London, which is unlikely. Now let me through!' she commanded imperiously.

'I suppose you're right. Perhaps one of the other men can go with you.'

'Thank you, but no!' She flashed him a smile to soften her words, pleased to have got her way, but she had no fancy for having one such as he dogging her heels. As he opened the gate she was through swiftly and running up the street before he could change his mind and come after her.

Philippa soon slowed down, her feet too sore to keep up such a pace, and the crowds in the streets impeded her progress. The Temple was beyond the Ludgate to the west, so she had some way to go, and she wanted to find her uncle and return to the house as swiftly as possible. She fretted at the delay the crowds caused. As she gazed about her, there was no sign of that hunger and fanaticism that had marked the faces in Canterbury, so perhaps everything would be all right, after all!

But as she neared the river she heard a great roar, similar to the sound in Canterbury cathedral, which caused her to stop in her tracks. For a moment she was unable to go on, then easing her shoulders and swallowing her fear, her feet took her in the direction of the noise. Worming her way through the crowd, she made the most of her small stature to force her way through the narrowest of spaces as far as the river bank.

At first the sun dancing on the surface of the Thames caused her to shut her eyes briefly before she could take in the full impact of the sight. The vision of colourful barges pulling away from the far bank and the mass of men on the other side burst upon her as she opened them again. It was true, then—they had arrived at Blackheath! Was that some of them in the barges? No! By the saints, it appeared to be Richard and several of his chancellors! Because of the din, she could not hear what was being said. Had some settlement been reached? Not according to the arrows that were winging their way across the water to the barges!

Where were Guy and Master Wantsum? Were they in this crowd? For the first time she thought of what Guy might say if he found her here, and her spirits quailed. Then, remembering her reasons for taking such a chance, she began to push her way back the way she had come until the crowd thinned.

The Ludgate was almost in sight, and she was just congratulating herself on getting so far without too much trouble when the thought struck her that the gate might be closed. What should she do? Continue or go back? Had Guy and Master Wantsum thought of that? Had he just soothed her with words to keep her quietly waiting in the house? Had he gone elsewhere with his friend and was not looking for her uncle at all? No! Surely he would not lie to her! She would go on and find out for herself.

So caught up was she in her thoughts that she did not heed the men coming alongside her. An elbow caught her sharply on the cheek, and she gasped in pain. The man turned and looked at her, and seized her shoulder before she could back away.

'Why, if it isn't Mistress Cobtree? Who'd have believed it possible to meet you here—and dressed for the rebellion, I see!' mocked the sneering hateful voice.

'Let go of me instantly, Tom Carter!' she said coldly, wriggling under his hard fingers, trying not to show her fear.

'I'll be damned if I will!' The arrogant unshaven face was thrust close to hers. 'Where's my sister?'

'Rose? She isn't with me.' She wrenched her shoulder from his grip. 'I thought her with you.' Her eyes were like chilly flames.

'No, the stupid bitch ran off, saying she was going to find you.'

'At least she has a sense of loyalty!' Her heart lifted momentarily.

'Loyalty!' He spat in the dust. 'I told her she was a fool and no sister of mine. You talk of loyalty, but what of hers to me—her own brother?' His brown eyes hardened, and he grabbed her arm cruelly. 'I've lost a sister and gained a mistress!' He roared at his own joke, his nails digging into her skin through the fabric as she stared at him, not struggling, although her knees were shaking. Suddenly he pulled her, so that she fell forward on her knees. 'You'd best come with me,' he snarled. 'You need someone to take care of you.'

'None of that now, Tom! Let her go!' A man in a grey tunic pushed into the space next to her as a crowd began to gather. He took her other arm and pulled her up, despite Tom's angry glare.

'Adam!' Philippa gazed at the ruddy face of the smith. He was a big man, much taller and broader than Tom, a freeman who had rented land from her father. Never had she understood why he had sided with the peasants. 'I never thought to see *you* here!'

'Nor I you. Best get away from here—could be a heap of trouble,' he said calmly. 'Don't reckon you should be involved.'

'Why don't you mind your own affairs, Adam Smith?' hissed Tom in a furious voice, attempting to elbow him out of the way.

''Tis my affair! Ain't you done enough? It should never have come to killing!' He pushed him away. 'You run, Mistress Philippa! Get out of London if you can!' He blocked Tom's swinging fist, shielding her with his bulk. She hesitated only a moment, then ran back the way she had come.

Her throat was tight with unshed tears. So they had got through the gates somehow. How many of her own people were in London? What had brought Adam, a good honest man, if blunt in speech, who had argued rights and equality in the past with her father without their falling out? What had driven him to join the likes of Tom? Could it have been Rose's brother who had killed her father? She limped along, frustrated rage surging, knowing that there was nothing she could do at the moment to bring him to justice. Rose! He had said she was seeking her, just as she had said she would. But how could they find each other in the warren of streets and alleys that made up so much of London—and in such crowds?

She was instantly aware that houses were being broken into, just as in Canterbury. Some of the citizens had even brought out barrels of ale and were bidding the peasants drink, to quench their thirst after their long march. Swiftly she quickened her pace, realising that soon the streets would not be safe. The peasants would soon be roaring drunk and even more dangerous than now.

It was like a miracle to find the Wantsums' house untouched by the happenings elsewhere, and she realised that she had given little thought since meeting Tom and Adam to what Guy would say if he had returned before her.

The guard greeted her with some relief and the news that the men had returned. Trepidation clutched at her stomach as she slowly went up the path to the house.

Both men stood listening to Beatrice's rather breathless voice explaining where she had gone. As she entered the hall, Guy whirled around, his expression one of relief, before a scowl darkened his face. 'Where the devil have you been?'

'I'm all right,' she insisted, limping over to them.

'You don't look all right!' He stood in front of her, staring down at the bruise on her cheek.

'I'm tired, that's all.'

He touched the bruise and felt her quiver. 'That's all? How did you come by this?'

'It was an accident . . . an elbow.' She wished Guy did not look so grim.

'Are you certain it was an accident?' He put a hand on her shoulder. 'Nobody hurt you?'

Her bottom lip trembled. 'Why should anybody hurt me?'

'Something's frightened you. I can feel you trembling. What is it, Philippa?'

'I—I saw two men from my manor, that is all.' She swallowed. 'One of them was Rose's brother—and I think he killed my father. Adam, the other man, prevented him from harming me.'

'From harming you! Then this was no accident!' The blue eyes darkened. 'You were mad to go outside, and you must not do so again. Not that the guard will let you through a second time!'

'But I must go out! I have to find Rose. Out there, she could be looking for me!' She bit her lower lip to prevent it trembling.

'Have you lost your wits? How are you going to find her?'

'I don't know, b-but I have to try. You could take me with you next time you go out.' Her green eyes shimmered as she gazed up at him.

Guy drew in a harsh breath. 'Take you with me? I'd not take a cat out there at the moment! As for looking for this Rose, we'll have a hard enough time finding your uncle.'

'You did not find him, then?' She sniffed hard, trying to stop the tears.

'No. And I presume you didn't?' His voice softened.

She shook her head. 'I didn't get as far as the Ludgate. I thought it might be closed.'

'It's open, all right. The Essex peasants were let in that way.'

She felt no surprise at the news. 'Perhaps tomorrow?'

'We'll try later. Not you.' His face grew gentle, and he brought her close. 'I am responsible to my brother for your safety. Be patient—perhaps tomorrow we can seek your Rose.'

'I'll try to be patient,' she answered in an uneven voice.

'Good lass!' A crinkle furrowed his cheek. 'Now go and change before we eat.'

She nodded, but before going upstairs, she apologised to the Wantsums for causing them anxiety.

'You mustn't be worrying, Mistress Philippa. Leave the search for your uncle to Guy and me. We shall do our uttermost to find him.' Master Wantsum was short and stocky, with an intelligent, square face beneath a russet liripipe worn like a turban wrapped about his dark brown hair.

'I'm sure you will, but I do not wish you to run into danger for my sake,' she replied soberly.

'I have no intention of doing so—but we shall take some of the men with us. We have to check the warehouse down by the waterfront, and Guy wishes to see if a ship has docked that is due any day now. There are also the Flemish weavers to see. Any trouble like this, and foreigners suffer.' He smiled kindly down at her. 'Now you go and change—we'll wait dinner for you.'

Philippa thanked him, liking him, and did as she was told. Not having eaten all day, she was hungry!

The two women sat over their wine in the hall. The men had departed, despite Guy's saying that he would not take a cat outside into the dangers that lurked there. It seemed that men could court such dangers, but not women. She said as much to Beatrice, who nodded.

'It has always been so. I worry for James, for he is an alderman and could easily be a target for those seeking to settle old scores. The London commons are certain to join the peasants.'

'When first I set eyes on Guy, I thought he had some sympathy for the rebels' cause.' Philippa's voice was pensive.

'That is likely true.' Beatrice hesitated, then said, 'It might shock you, Philippa, but our great-grandfather was a serf.'

For a moment she made no reply, only glancing about the hall. It was better furnished than her father's had been: the tapestries were finer, the trestles and settles not so crudely made. 'That does surprise me.'

Beatrice smiled. 'Our grandfather it was who made the family's rise possible. He was clever, and the priest recognised it and took it upon himself to educate him a little. Because of his aptitude, he was brought to the attention of the steward on the manor. It was not long before he had the bailiff's job, although he was quite young.' She paused, and took a drink.

Philippa rested her elbows on the table, interested in anything that involved Guy.

'When the wars in France began, the steward went off to fight and left the manorial affairs in my grandfather's care. Normally his wife would have taken charge, but she had died a few months earlier. Under my grandfather's hands the manor prospered, and when the steward returned with his master, Henry of Lancaster...'

'The Duchess Blanche's father?' interrupted Philippa, her eyes bright. 'I understand now the connection between the Milburns and the Lancasters. Their riches are legendary!'

Beatrice nodded. 'To cut a long story short, our grandfather's aptitude for business led him to making enough money to buy his freedom, and to rent a parcel of land. Upon that he managed to live reasonably well with his wife and two sons. One was my father, who crossed the Pennines and married a Lancashire widow. The other was Guy's father, who went to France and met your father. Because of the fortunes of war, and the capture of certain French noblemen, who were ransomed, both came back the richer.'

'From rags to riches,' murmured Philippa, her face rapt. 'It makes a good tale.'

'It couldn't happen today,' sighed Beatrice. 'The ransoming, I mean. Guy and Hugo tried it. But now Guy and James are going into business together. They are in touch with some Flemish weavers and are considering not exporting all the wool, so as to avoid paying taxes.'

'Guy mentioned it to me. It is a good plan, and I hope it succeeds for him—for both of them.'

'So do I! Not that I have a head for business. James's mother did. After his father died quite young, it was she who kept their grocery business going until he was old enough to take over. One has to have a streak of ruthlessness and determination to get what one wants in this life.'

'That is true, and I don't know yet if I have such traits,' murmured Philippa. 'But then I have never had the opportunity to find out. Or even to think exactly what it is I want. Always I had to obey my father.'

'That is how it is for most women.' Beatrice put down her goblet and went over to the window. 'Shall we go outside in the garden? It is such a lovely day.'

'If you wish.' Philippa crossed the hall to stand at her shoulder, and suddenly she sniffed. 'I can smell smoke!' Her hands clenched into fists.

'They set the Marshalsea on fire,' muttered Beatrice, going pale. 'Let us go upstairs. From the windows we might be able to see what is happening in the city.'

'If you think we should.' Philippa had begun to quake inside, but she fought to conceal her fear.

When they went upstairs to the front chamber, they could see a pall of smoke in the sky over the buildings to the west. Then there came a muffled roar, and they clutched each other.

'By all the saints, what was that?' whispered Beatrice, her plump face quivering. It seemed to come from beyond the Ludgate, and more smoke was billowing, darkening the skyline.

'Come away,' cried Philippa, the colour draining from her face. 'There is nothing we can do but pray that they will be safe. We must stay calm.'

'Easier said than done,' said Beatrice shakily. They both sat down on the chest in the large bedchamber.

'Have you noticed that the shouts and cries of the rioting are clearer up here?' Her words were clearly enunciated, for Philippa was making great efforts not to panic, or to dwell on how it had been the day her father was murdered, or to think that somewhere in the area whence the smoke rose Guy might be looking for her uncle. Were more people burning with the buildings? Was Tom involved? A spurt of hatred set her pacing the floor. 'I wish we knew what was happening!' Hugging her breasts, she halted abruptly in front of Beatrice, then her expression changed. 'They should be safe. They could be at the docks.' She gave a limp smile.

'Ay,' said Beatrice, standing up. 'Let's go to the solar. It will be quieter there.'

It was quieter. Philippa stared over the garden to the rear of the house, laid out with lawns and paths, borders of roses, gillyflowers, marigolds and poppies. Then unexpectedly its peace enfolded her, soothing her spirit, and she seemed simply to exist in a golden moment of quiet in the sun that winked and sparkled through the glazed windows. The only disturbance came in the shape of one of the maids, who asked whether they wanted supper laid, but dinner had been late, and both shook their heads.

It was a period out of time, thought Philippa, and the peasant army might never have existed. But gradually she found herself becoming fidgety and tired, but could not rest. Tomorrow, if possible, she would insist on going with Guy wherever he went. She must find Rose! While Beatrice dozed, she paced the floor. Dusk fell, filling the room with shadows. The door opened, and the maid entered at a run.

'The master's home, and Master Guy has a cut on his head, but they seem unhurt otherwise,' she declared excitedly.

Beatrice woke with a start. 'What's that?'

The maid repeated her words.

'Oh, praise the holy Virgin, and here's me sleeping!' she cried, moving swiftly, her red skirts swishing on the wooden floor.

'She said Guy was hurt!' Philippa's hands shook as she pulled the door shut behind her.

'But it doesn't sound too serious.' Beatrice pressed her hand, and went before her.

Guy was sitting in the large carved oak chair normally occupied by James. There was blood on his cheek and at the corner of his right eye, which was swollen.

'A blow with a cudgel,' stated James, his dark brows lowered. There was a bowl on the table, and he was squeezing out a cloth. 'They had us hemmed in in one of the warehouses, but we managed to fight our way out and reach home.'

'Let me do that!' Philippa took the cloth from James, not seeing him exchange glances with Beatrice over her head, before going to sit beside her on the bench. He rubbed his chin against his wife's hair.

She wiped the blood from Guy's cheek. There was a long graze that must hurt, but he made no sign of it, suffering her touch. The eye was a different matter, and was already closing. She dabbed at the blood, gripping his chin with her other hand, overcome by an extraordinary calmness.

'Does it look as bad as James said it does?' he asked.

She jumped when Guy spoke, and raised her head to see his face. 'I'm sorry if I hurt you.' Her legs felt weak, and she had to force herself to be busy with the cloth and water.

'I have some goosegrease salve.' Beatrice handed her a tiny jar, and Philippa sank down on the edge of the bench, and with shaking fingers smoothed it on the cuts while Guy rested his head on the back of the chair.

How tired he looked! His eyes flickered open and met hers, and warmth flooded her.

'Pour some ale, there's a good lass!'

She filled the two cups near at hand and gave him one. For a second he gazed into its depths and then raised it in a salute before taking a long draught that emptied the vessel. Then he handed it back, asking her for more. The servants came in and set food on the table.

'I could not find your uncle.' Guy dug his spoon into a mound of rice and diced chicken in an onion sauce.

'You asked for him by name?' Philippa took a mouthful of food. Rice was an unexpected treat!

'I asked after him where I could,' he said, hesitating. 'All the lawyers and students had fled. I did not know where else to seek him after this second time, but I could try other places tomorrow. James knows several people who might help to find him. I am very sorry.'

'The blame is not yours.' Aimlessly Philippa pushed the food round the bowl. 'Thank you for trying, but it seems hopeless. As hopeless as my desire to find Rose.'

'Don't give up, Philippa.' Guy covered her hand with his, pressing it gently.

'What shall we do if we cannot find him?' Her fingers quivered under his, soothed, even as his touch sent a thrill through her.

'Then we shall have to go to Yorkshire.' He removed his hand.

'What of Rose?'

'We cannot search for a maid who might not even have reached London. How could she have kept up with the men?'

'I—I never thought of that,' she said slowly. 'But she is strong in body and spirit, and could do it. Did not I almost walk to London? She could come later.'

'Perhaps. But the sooner you are safely delivered to Hugo, the easier it will be.' His expression was stern, with no hint of the warmth that had been there a moment ago.

Her appetite deserted her. What a foolish chit she was to want more from him! She was merely his brother's betrothed—and he wished to be rid of her as soon as he could. The emotions that he stirred within her must be quashed, for there was no future in dreaming that there could be anything between them!

CHAPTER SIX

PHILIPPA SOUGHT for words to fill the sudden silence, and to take her mind from her dismal musings. 'We saw smoke in the west, and were anxious. Do you know what caused it?'

'The Savoy was set alight.' Guy grimaced lopsidedly, tearing a lump from the bread.

'John of Gaunt's palace?' She stared at him, her green eyes wide with dismay. The Savoy stood about a mile outside the western walls, where fields and gardens sloped down to the riverside from the Strand that linked London to Westminster. It was said to be furnished from the plunder of France.

'Did you say the Savoy was destroyed?' Beatrice's voice broke into her thoughts. Guy nodded. 'James, why did you not tell me? What a waste! It was such a beautiful place. How could they do such a thing?'

'Because they hate Duke John, that's why, my love. They feel they have an ancient score to settle with him. It's not only the peasants rioting—they have been incited to greater violence by the rabble in London. They've set light to those new houses and shops in Fleet Street, which seems utterly senseless to me.'

'What is the council going to do, James? They must do something, surely,' she said indignantly.

'They'll probably be deciding at this moment, love, but you must not fret. Now give me a smile, and as soon as supper is over we'll go to bed. Likely we mightn't get much sleep, but we shall rest more easily there than waiting for something to happen.'

'That is a good idea.' Beatrice forced a smile as James kissed her cheek before turning to Philippa.

'I am sorry we could not find your uncle. Perhaps tomorrow?'

'Perhaps—I hope,' returned Philippa, smiling slightly, before rising to her feet. Always it was tomorrow and she did not intend that the men should get an early start on her. If they were to go out, she would go also. 'I think I shall go to bed now.'

'You have had enough to eat?' asked Beatrice, gazing at her worriedly.

'Enough, thank you.'

'I'll escort you up.' Guy got to his feet, taking a candle from the table.

'It is not necessary, thank you,' said Philippa in a stiff voice. 'I know the way.'

'I'm tired too,' he said softly.

She nodded. Probably he was more than tired. Perhaps his head hurt? But she had no desire to be caught up in a senseless debate over whether it was safe for her to go out with him or not. She would rise earlier than he and be ready and waiting when he got up.

The candle set shadows scurrying up the narrow staircase. Guy's arm brushed hers and she was intensely conscious of the excitement such contact caused. What was it about this man? Needing to break the silence that seemed to wrap them round in a strange intimacy, she rushed into speech. 'Do not feel you have to go out for my sake, Guy. I don't want you to take risks.'

'Don't you?' She caught the glint of his teeth. 'Yet you would take risks yourself.'

'There was little risk. You faced more danger than I,' she flashed.

'I'm a man, and there's the difference.'

'I know the difference! But when it is my affairs you are about, I don't see why I can't come with you. Was it any different when we ran before the peasant army?'

'That was necessity,' he replied impatiently. 'It is worse out there now. Tomorrow I go out on business other than yours. There is a ship due from Calais, but it has not arrived yet. I have hopes of finding a passage to Kingston-on-Hull, and thence home.'

They came to her door, having passed through his chamber.

She tried a different tack. 'I have never been aboard a ship.' Her back was to her door. 'It should be safe enough at the waterfront for me to come with you.'

'Dammit, Philippa, doesn't anything frighten you?' He ruffled his hair with a jerky movement.

She hesitated, then said, 'Ay! And my fear is made worse when I am left behind waiting—waiting. When I see smoke...' She swallowed, unable to go on.

'I understand.' He touched her hair lightly, then his fingers brushed the curve of her cheek. 'I pray that the ship will be there. My one thought is to get you away from the dangers here in the city. Despite sea voyages having their perils, I want us to take that ship. You have spoken such good sense on several occasions, Philippa, so speak it now. Accept your limitations as a woman.'

'They are only limitations that men have set on us,' she said unsteadily, experiencing again a jumble of emotions.

'For your own good,' he said quietly.

She made no answer, knowing that some of what he said was true, and that there was little point in arguing about the rest. To say that she had a yearning to make her own decisions would sound like madness to him. Most men thought women utterly incapable of doing so.

'Thank you for tending my wounds.' He handed her the candle. 'Good night, Philippa. If anything disturbs you, just call, and I shall hear.' He turned away.

For a moment she stood there, staring at his retreating figure, then she fumbled for the handle and went into her chamber, undecided what to do.

* * *

'Philippa!' Beatrice's call sounded loud in the room, causing her to sit up swiftly. She yawned, and peered bleary-eyed at the older woman. Dressed in blue linen, and with her hair neatly bound up in a net, she yet managed to look jaded.

'What is it? Did you not sleep well? What has happened?'

'Does it show?' Beatrice gave a mirthless laugh. 'The men have already gone out. They were up at dawn! I could not bear my own company any longer, so, self-ishly, I came and woke you.' She sat on the bed.

'They have gone already? How could I have slept so long!' Philippa snatched up the white shift and green gown lying on the bed. 'He knew I wanted to go with him,' she stated vehemently.

'Guy?' Beatrice's brow wrinkled. 'He might have taken you with him, only a message came for James saying that the king is meeting with the peasants at Mile End this morning. Some of the other aldermen are going with him in the hope that they can come to an agreement with the peasants and persuade them to go home.'

'Oh!' Moodily she hunched her knees, resting her chin on them. 'I don't think that will happen.'

'It is possible. Perhaps they will listen to the king. According to Guy, they have a great affection for Richard, believing he can put right all the evils in the country.' There was a note of hope in her voice.

'They have not come all this way to be so easily per-suaded!' Philippa pushed back the bedclothes and pulled on her shift before getting up. Going over to the window, she flung back the shutters, gazing out on the new day. It was going to be hot. 'They will make demands that perhaps Richard cannot concede.'

Beatrice's smile faded. 'You're right, of course. But at least they are talking. I would that life could return to normal,' she said gloomily.

Philippa went over to the washstand. What was normal? Her normality had ended a few days ago, and now she felt like a leaf drifting down-river to the sea, waiting for the waves to reach out and take her into further experience. Waiting? Already she had altered from that girl who had trembled in the hall waiting for her father. Inside her, fear still lurked, but also there was a core of steel that made her face that fear.

'If you have a mind for work, Philippa, I would appreciate your help in repairing a tapestry,' said Beatrice, handing her a towel.

'Work?' Her eyes were shadowed. 'I'm not sure... Did Guy say he was going down to the river after...'

'Why do you ask?' Beatrice's voice was wary.

'He just mentioned that he might—that's all.' She picked up a comb.

'If that's all, I'll leave you. Follow me when you are finished. I'll be in the garden.'

Philippa nodded vaguely, staring into the metal mirror, grimacing at the freckles on her nose. Nothing seemed to dim them. Would she be able to get out of the gates? Why could Guy not see she had an interest in what happened at Mile End? How strange she had felt when he had been hurt. It still pained her to think of how his face looked. She frowned. He was devious—he could have woken her! If they thought it safe enough for the king, it was safe enough for her. He just did not want her with him. And she—she must stop her wayward thoughts dwelling on his attractions. Without more ado she braided her hair and left the room.

'No! It would be more than my job was worth to let you through again,' said the guard determinedly, his fingers tightening about his pike.

'All right! I don't want you to lose your job.' Philippa forced a smile and turned to walk back towards the house and thence to the garden at its rear. She had not really thought he would let her out but had wanted to convince herself that it was worth the try. Truly, though, she did not want to be out on the streets alone—yet she hated the thought of Rose perhaps being out there seeking her and not knowing where to find her. Neither of them had given proper thought to the difficulty of searching for someone in London. But then everything had been done in such haste.

Beatrice was sitting on a bench near the dovecot at the far end of the garden, sewing. Looking up, she smiled. 'For a while I was anxious.'

Philippa felt guilty. 'There is no need for you to worry over me.' The air was sweet with a heady fragrance that soothed her restlessness, yet she could not keep still for long.

Beatrice had left her sewing and was snapping off a dead rose-head. 'I do understand how you feel, you know. Waiting is terrible.'

'Perhaps the guard would let you out with me?' suggested Philippa with a mischievous smile. 'Why should we always be left behind like children.'

'I know! Yet what could we do at Mile End, but be squashed by a crowd, perhaps? And I doubt we could see much. It might all be over now.' She paused. 'If so, they should be back soon.'

Philippa nodded and sauntered over to the dovecot. As she put out her hand to one of the birds, a scrabbling noise drew her attention to the wall, and her heart seemed to climb into her throat. A hand, then a leg clad in tattered hose, was visible. Next came a face—a moment, and the man was sitting astride the wall, looking down at them. Swiftly her eyes went to Beatrice, whose face was a mask of disbelief. Then the older woman picked up her skirts and fled towards the house.

The man's darting glance followed her movement before jumping at Philippa as he slid slowly from the wall. Just as another man appeared on top of it, he advanced towards her. She backed away until she felt the hard wood of the bench behind her knees. Her fingers sought the tapestry that Beatrice had worked, found it, and flung it at the man as she came to her senses. Then she ran.

Through the doorway she went, turning swiftly to shoot the bolt, only for someone to fling themselves against the door before she could shoot it fully. An arm appeared, and she pressed against the door hard. There was a harsh grunt. Whirling round, she raced up the short passage to the kitchen. It was empty! Beatrice must have warned the maids. Philippa picked up a knife from the table almost at the same instant that the guards burst into the kitchen.

'Down the passage!' she yelled. Her relief was overwhelming, for they could have been raped or had their throats cut. Her fingers felt the edge of the blade and she rammed it in her girdle, gaining a sense of security from it. Peasants tumbled into the kitchen, stopping warily at the sight of the men.

'Out of here, mistress!' One of the guards seized her arm and thrust her through the doorway into the hall. It was closed firmly behind her, and she was glad.

'A goblet of wine, Philippa.' Beatrice's voice was firm, but her hand shook as she handed the vessel to her.

'Thank you.' She sat down abruptly on a bench before taking a deep gulp of the liquid.

'Well! It seems we aren't safe even in our own house,' muttered the older woman. 'Who would think of them climbing the wall—the height it is!'

'None of the men did. It was fortunate that we were out there,' stated Philippa, taking a more cautious sip of the wine, and listening with half an ear to the grunts and yells coming from the kitchen.

'Was that man armed?'

'There was more than one; two at least. What did they think to gain?' She was feeling better now.

Beatrice shook her head and looked towards the kitchen. The two maids who had been preparing dinner sat at the far end of the bench, their interested gaze on the kitchen door as it opened and a serving-man entered.

'Shall we lock them in the cellar, mistress? Only four of them, and scared that we'll run them through! Said they came looking for food—and drink. Skinny-looking bunch, who've not eaten much for days . . . so they say.' He shook his head dubiously. A big strapping fellow, who reminded Philippa of Adam.

'Certainly lock them in the cellar, and give them something to eat,' said Beatrice after a moment's hesitation, before turning to Philippa and saying almost apologetically. 'I don't think they are all bad.'

'No,' she murmured, 'not all.'

They both fell silent, drinking their wine, and Philippa remembered that she had had no breakfast. Her stomach felt hollow, yet she had no desire for food. If men could get inside the house, what could they be up to outside at Mile End or on the streets? Getting to her feet, she crossed the hall towards the front door.

Beatrice rose swiftly and followed her, her goblet still clutched in her hand. 'Where are you going?'

'Just to look . . . to see what goes on outside the gates.'

Beatrice nodded and slipped her hand in her arm. 'We'll go together.'

Philippa smiled soberly. 'Don't you trust me? I'm not such a fool as to go out alone, even if it were possible!'

'It is possible. The guards are in the kitchen or the cellar.' Determinedly Beatrice stuck with her as Philippa strolled to the gates.

From the distance, shouts and an indistinct murmur of activity could be heard. A sudden hideous cry split the air, making them exchange swift glances. There was nothing much to see outside the gates, despite their apprehension.

Philippa breathed more easily. There had been a terribleness in that cry that had caused her blood to chill. 'Let's go back.'

Beatrice nodded, but just as they turned away, there came the tramp of feet. Then shouts and jeers, catcalls and chanting.

'John Ball for archbishop! Let all be held in common! Down with all traitors!' As if pulled by a thread, both women faced the gates again. Beatrice screamed, but Philippa's mouth went dry and she could not speak.

Carried on pikes were several heads. Fists were shaken at the women or kisses blown, as the marching men passed, but no move was made to assault the gates.

'It's Archbishop Sudbury,' whispered Beatrice, crossing herself rapidly. 'And old Lyons, the treasurer.'

'Were they at Mile End, I wonder?' croaked Philippa.

'Surely not! They would know the mob would be after their heads!' Beatrice put a hand to her mouth and hurried back to the house.

'Oh sweet Jesu!' Philippa eased her aching throat, then followed stiffly as though her limbs had turned to wood. Then suddenly, as she reached the hall and there was no sign of Beatrice or anybody else, she began to run. Up the stairs she went until she came to her bedchamber. There she flung herself on the bed, clutching feverishly at the covers.

'What if Guy were dead? What if the king is dead?' She voiced the words aloud, so that they seemed to shout back at her. She did not want to believe it was true, but what if they did not return? What had happened at Mile End? Why did they not return if they were safe? What of Beatrice and herself? They were not safe anywhere, it seemed!

How long she lay there allowing her fear to spiral out of control, she did not know, but eventually some remnant of common sense asserted itself and pushed down the terror. At last she sat up, pushing back her braids. She would go and find Beatrice. Shivering still, she rose and went first to her bedchamber. Not there! Then to the solar. Beatrice sat there—to all appearances calmly sewing and in control. Then Philippa noticed that the fabric shook slightly. Not so collected, after all! It gave her comfort, somehow, to know that her own fear was shared.

'You will have something to drink and eat, Philippa?' Her voice quivered.

'Nothing too heavy, thank you.' Philippa sank on to the settle.

'I'll go and see to it... Something to do. Stop me thinking.' Beatrice smiled wanly. 'I won't be long.'

'Thank you.' Philippa could think of nothing else to say.

Soon Beatrice returned with a tray, on which were set some spiced wine and a platter of darioles. They drank and ate in silence. Philippa, feeling her nerves stretch as the silence did, broke it to ask for the recipe. 'I have never had these before.'

'One can have them only in the summer,' said Beatrice brightly. 'Strawberries are available then, but dates are difficult to obtain. The cream and wine are not so.' Her face showed a touch of animation. 'I'm so blessed in having a grocer for a husband, for he manages to obtain so many rarities.' Then the light died in her eyes. 'How much longer do you think they will be?'

'Who can tell? Surely not much longer.' Philippa poured out another cup of clary for each of them. It was spicy with nutmeg and sweet with honey.

'You don't think...'

'No!' Philippa burst out. 'No, we would have heard. We shall not think on that.'

'No,' murmured Beatrice. 'You are right.'

As twilight began to fall, there was a red glow in the sky that was not due to the setting sun. Fires must be burning somewhere! The silence sat clammily in the shadows, and seemed to press in. Then unexpectedly the door opened and men's voice sounded. Whirling round, Philippa stared across the darkening room. It was Guy and James, bearing lights.

'Sitting in the dark?' James's deep voice was all that was needed for Beatrice to fly into his arms.

Philippa's gladness could only soar inside her as she gazed at Guy, examining his face for any further sign of injury. 'You have been so long!' Despite all her efforts, her voice shook.

Guy came closer. 'I'm sorry—and I do not even bring you the news you desire about your uncle.'

'Is that what delayed you?' She clasped her hands in front of her to stop them trembling.

'We did not intend to stay out all day. But what with Mile End, to begin with...'

'What happened? We saw...Sudbury... His head...'

'How? You haven't...' He seized her arm.

'No! Through the gates, as they marched past. There were other men...I didn't know.'

'They broke into the Tower. Hundreds of archers were there—but they got in,' Guy said hoarsely. 'The king refused to hand them over, you see, so they went and took them. I can only believe it is the very weight of numbers that causes people to throw down their arms. They frightened the life out of the king's mother! One kissed her, but they offered her no other harm.' He smiled faintly.

'The king is safe, then?'

'Ay!' He paused. 'And you both are too, despite what one of the guards told me—that serfs climbed the wall?' he said stiffly.

'You can see we are.' Philippa gave a brief laugh. 'It is not so safe here, after all, you see. But still you have not told me what happened at Mile End?'

He released her slowly. 'The king did his best with them—and, to give the commons their due, they were prepared to listen—and welcomed him and swore allegiance.'

'But they haven't gone home.'

'Some have already left—those that trust the king to keep his word . . . those who are tired of the whole thing.'

'Some? What did the king promise?'

Guy scrubbed at his nose. 'Most of the peasants there were from Essex. He gave pardons to them, but refused to let them deal with those they considered traitors. And you know what happened there.' He sighed. 'They want serfdom abolished—and to be free tenants paying low rents.'

'And did he promise that?'

'What would you do surrounded by thousands of serfs?'

'I see. What happens next? What of the Kentish men and the London commons?'

Guy gave a bitter laugh. 'Who knows? They are slaughtering foreigners on the streets. A couple mocked my northern accent—they asked me to say "a little bread and cheese". The Flemings can't say it properly, you see! I was able to convince them I am an Englishman, despite my northern accent—although I am not very proud of my countrymen at the moment.' He leaned against the wall, anger playing over his features. 'Tomorrow, or the next day at the latest, I shall get you out of London.'

'The ship has docked?' Philippa's heart quickened its beat.

Guy nodded, pushing himself away from the wall. 'As soon as it unloads some of its cargo and takes on more, we'll be on that ship.' He moved his candle so that she could not see his expression clearly. 'Hugo will be getting impatient.' He sounded disgruntled.

'He kept *me* waiting long enough!' She did not want to dwell on the thought of Sir Hugo claiming her as his wife, which was what Guy's words instantly conjured up. Not when she was with him!

'A mistake,' Guy said roughly. 'He should have wed you years ago. It would have saved much trouble.' His body swayed so that he had to lean against the wall again to stay on his feet.

Philippa was upset. 'I would have preferred the last few days to have been different. If my father...'

'I didn't mean the last few days.' He blinked at her wearily; his eye was hurting, and he was almost asleep on his feet. 'You don't know what is between my brother and me—that's how it should be. But I'm too tired to talk any more now—or even to eat. It's bed for me.' The words were slurred, his eyes almost closed.

'I'll light the way for you,' Philippa said abruptly, picking up the candle, having no notion of what he had spoken. Unless it was something to do with being his brother's steward? 'I'm not hungry, and you might fall down if you go up with your eyes shut.'

Unexpectedly he did not argue with her, and after a few words with the Wantsums they left the solar. Without lingering at his door, she whispered a swift good night and passed into her own chamber.

She settled herself to sleep, determined not to dwell on the happenings of the day, but her thoughts were a churning jumble of pictures of the events not only of that day, but of the preceding days. At last she drifted into a semi-conscious state, in which her father's face stared at her from out of the flames, and a skeleton hand beckoned her to come to him. Not wanting to go, she tried to run, but again Tom was there—and those men, with their rope. Knowing what was to happen, she turned to look for the stranger, but he was not there this time. Why? Why? She was being dragged along the ground towards the burning house.

Philippa woke in a lather of sweat to find herself on her stomach on the edge of the bed; overbalancing, she fell on the floor with a thud. Her legs were shaky when she stood up, and it took a moment for her to straighten up. A warm orange glow flickered about the room, and realising that she had not closed the shutters, she stumbled over to the window.

Shock held her there, gripping the sill so tightly that it hurt her hands. Wherever she gazed, there were fires. The smell of charring timbers and smoke was in her throat and nostrils. There was no escape in waking, this time. She would burn! She screamed, and kept on screaming. The door opened, but she did not hear it—nor was she aware of the thud of feet.

'Philippa!' She was whirled round and roughly shaken. 'Philippa! For God's sake, stop it!' commanded Guy.

'Lon—Lon—London's burning!' she cried, 'and we'll all burn with it!' Her eyes stared wildly into his face. 'We will, Guy!'

'No!' He shook her again, and she clutched at his arm. 'No, we won't.' His fear for her sanity was a tightness in his chest.

'It's some sort of jest, isn't it? A diabolical jape? We ran all the way here, thinking to be safe!' A sob escaped her.

'You are safe. You are with me!' he insisted emphatically.

'I'm not! I'm not! You'll die too if you stay with me. You must go.' She made to push him away, but he held her arms tightly.

'Philippa, listen to me! There are gardens and a wall surrounding this house. But, believe me, the flames are not close. It only appears so because it is dark. If any peasants attempted to invade this house with torches, we would be warned and could escape.'

There was such assurance in his voice that some of her fear abated and she looked up at him. His nose and cheekbones were highlighted by the flames outside, and a lock of dark hair curled on his forehead. He looked worried.

'You do believe me, Philippa, don't you?' His chin brushed her hair as she dropped her head on his chest.

'I was so frightened.' Her voice was muffled. 'I'm sorry I woke you.'

'That doesn't matter.' His arms went about her. 'You do believe that you are safe?'

Philippa was silent. While he held her, she felt secure, but when he left the room, she was certain the dark fears would crowd in. Her fingers curled on his chest, and she realised it was naked. Her heart gave a peculiar lurch, and warmth swept over her like a tide and she trembled, glad that this night she had put on her shift.

'Don't be frightened,' urged Guy. The back of his hand brushed her cheek.

Slowly she lifted her head, and some of her timidity eased. The cut on his face and the almost closed eye made him appear unusually vulnerable. A desire to re-assure him kindled in her heart. 'I'm not frightened now.'

'Good.' He gave a crooked grin, then winced. 'When you screamed, I thought that one of the peasants had escaped from the cellars and somehow entered your room.' His finger traced the curve of her cheek, feather-edged the corner of her mouth, causing her lips to quiver. 'Thank God it wasn't so.' His finger stilled on her dimple.

Philippa swallowed. His caress induced a thrilling headiness that she was unused to, and she had no desire to move away, even though she knew she should. 'I—I was dreaming, and when I woke, it seemed that my dream was reality.' Of its own volition her hand reached up to smooth back a strand of black hair sticking to the dried blood at the corner of his eye.

Guy caught her hand and held it. 'You're still having that dream?'

'You know of it?' She smiled. 'But of course—you are the stranger in the shadows who tries to save me but can never reach me.'

'You dream of my saving you?' The note in his voice puzzled her, even as it sent a stir rippling through her nerves. 'Dammit, you shouldn't do that!'

'Why? I have no control over my dreams.'

'Well, you should have.' His hand trembled as it curved about her jaw. 'I am no dream lover, Philippa,' he added harshly, bringing her mouth up to meet his.

It could have been a kiss to comfort, but there was nothing calming about it, rousing her to respond hungrily as it did. Even when he took his hand from her face, she made no effort to free herself, but stayed still. Perhaps it was the light from the fires that caused his eye to gleam with a sudden awareness, and before she could move away he had kissed her again. The third time he kissed her she floated—or felt as if she did—for the strength in his embrace swept her off her feet. To struggle seemed out of place as he carried her, breast to chest, mouth against mouth, over to the bed. He was lying with her beneath him before she thought of any danger. Words spoken by him when they had talked of Lancaster and his mistress—words about not blaming a man for trying to have it both ways—a wife and a mistress—love and lust—the words rang in her head like a clarion call. She struggled, and he released her mouth.

'Guy, please.' The words were barely audible; but he heard them.

'Please what?' he whispered, rolling her over so that they lay side by side. 'Please, Guy, kiss me again and forget Hugo who lies between us!' His tone lashed her unexpectedly, seeming to lay on her the blame for what was happening.

'No!' she cried before his mouth found hers again, silencing her protests even as his hands ranged down her spine in a tingling path then up to seize the shoulders of her shift and bare her skin. She gasped as he pressed his mouth on her collarbone and struggled as he slid over her again. His lips took a descending path, touching hollows and pinnacles that no man had ever seen.

'Damn you, Guy Milburn!' There were tears in the whispering curse. 'I hate you!'

'Good!' he muttered, stopping abruptly. 'You've come to your senses.' His breath came unevenly. 'Go on hating me, but don't think of me as some kind of saviour or a courtier who would worship at your feet. I'm not that breed of man.'

'No!' She took his hands and removed them from her breasts. 'No, you aren't.' Again the tears were there. Despite all her seeming common sense she had dreamed of him as a knight—but in all her fantasies her knight had stopped at a chaste kiss. Reality was far different from the dream, and what was so terrible was that in some ways she preferred the reality—in many ways! 'You— You had . . . better leave.'

'Ay!' He pushed himself up, staring down into her face. 'If I were that kind of man, I would not even think of you in a tender way. There's the trouble, Philippa! You should feel flattered, for it's a long time since I wanted any woman. So don't go to Hugo thinking yourself without attraction.' There was a touch of anger in his voice.

'I don't understand.' Emotion made the words harsh.

'No, I don't suppose you do.' He got up and went to stand by the window. He closed the shutters on the fires still burning outside, still wanting her, furious with Hugo for having beguiled him with a promise that had sent him to fetch such a maid, only to hand her over!

'You will be all right now?' His voice was smooth as he faced her.

'Ay!' The word sounded a discordant, bitter note in the now dark chamber. 'You have made me learn my lesson all the swifter.'

'Good! Most men are beasts, sweet Philippa,' he mocked. 'Don't trust even the best of us.'

She made no answer. His words were confusing her again. One moment it seemed that he blamed her for what had happened—the next, himself.

'Good night, then.' Guy moved away, but she did not look up at his leaving, and he smiled sardonically at his own desire that made him want her to as he closed the door behind him.

For a long time Philippa lay there, a chill at her heart, before she sat up, and leaning forward, dragged the covers over her. Huddling beneath them, she sought forgetfulness, but it did not come, and she was still awake when dawn lightened the sky.

CHAPTER SEVEN

A THRUSH WAS trilling in the bush beneath her window as Philippa flung back the shutters. Perhaps it was a good omen? A wry smile puckered her lips. There was no bright-dream-come-true-future for her. Having no desire to stay in her chamber with her thoughts any longer, she washed in cold water, dressed and opened the door, wondering how she was to face Guy. Squaring her shoulders, she shut the door firmly on her dreams but not on the reality of what it might have been like to have a dream come true.

Guy still slept when she peeped in. All she could see was a tousled mop of dark hair and a bare arm sprawling across the pillow. The thought that he had not lost sleep over what had happened angered her and made her determined not to yearn for the unattainable.

It was so early that she did not expect anyone but servants to be about. In the garden, she was surprised to find Beatrice, who was cutting sprigs from a large clump of sage.

'What a beautiful morning it is,' said Philippa, giving a bright smile. 'Did you sleep well?'

'Not so well,' Beatrice murmured unenthusiastically. She straightened up, and shuffled the stems in her hands, not looking directly at her.

Philippa was suddenly uneasy. 'Is anything wrong? Master Wantsum?'

'He is still sleeping.' Beatrice pulled off a leaf and rolled it between her fingers. She sniffed at the bruised herb, her face screwed up. 'Have you given any thought to when you will wed? I think it should be as soon as you arrive in Yorkshire.' The leaf fluttered from her fingers.

Philippa stared at her, puzzled. 'Surely Sir Hugo will be willing to wait until I finish mourning my father?' She sat on a bench, her palms resting lightly on the wood each side of her. 'He has kept *me* waiting a long time. But why do you ask me now? You have mentioned Hugo hardly ever, all the time I have been here.'

Beatrice licked her lips and placed the sage on the bench with great deliberation. 'I did not sleep well last night and I heard screaming, recognised that it was you and went to see if you had need of me.' She paused. 'Neither of you heard me, so I went away again.'

There was a silence.

'It wasn't how it appeared.' Philippa's cheeks burned.

'Wasn't it?' Beatrice sat beside her. 'Catalina caused disharmony between my cousins, and I would not like you to do so, Philippa.' She put her hand over one of hers. 'You have been through much with your father's death—your home destroyed—and Guy must appear to you...'

'What did Catalina do?' interrupted Philippa ruthlessly, not wanting Beatrice's sympathy or to excuse her behaviour. Her conscience squirmed uncomfortably enough.

She remained silent so long that Philippa grew impatient. 'You have said too much or too little, Beatrice. Do not heed my feelings—you might as well tell me the whole tale. I have long realised that Sir Hugo considers me of little worth, else he would have surely claimed me before now.'

'Perhaps it is best that you do know.' Beatrice's face was troubled. 'Catalina was a maid in the train of the Duchess Constancia of Castile—the one who is wed to the Duke of Lancaster. She was a young girl far from her own land. Hugo...seduced her—or she him, who knows, and he got her with child.' A tiny gasp escaped

Philippa, but before she could speak, Beatrice continued, 'Guy fancied himself in love with her also, so when Hugo revealed what had happened, Guy wed Catalina.'

'So there is a child?' Philippa's thoughts were in confusion.

'The child came before time, and died. One would have thought that that would have made matters easier, but…' She shrugged. 'I consider Hugo's feelings towards Catalina were strong—that he truly cared for her. He panicked, though, over the child, because he was betrothed to you and feared his father's anger. He was glad when Guy relieved him of that trouble, but afterwards jealousy got the upper hand with him. He behaved badly to Guy.'

Philippa moistened her mouth. 'What do you mean— he behaved badly to Guy? To Catalina and myself, ay!'

'My uncle was furious when Guy wed a foreigner— and without his permission. There was another maid he had in mind for him who would have brought more land to the Milburns.'

'What happened?'

'My uncle refused to receive Guy and his wife when they travelled to Yorkshire, and even tore up the message he sent to him. Hugo could have made it easier. He could perhaps have told the truth and trusted him, for my uncle was not without warmth of feeling. Both sons had returned from a disastrous expedition in France and were ripe for a different kind of adventure. Hugo was his heir, and while he would have been furious at first, it is likely he would have been able to deal with the matter better than they did.'

'I can guess what happened next,' murmured Philippa, her eyes dark. 'His father made no provision for Guy after his death.'

'Guy told you?' Beatrice sounded surprised.

'Ay! When we talked about sheep once. It seems unjust.' Her brow creased. 'Could Hugo not have passed some of the land to him?'

'Of course he could. But Guy had Catalina, so *he* couldn't have her. Guy wanted the land, so Hugo reacted by not giving him what he desired. Moreover, Hugo is a man who holds on to what he considers is legally his.' Beatrice leaned forward, her expression sympathetic. 'He regards you already as his possession, and your manor also.'

'Does he?' Philippa's eyes clouded and her mouth tightened. 'Just as Guy does! You don't have to worry about my coming between the brothers, Beatrice; I know exactly where I stand with both of them.' But did she? A voice mocked in her head. 'Besides, I do not possess the sort of beauty men fight over.'

'No? Yet Guy is attracted to you. I know my cousin. There was a time when I fancied myself in love with him—and he with me. A long time ago, that was.' Beatrice picked up the sage and placed it in her lap. 'If Hugo guesses that you and Guy have even kissed, the rift that has been closing since Catalina's death will open again,' she said earnestly. 'They were close once, and I would have it so again—and so would they, I believe. Do not think there is no good in Hugo—there is. His greatest sin is that he hates being put in the wrong, and he will not admit when he is. He is quick-tempered, and grew up expecting always to get his own way. But he can be generous and kind, although he does not suffer fools gladly.' She stood up, and there was pity in her glance. 'I am not unaware of your situation, Philippa, but I thought you should know what it is like between the brothers.'

'And you are right,' muttered Philippa, getting to her feet. 'I should be grateful for all you have said.'

'But you aren't!' Beatrice smiled sadly. 'If you don't feed your emotions, my dear, they can die. Harden your heart against Guy's charm. You are not the first to fall under its spell, and I doubt you will be the last.'

'I suppose so,' she retorted, yet even as she spoke, she knew it was too late. A sore heart was to be her burden for caring where she should not. But as for pining, that was not going to be her way at all!

The two women went indoors, Beatrice to the kitchen, saying that she would join her in the hall presently for some collops of bacon and eggs. Philippa sat down on a settle, wondering what the day would bring. Despite her determination to curb her feelings, when Guy and James came into the hall a warm surge of emotion leaped inside her at the sight of Guy.

'Good morning, Philippa. I trust you slept well?' His long-lashed, still very much wide-awake, eyes surveyed her with a certain inscrutability.

'Not really,' she replied honestly in a cool voice. 'I had much on my mind. And since I did not want you to go out without me, I rose early,' she added imperturbably.

He raised a dark brow, went to speak, but at that moment the sound of a commotion in the courtyard drew their attention. The two men exchanged swift glances, and without speaking, went outside. Philippa followed.

'What is it, lad?' James demanded of the young squire who was dismounting.

'You were missing from council last night, Master Wantsum, and your presence is requested this noon at Smithfield. It was decided that the king will make another attempt to reason with the peasants. They have agreed to meet him.'

James's eyes lightened. 'I'll be there. Where is the king now?'

'At Westminster, praying. He will go from there to Smithfield.'

James nodded. 'Go into the kitchen, lad, and ask for some ale.'

The squire shook his head. 'Thank you, but I have others to visit.'

'God go with you, then.' James raised a hand in farewell as the lad mounted, before turning and walking swiftly back to the house, his brow crinkled in deep thought.

'Well! So there is to be another meeting. Will you go, with or without the king's invitation?' Philippa faced Guy determinedly.

'I might,' he said lazily. 'But please put aside any thought of coming with me.'

'Why should I not go?' Her green eyes flashed fire, and she put her hands on her hips, her whole diminutive figure bristling.

'And what do you think you can do if you go?' He eyed her derisively. 'Fight the whole peasant army single-handed?'

She flushed. 'No, but I would fight, this time, not hide or run away! Or wait to hear news of death! Or to have to face raiding peasants here if the king fails to pacify them. I have not forgotten the fires of last night!'

'You have little faith that the king will succeed,' he said softly. 'Pray, Philippa—that is a woman's task at such time as this.'

'Pray? Do you not think I haven't? If you have such faith, then allow me to come with you. Should danger threaten, I promise I shall leave. But do not tell me to be calm and wait and pray because I am a woman! I have a knife,' pulling out the one she had taken from the kitchen, 'and I would use it.'

There was a moment's silence before it was broken by Guy's laugh. 'Sweet Jesu, I believe you would! Do you know what you might have to face, little fool?'

'Ay! More than you and Master Wantsum am I involved in this conflict. My father was foully murdered! I—I buried him with my own hands! I...'

'All the more reason for you not to be hurt any more.'
His face softened, and his voice was hesitant when he
spoke again. 'I admire your courage, Philippa, but what
you suggest ... I would be doing you a disservice ...'

'Am I of more value than the king?' she demanded.

'You don't know what you are asking,' he said tersely.
'Hugo ...'

'Hugo has no need to know. If he is aware of what
is happening in the south, he will accept that there is
danger here for me.'

'Ay! But not that I would deliberately take you into
a perilous situation. James and Beatrice would consider
both of us to be mad!'

'The world has gone mad, Guy! The world I know—
that I am part of.' She paused, not questioning why it
was so important to get her way on this. 'I would climb
the wall, as the serfs did, and find my way to Smithfield
on my own,' in a soft voice, 'once you were gone.'

'I could lock you up,' he retaliated, frowning.

'In the cellar? There are serfs there who broke in while
you were gone, remember?'

'This isn't a game, Philippa!'

'No.' She was instantly serious. 'It isn't amusing, either
to play at patience while you and James are in danger.'
She sighed and rested her case, considering she was not
going to win.

'You will do exactly as I tell you?' said Guy, wondering if he was running mad.

'You—You *will* take me with you?' Her eyes widened
in amazement.

'Isn't that what you want? And at least I shall have
you under my eye and shall know what you are doing!
I only pray that we both won't regret your persuading
me.' His eyes narrowed thoughtfully as he stared at her.
'You'll have to think of something to tell Beatrice. As
for James, it is likely that he will ride with the council.
I'll tell him that I'm going to the waterfront first and

will join him later at Smithfield. There's no need to tell them the truth of the matter yet.'

'No. I'll tell Beatrice I have the headache and intend staying in bed.'

'Hmmm! Make it convincing. I'll meet you in the stables in about an hour. I'll bring one of my caps to hide that hair of yours—and you can envelop yourself in my dark cloak!'

She nodded. 'Whatever you say. I want to go!'

'I'll keep you to that. If it gets dangerous, you must leave. Your word and your hand on it, lass.' He held out his hand.

She put her small one in his larger one and they shook hands solemnly. It was hard to believe that last night they had been in each other's arms—but perhaps it was better this way.

Philippa marvelled at how easy it had been to follow their plan as she rode beside Guy through green fields. The guard had given her only a perfunctory glance as she passed through the gates with Guy. Perhaps he thought her one of James's new grooms. They had done as he said and visited the waterfront first, where he spent a brief time in conversation with the master of the ship. Then they had caught up with a cavalcade of some two hundred men just outside the city walls. Where James was she had no idea, and Guy had not gone to seek him but had stayed to the rear of the horsemen. He had spoken little to her, and she wondered whether he was regretting having given way to her.

The cloak made her hot, and the curls beneath the cap were damp with perspiration. She would be glad to reach Smithfield, for tension was in the very air she breathed.

As they neared Saint Bartholomew's, she could see and hear the huge crowd of peasants standing in lines ahead, and her heart misgave her for a moment. Some had already returned to their homes, but there were still thousands of them, it appeared. The cavalcade of men were spread out on each side of the king, so that now she could see better what would take place between Richard and his rebellious subjects. A hush fell over the field as a man went forward towards the peasant lines.

'It is William Walworth, the mayor of London,' whispered Guy in her ear. 'Probably he is giving the rebel leader leave to come forward and speak to the king.'

She nodded, all her attention on the youthful fair-haired Richard, who had brought his horse a little away from his own side. His robe was trimmed with ermine, and he showed no sign of fear.

A rough-looking man approached him on a pony. He dismounted, but did not doff his hat or drop to his knees, but only half bent one knee, and taking the king's hand, he shook it roughly. 'Brother, be of good cheer, for in the fortnight that is to come, you shall have 40,000 more commons and we shall be good companions.' Then he stood back, tossing a dagger from hand to hand.

A murmur rippled through the king's men, and Philippa drew in a breath. He was close enough to stab the king, if he had a mind to! 'Is that Wat Tyler?' she asked Guy and he nodded.

'Why will you not go back to your own country?' asked Richard calmly.

Tyler muttered something she did not catch, then said, 'Not until we have our charter, will we go. And if it is not done swiftly, then the lords of England will regret bitterly that the demands of the commons have not been met.' Then he recited all the demands made at Mile End, and added several more.

'No man shall be outlawed! No lord should have any lordship except the king. The wealth and lands of the church should be taken away and divided among the people!' There was a roar of approval at this. 'There should be only one bishop!' He glanced about him as for another roar of agreement, and a cheer went up. 'The commons should be free—to fish or hunt in all water, fishponds, woods and forests.' Another roar.

Philippa and Guy exchanged glances. 'They want the impossible!' he murmured. 'But they are in a good bargaining position at the moment.'

She nodded, but remained silent as the king spoke again. 'The commons shall have all that they asked which I your king can grant by the law of the land,' replied Richard quietly. 'Now you must return to your own homes.'

Wat Tyler stared at him, frowning, then called loudly, 'Bring me a jug of water!'

A man came forward from the crowd of peasants. Wat rinsed his mouth and then spat at the king's feet. A murmur of anger went up from the king's men, but Richard made no sign of having noticed.

Wat eyed him thoughtfully. 'A jug of ale,' he called. He drank it at one draught before climbing on his horse.

Then unexpectedly from among the king's men a voice rang out. 'This man is the greatest robber and thief in Kent!'

Heads turned, and Philippa craned her neck to see who had spoken. The men about her were muttering now. Her horse stirred uneasily, and Guy's hand went to her bridle.

'Put that weapon away in the presence of the king!' shouted the mayor of London.

She looked quickly towards the king and the peasant leader, who was brandishing his dagger as he approached the king's line. The mayor came forward swiftly, and Tyler launched himself on him and stabbed him. Walworth reeled, but drew his own dagger and struck Tyler in the neck and then in the head. There was a scuffle, and another of the king's men ran forward with a drawn sword and ran the rebel leader two or three times through the body. Wat gasped, and leaning dangerously low in the saddle, managed to spur his horse and ride towards the peasant lines, but he fell to the ground before he reached them.

A great cry went up from the peasants. 'Treachery! Our captain is dead—slain by treachery. Let us avenge his death!'

Guy's face was dark, as the front line of serfs began to pull out arrows and fit them to bows. 'Away with you now!' Pulling on the bridle, he started to turn Philippa's horse.

'Not yet,' she cried. 'The king! See, Guy!' She pointed. He hesitated and looked to where she indicated.

'Is he mad?' muttered Guy, yet managing to infuse a note of unwilling admiration in his voice.

The young king was cantering towards the furious crowd, and right among them he went. 'Sirs, will you shoot your king? I will be your chief and your captain and you shall have from me all that you seek, only follow me into the fields without.' He pointed to the open fields near the burnt-out remains of Saint John's priory, which had been destroyed by the peasants the day before. Slowly he began to ride in its direction. After a moment's hesitation, the crowd slowly began to stream after him in a bewildered fashion.

'Good God,' breathed Guy. 'I always thought they meant him no harm.'

'They might still kill him,' murmured Philippa. 'What do we do now?'

He stared at her. 'You don't do anything but go home,' he ordered. 'You won't be alone,' he added drily.

She saw that already some of those who had come with the king had turned tail and were making for London at a gallop. 'Then there is danger—they could still...?' She moistened her mouth. 'Do you come with me?'

He shook his head, his blue eyes extremely bright. 'Farewell! Now is the time to seek out James. God willing, we shall meet again this day.' His hand smacked her horse's rump, and she was away.

Tears blurred her vision so that she could hardly make out the road ahead, and part of her wanted to turn back, but she had given her word and that was an end to it. It was not until she reached the gates of the Wantsums' house that she thought of sending the guards to the help of their master, and their king. Pulling off her cap, she let her hair cascade over her shoulders as the man looked up at her.

'I have been to Smithfield, and Master Wantsum has need of you all. The rebel leader is badly wounded, and now is the time to fight for your king.'

'A fight?' Another man sauntered out of the guardhouse and surveyed her with some humour. 'Not before time! The master sent you, did he, mistress? Now that does surprise me!'

'Of course not! He did not know I was there. Master Guy sent me here.' Her eyes smouldered. 'Well, why are you standing still? Go to help your king!' Her voice rang loudly in the street.

The two men looked at each other, and one opened the gate swiftly, while the other ran back into the guardhouse.

Philippa did not wait to see whether they obeyed her, but made her way to the stables. When she slid from the horse, she realised that her legs would not hold her, and sat down abruptly. There was a sick feeling in her stomach, and for what seemed a long while she stayed there, her head buried in her arms.

'Are you all right, mistress?'

She lifted her head and looked into the groom's concerned face, and nodded. 'Could you see to the horse? But first help me up?

He did as she asked and left her leaning against the wall. Although she stayed listening for any sound coming from the hall, she could not hear Beatrice's voice, and taking several deep breaths, she slowly made her way indoors. Fortunately the hall was empty, and now that she was moving again, her legs felt strong enough to climb the stairs. Once in her chamber, she lay down on the bed, gazing up at the rafters. She prayed soundlessly, while expecting to hear the roar of the peasants. But no such sound came. The day wore on, and at last she stirred and changed her dusty gown into a pale green one, the gift from Beatrice.

Her hostess was gazing out of the window when she entered the solar, but turned when she heard her feet. 'You are feeling better?'

'Much better.' Philippa crossed the chamber and stood next to her. In the past few days, how many times had she stood at this window, looking out and worrying? Always they had returned. God willing, they would return this time. Even as she thought of them, there came the noise of voices, the whinny of horses and the scraping of shoes on the step.

Beatrice flew downstairs, but Philippa followed more slowly, unbelievably weary.

'James, tell us quickly—what has happened?' his wife blurted out as she entered the hall.

'A drink of ale, then news, good wife.' James kissed her, and then sat down with an air of relief.

Philippa stared at Guy, who cocked a brow, smiled faintly, and then reached for the jug of ale himself before Beatrice could get a hand to it. The first brimming cup he gave to James, then filled another for himself. Both men drank deeply. Guy finished first.

'The king has won the day.' He addressed Philippa. 'Master Walworth, who fortunately wore armour under his garments, rode back to London and called on all those willing to fight. Sir Robert Knolles, an old campaigner from the French wars, brought a company of lancers and rode straight through the peasants to take up a position with us by the king's side. But the king

already had them perfectly under control. How he did
it I don't know, but they were on their knees to him.
They were soon surrounded, and some of the military
were for slaughtering half of them in order to teach them
a lesson!'

'The king would not have it,' James interrupted. 'He
said that most of them had only been brought to London
by fear and threats, and gave them leave to go home.'

'Home?' cried Philippa, starting forward.

'Most of them have already gone. Some of the ring-
leaders have been taken in charge. Some fled, and are
being hunted down. The men of Kent have been escorted
through London and over the bridge.'

'What of their leader?' asked Philippa.

'He's dead,' replied Guy. 'Old Walworth dragged him
out of Saint Bartholomew's, where he had been taken,
and...' Graphically he drew a finger across his throat.

'Then it is over,' said Philippa, sinking on a bench.

'For us, it is,' Guy murmured. 'We leave within the
hour, for the evening tide takes that ship I spoke about.
You had best make haste and pack what you can take.'

'Within the hour?' Her voice rose to a squeak. 'But
you have not eaten.'

'I can eat later on the ship. Beatrice, would you be so
kind as to provide us with some bread and meat—
whatever you can spare?'

'Of course! But so soon, Guy? And just when Philippa
and I could see the sights of London without worrying.'
She frowned.

'It can't be helped.' Absently he dabbed at his cut eye,
which was bleeding a little. 'I must wash and change and
pack, in that order, immediately. Will you come,
Philippa?'

She nodded and rose, to meet Beatrice's searching
glance. It seemed an age since their conversation that
morning. But once again she was reminded that it was
Hugo to whom he was taking her—Hugo, who was her

future husband. They were both silent as they went up the stairs. She packed the little she had, and then knocked on entering his chamber.

His dark hair was damp, and he had changed into a burgundy doublet with slashed sleeves that showed blue, over which he wore a burgundy surcote. No longer did he look tired, but rather as though filled with impatience.

'You are ready?' He took her bundle from her hand.

'As ready as I ever shall be! You were not hurt at all?' It was she who opened the door, not loitering.

'No. I gather you did not tell Beatrice? And it was you who sent the men?'

'Ay! And she had not noticed that I had been missing. You told James?'

'No! Although it might come out that the men were sent by a woman. I thought to ask—but James didn't, presuming it was Walworth's doing.' His arm brushed her shoulder. 'It was well thought of—and no harm came of your being there. Although... Did it serve your purpose, Philippa?'

How could she answer that? She was still not sure what her purpose had been. 'I have seen history in the making,' she said slowly. 'I saw my king vanquish a foe by bravery! Do you think he will keep his promises to the serfs?'

He hesitated. 'He might want to keep some of them. One could not help pitying many of those men, with their ragged clothes and half-starved bodies. It isn't justice that so few have so much and so many have so little, but I doubt that those round the king will let him do what he wishes. They've had a fright; they have seen what it is like if the commons are allowed power—to have a say in what should be done, for justice's sake. But always there must be the thought that had Tyler not been killed, what would have happened? They lost a leader who had audacity and ability—greed and courage as well, I should think—who would have swept away all that those who value order had built up. They hate lawyers—yet without law there would be lawlessness. We shall never know what would have happened if they had won and the king had lost.'

'Then you think everything will go on as before? That my serfs will return...'

'Most likely. But I doubt if it will be exactly the same. They have felt their power also, and will not forget the feeling. To take away that which they hate the most is the only way to prevent such a rebellion again. Men should be free to choose their own destiny—but that day will not come for a long time.'

They were both silent as they came into the hall.

'It is sad that you must go when all is safe,' declared Beatrice, coming over to her.

'I shall see you again, perhaps,' responded Philippa, giving a quick smile, not really believing it. 'Thank you for all your kindness, which I appreciate more than you can realise!' She kissed the older woman's cheek.

'So...little I could do for you, really.' Beatrice hugged her. 'How I wish all could be as you wish!' She drew away. 'May the saints go with you. Have a safe journey.'

James said, 'Go now—the tide will not wait.'

The Wantsums went with them out into the courtyard. The baggage was loaded on a horse, which one of the men would bring back. She was helped on to a pillion seat, then Guy hoisted himself up before her. Farewells were called, and they clattered through the gateway and out into the street.

Philippa looked about her. Already people were setting about the task of clearing rubbish, and vendors cried their wares. Within days, she supposed, a semblance of normality would have cloaked the happenings of the last few days, but never would they be forgotten.

CHAPTER EIGHT

It was as they neared the river that Philippa noticed the girl. There was something familiar about the stumbling figure, although her fair hair was matted and loose about her drooping shoulders. As they passed, she twisted round to see the girl's face.

'Stop!' she cried, seizing Guy's shoulder. 'There is someone I know. I must speak with her.' Urgency sharpened her voice.

'There is no time, Philippa. We have a ship to catch,' snapped Guy.

'One moment, that is all!' Already she was swinging her leg over, and sat precariously for a second before sliding from the horse as he pulled hard on the reins.

The girl walking towards her would have gone past if she had not seized a handful of the torn and filthy gown. 'Rose!' she cried frantically. 'Don't you know me?'

The girl lifted dazed eyes. There was a smudge on her cheek and a bruise darkened her chin. She put a shaking hand on her arm. 'Mistress Philippa, is it really you?'

'Ay, 'tis me, Rose.' She clasped her fingers tightly. 'We have found each other at last!'

A smile broke on the maid's face. 'I had given up hope of finding you. But here you are, praise the saints!'

They stared at one another, then Rose's eyes went to the man sitting on the horse. 'Where are you going? This man . . .'

'He is Sir Hugo's brother, Master Guy Milburn—you must remember them?'

'I remember them. But what a fate—a kind fate—that brought him to you at such a time,' said Rose in awe. 'Did you meet him here?'

'It is a long tale, Rose, and I have not the time to tell it now. We are in a hurry.'

'Where do you go? Back home?' Her throat moved. 'You will not be finding Tom there.'

'You have seen him, Rose? I did. Has he told you he remains in London? Does he hope to avoid being brought to justice by doing so?'

'He is dead, Mistress Philippa. I met some of the men, and they told me. He went to John of Gaunt's palace of Savoy and was blown to bits.'

'Oh, Rose,' whispered Philippa. 'I heard the explosion—saw Tom a short time before—but never thought...'

'Ay! What an ending to his dreams.' Rose threw back her head and gazed at her from feverish tear-bedewed eyes. 'But it was no worse a fate than that which he dealt your father. It was he who killed him—and then to hang and burn his body...' Her voice faltered, and she plucked at her filthy skirts and lowered her eyes.

'We go north, lass. Do you come with us?' Guy's voice tore the sudden heavy silence. 'Your mistress could do with another woman's company.'

Rose lifted her head and looked at him. 'North, you say?' she said huskily. 'I hear they're a wild lot up there.'

'No wilder than down here—less wild, if the last days are anything to go by.' He smiled at her.

A glimmer of response warmed Rose's face and she stood arms akimbo. 'You look a wild one, if that eye's anything to judge by.'

He grinned. 'I swear I'm a respectable merchant and farmer. Come, lass, we must catch the tide. If you are coming too, get up behind the baggage.'

'The tide,' said Rose doubtfully. 'I don't know.'

4 BOOKS PLUS A CLOCK AND MYSTERY GIFT

Here's a sweetheart of an offer that will put a smile on your lips . . . and **4 FREE** Mills & Boon Romances in your hands. **Plus** you'll get a digital quartz clock and a mystery gift as well.

At the same time, we'll reserve a Reader Service subscription for you. Every month you could receive 6 brand new Mills & Boon Romances by leading romantic fiction authors, delivered direct to your door. And they cost just the same as the books in the shops — postage and packing is always completely FREE. There is no obligation or commitment — you can cancel your subscription at any time. So you've nothing to lose! Simply fill in the coupon below and send this card off today.

Please send me 4 FREE Mills & Boon Romances and my FREE clock and mystery gift.
Please also reserve a Reader Service subscription for me. If I decide to subscribe, I shall receive 6 brand new Romances each month for £7.50, post and packing free. If I decide not to subscribe I shall write to you within 10 days. The free books and gifts will be mine to keep in any case.

I understand that I may cancel my subscription at any time by simply writing to you. I am over 18 years of age.

9A8T

NAME_____

ADDRESS_____

_____

_____POST CODE_____

AS A READER SERVICE SUBSCRIBER, YOU'LL ENJOY A WHOLE RANGE OF BENEFITS. . .

This attractive digital quartz clock — Yours Free!

★ Free monthly newsletter packed with competitions, recipes, author news and much, much more.
★ Special offers created just for Reader Service subscribers.
★ Helpful friendly advice from the ladies at Reader Service. You can call us any time on 01-684-2141.

So kiss and tell us you'll give your heart to Mills & Boon.

------------✂------------

**Reader Service
FREEPOST
P.O. Box 236
Croydon, Surrey
CR9 9EL**

POST THIS CARD TODAY!

NO
STAMP
NEEDED

'We must go,' said Guy, holding a hand down to Philippa. She took it, but hesitated.

'Rose, please?'

The maid heard the plea, thought of the past—and the future with a big question hanging over it. 'I'll come.' She bounded forward as Guy pulled her mistress up, and was dragged unceremoniously on to the baggage by the groom. They set off at a gallop. The tide could not wait any longer.

The single sail bellied out in the wind as Philippa passed beneath it, and she clung to the side of the ship as it dipped and rose. Waves slapped and surged, sending spray flying. The wharves and buildings of London were dark against a gilded sky. Rose was below in their cabin, tired out by the events of the last few days. There had been little rest from walking for her, so she had told them. But Philippa was too restless to sleep, weary as she was.

'I thought you would be asleep.' Guy spoke at her shoulder, and instantly she was remembering all that was between them.

'I decided to come and see what the city looks like from out here.' She jumped as his elbow brushed hers.

'The fairest of cities, she's been called. And if the Savoy still stood, one could see it. It's a pity,' muttered Guy.

She did not look at him but stared out over the sparkling gold-edged waves. Gazing upon his bruised face made her feel a need to reach out and touch him.

'I'm glad we came upon your Rose. She will provide you with the company you need. It was necessary for you to have somebody.'

'Necessary?' She felt breathless, insecure, furious with him for making her feel so.

'I'm a wild one,' he mocked. 'Didn't you hear your maid say so? But you don't need her to tell you that, do you?' She looked at him quickly and away, and would have moved but the shifting deck only served to bring them closer. 'You don't agree with your maid?'

'I know that you are no saint,' she muttered. 'But saints live in Paradise, so I would not expect to find one on earth.' He was much too close for her comfort.

'No temptation to drive them wild—no Philippa?'

'I don't drive you wild!' protested Philippa desperately. Butterfly wings of sensation were fluttering uncontrollably up and down her spine. 'Like a sister I shall be to you.'

'A sister? Ha!' he responded, suddenly grim-visaged. 'You did not behave like a sister to me last night!'

You didn't behave like a brother!' she fired back, seeking to push past him, but she had not found her sea legs and stumbled over his feet as he turned.

His hand shot out and prevented her from falling, but brought her close to him. A moment he gazed, then his mouth sought hers and found it. Hard and punishing was his kiss, and she resisted. Then unexpectedly his hold slackened, his fingers moved up and came to rest about her throat. He caressed tenderly the place where the pulse beat rapidly, and his lips buffed hers more gently, causing her to question such tenderness in a wild man. Her mouth opened beneath his, and she swallowed painfully. 'I am betrothed to your brother.' She said the words as if she had committed them to memory—just as she had her prayers when a child. There was silence except for the waves slapping the sides of the ship, and the shout of a seaman.

'Bear that in mind, then—always,' he whispered against her mouth.

'I have, since I was ten years old,' she replied in a barely audible voice. 'Perhaps you should remember it also,' she added with a touch of spirit, and a hint of a sparkle in her eyes.

'I try.' His expression clouded, and releasing her, he turned away across the unsteady deck.

She stared after him, before swaying and stumbling in his wake. Hampered as she was by her skirts and stinging tears, she nearly fell down the ladder that led to her cabin. When at last she lay on the lower bunk, she could only pray that being in love was a passing phase and that tumbling out of it was as easy as falling into it. Then she could face meeting the man who awaited her in Yorkshire—could face being his wife.

Sitting on the deck the next morning with Rose, eating a breakfast of smoked bacon and rather hard biscuit, Philippa tried to keep her attention on the scene about her, while not allowing her eyes to wander too often to where Guy stood on the poop deck conversing with the master. His longish black hair beneath the turbanned liripipe was whipped about his face by the strong breeze that filled the sail. Only once had his glance washed over her when she came on deck. A brief nod in so doing, and that was all. Her spirits were low but she was determined to appear cheerful.

Now that they were out of the estuary and into the North Sea, all the tales she had heard about sea monsters and pirates were more real and believable. Mermaids, sea serpents that could drag a ship to the bottom, and fish as large as Jonah's whale were said to frequent these waters! Pirates were said to abound, who were not necessarily French or Spanish, or even Scots. There was hostility and rivalry enough between the different seaports that dotted the English coast to turn the crews from the harbours to piracy. Earlier that morning she had prayed and included a prayer to Saint Nicholas, the patron saint of sailors, and just for added security she had sent a petition winging to Saint Thomas, who was believed to take an interest in those who dared the dangers of sea voyages. Hopefully the saints would not be kept busy on her behalf, she thought sardonically, suddenly thinking of her father's death.

She frowned, and scanned the deck once more. The gentle low clucking of several hens confined in a cage to provide food for the journey attracted her attention. Their voice was so familiar that it soothed. The deck dipped and rose, dipped and rose, seeming to go deeper each time as the day wore on. Spray flew high, scattering myriad icy droplets over them. Philippa pulled her blue surcote tighter over the scarlet gown.

'Mistress Philippa!' Rose spoke suddenly, disturbing her thoughts. 'Master Milburn is signalling to you.'

She looked up. 'You go, Rose, and see what he wants.'

The maid nodded and went. Listening to her feet, Philippa was tempted to watch her progress across the deck and her meeting with Guy, but resisted. It seemed an age before she returned.

'Master Milburn says there's a squall coming up, and that we are to go to the cabin,' declared Rose, clutching at the cargo lashed to the deck, which was sheltering them from the worst of the wind.

'You have been all that time just to tell me this?' said Philippa crossly. The wind had whipped colour into Rose's face, and clad in one of the more serviceable gowns Beatrice had given her, she looked extremely pretty.

'He was asking after your manor—wanting to know the number of labourers in the fields, and the craftsmen our village could boast.'

'If he wished to know more about my manor, he should have asked *me*.'

'But you sent me to him,' Rose parried irritably. 'He said I had a good grasp of manorial affairs.' She smiled slightly.

'Is that so surprising? You sat with me when my father discussed such matters.' Why she was so annoyed she could not quite understand, but then as she looked at her, she wondered if Guy had deliberately kept her talking. Rose did not have freckles, and her eyes were a lovely hazel, brown and green flecked. Her nose was dainty, and there was a hint of a cleft in her firm round chin.

The sun suddenly vanished, and she looked up. A heavy mass of black cloud was being tumbled across the sky in their direction. Another curl of spray arched and flung water, drenching them both. They gasped, and instinctively clung to each other as the next wave slammed the ship.

'Let us go below,' cried Philippa, rising with a shiver, and clutching at the tarpaulined cargo.

The rain came suddenly, mercilessly heavy as it poured down in great sweeping sheets. They slipped and slithered as they moved towards the raised stern, needing to hang on to what they could—rope—beam—cargo. Past the squawking, wing-flapping hens they went, and for a fleeting second Philippa pitied them, but at least their cage was firmly wedged between a couple of beams. The sail was being lowered. Guy was with the seamen, his hat gone, and wet medusa-like locks clinging to his neck. His attention was on his task. She saw the wet material tight over the muscles at his shoulder, arm and leg. Then they reached the ladder. As she climbed down, first and uppermost in her thoughts was relief at being out of the worst of the storm, and they both sank on the bottom bunk.

'We'll have to get out of these wet clothes,' stuttered Rose, 'or we'll catch our death.'

'I know,' shouted Philippa. She got no further, as the plunging ship flung them to the floor. It righted itself a moment later, and they slid across towards the bunk.

Philippa hoisted herself back on to it, and lying flat, she began to peel off her gown beneath the cover of one of the blankets, more for warmth than out of modesty, for Rose had often dressed her. She wrapped herself in a blanket, and her maid followed suit, sitting, her feet outstretched, at the bottom of Philippa's bunk. They were both exhausted.

The storm continued, until eventually the movement of the ship appeared to be less violent, and Philippa began to stir. Some time later the dull thud of feet shook the ladder, and half dazed, she sat up, pulling the blanket closely about her. Rose still slept.

First Guy's sodden hose-clad legs appeared, then the rest of him. He stood, swaying with fatigue.

Philippa got up from the bunk. 'You look exhausted!'

'I am. I just wanted to make sure you were all right, and to reassure you that the storm hasn't caused too much damage to the ship,' he muttered in a dull voice. He swayed again, putting out a hand to steady himself, but missed the ladder completely. Philippa made a grab for him as he lost his balance, only to trip over the blanket. They both fell in a tangle of arms and legs.

'Damn!' the utterance came from Philippa as she struggled to rise, but Guy was beneath her, lying on an end of the blanket.

'Such language from a lady—but ouch!' he groaned, trying to move. Raising himself on an elbow, his blue gaze fixed on her.

'I wish you could get up from my blanket,' she said in a whisper, her cheeks pale.

'So do I.' There was the slightest hint of laughter in his eyes. Their glances locked, and she experienced a honeyed sensation that melted her limbs. He reached up and pulled her down on top of him. 'I think you'll have to help me...perhaps if we rolled over together?'

Philippa nodded, unable to trust her voice to reply. His doublet was damp against her skin, roughening it, when his arms suddenly tightened as he rolled with her.

'You pull part of the blanket free,' he murmured, giving a yawn.

She carefully obeyed him, attempting to stem the treacherous wave of colour, and praying that Rose would not choose this moment to wake up. Part of the blanket worked free, so that she was able to bring a fold of it across her breasts. It took a few minutes, and when she looked at him once more, his eyes were closed. Exasperated, she groaned. If Rose should wake! 'Guy,' she whispered, putting her mouth against his ear. 'We can't stay here. Wake up.' She could not bear any more emotion!

His one good eye blinked open sleepily, and rested on her face. 'Where...? Damn! Beg your pardon, Philippa. Almost asleep.'

'I do have eyes, Guy,' she muttered. 'Could you move off the blanket so that we could both get up now?'

'Get up?' He grimaced. 'Just when I'd found a warm dry spot!' He did not make a move.

She expelled a long breath. 'Master Milburn,' she snapped, 'I cannot believe you are comfortable like this! I can't believe we are having this conversation—not after last night!'

'Last night?' He blinked, then suddenly seemed to pull himself together. 'Of course! Brother and sister! Hell!' He reached out and managed to grasp the ladder and pull himself off the blanket. Then, staggering to his feet, he leaned against it. His expression was sombre as he stared down at her, swathing herself in the blanket's folds from neck to feet. 'You know, Mistress Cobtree...' he paused to yawn, 'the only way we seem able to stay out of each other's arms is by keeping away from each other.' His tone was derisive.

Philippa stared up at him. She had to agree! 'I think I understand what you are saying,' she returned brusquely, 'and I will do my best to stay out of your way while on this ship.' Awkwardly she got up, folding her arms across her breasts.

'It would be wiser, perhaps.' He sighed, and turning away, was soon out of her sight.

Her throat aching, Philippa crossed the short distance to her bunk. She was suddenly near to tears, and had to swallow them back.

'Well!' Rose's hazel eyes were wide with interest.

'How long have you been awake? No! Don't tell me!' commanded Philippa, determined not to consider that Rose had heard and seen all that passed between her and Guy.

'I think that perhaps you should have been betrothed to this brother, Mistress Philippa! I wonder what Sir Hugo would think...'

'That's enough, Rose! Get off my bunk.' She swept the maid's legs down with an angry gesture.

Rose moved hurriedly without saying another word, and climbed up to her own bunk. Philippa stretched herself out, thinking that it was going to be a long voyage if she was going to steer clear of Guy Milburn—and difficult—but somehow she would do it. She had to, for it was just as he had said. Distance, perhaps, would lend disenchantment to the feelings she had for him, and then she would find it easier to recover from them.

'Mistress Philippa, you can't go on like this,' declared Rose in a rough voice. ''Tis pleasant on deck. The sun's shining, and the sea's reasonably calm. There's even gulls overhead now. You've spent too much time down in this cabin—it can't be healthy!'

'Don't talk nonsense!' Philippa raised her head. 'Is *he* on deck?'

'You mean Master Guy?' the maid responded in a sly voice, smiling slightly. 'He is, and he admired my gown.' She smoothed her skirts with a caressing hand.

'Then I shall stay here,' murmured her mistress, adding, 'When did he say we would reach Kingston-on-Hull?'

'Some time this evening,' replied Rose affably. 'You'll have to speak to him then, and be in his company. Over a week, and not a word exchanged between you.'

'It's none of your business, Rose!'

'He asks after you.' Rose sat down on the bunk, staring measuringly at her mistress. 'Whenever I go on deck, his face lightens, until he realises it's me and not you. Why should he do all these things if he doesn't feel something for you?'

'Because he is responsible for me, and wishes me to be in prime condition when he hands me over to Sir Hugo. And maybe, Rose, he is pleased to see you—and does not think about me at all.'

'I don't believe that,' Rose laughed, 'or he would be more pleasant instead of so grim. That is, when he's not passing the time telling tales to the mariners.' She closed her eyes, and a dreamy expression came over her face. 'They're of knights and fair maidens—of giant beasts and battles. Of Paradise he speaks also,' she declared in admiring tones.

Philippa's face clouded. 'I think he's bewitched you! What else does he speak of?'

'We talk about my life and yours on the manor. If you care for hunting, or whether you like music. I told him you can't abide hunting, but play the lute prettily. He seemed pleased.'

'And you think he is concerned about me?' snapped Philippa, her green eyes dilating. 'He doesn't want me to be happy.' She swung her legs to the floor.

'Perhaps he doesn't,' murmured Rose pensively. 'He's a good man, is Master Guy. He cares about people— even me. But I don't think he's happy.' She toyed with the plaited leather girdle about her hips.

'You say he's good, and yet at the same time you don't think he wants me to be happy? Where is the good in that, Rose?' She gazed at her thoughtfully. She was pretty! And Guy had admired the gown she wore. A twist of jealousy curled inside her. 'Has he kissed you, Rose?' Her tone was sharp.

'Kissed me?' Rose frowned. 'That he has not! What are you thinking of, Mistress Philippa, when you know it is you he wants,' she said boldly. They exchanged glances.

Philippa flushed. 'Don't say such things! Forget what you overheard the night of the storm.'

'I don't think *he* has,' said Rose softly, her eyes on her mistress's face. 'I think he would have liked to spend the night in your arms.'

'Rose!' She went over to the ladder, suddenly in need of fresh air.

The sun was shining, just as Rose had said, when she came out on the deck in a swirl of scarlet skirts. How good it was to be out of that cabin! Deep breaths of salty air refreshed her lungs. She climbed over a coil of rope and stood gazing towards the distant coastline. Guy was on the poop, his arms resting on the rail—she had taken that in when emerging on deck.

'At last!'

Philippa started, although she had heard his footfalls. 'I had the headache—and thought some fresh air...' Her voice was cool, her manner composed, despite the swifter run of her blood.

'Sensible of you. You look pale.' He had missed her company and the sight of her diminutive figure, her smile—and the way she sometimes met his eyes with hers, and they lit up. Had she been dreaming lately, he wondered, not wanting to ask, in case his words triggered off the bad memories.

'Perhaps that's just as well. Only a week ago I was quite burnt by the sun.' She turned and looked at him. The bruising and swelling had all but vanished, only a faint smudge of yellow under his eye and a healing scar on his cheek remained. It was a mistake coming on deck, she realised instantly. Nothing had changed. That tug of attraction was still there, and the look she gave him held a hint of greed as her eyes took in every feature of his face.

'You still have your freckles.' He smiled slightly.

Her mouth curved just a little. 'They are the bane of my life! Nothing will banish them.' It seemed a strange conversation after not seeing each other for a week, but it was something to be talking to him. 'Rose—Rose has been telling me how you kept the crew—and herself— spellbound with your tales.' She moved slowly away, towards the prow.

'Has she?' He walked at her shoulder. 'You dressed her up just like a lady, Philippa, but why? She has a look of you, but she isn't you,' he said ill-humouredly.

'What do you mean by that?' she countered, her brows knitting. 'She could no longer wear the gown she had when we found her in London.'

'Is that the only reason you sent her to me dressed so finely?' His features were serious.

'What other could there be?'

Guy pulled a face. 'I thought you might have sent her to me instead of you. As a replacement, you understand?' She stared at him. 'To satisfy my carnal lusts, so that I don't bother you,' he added softly, a flush darkening his cheeks. 'There is no need, you know. I won't bother you again.'

'You think I could do that to Rose?' she asked, her voice furious. Her face was upturned to his, and the green eyes sparkled. 'I never sent her.'

Guy gave a twisted smile. 'It seems that I was wrong again!'

'I have known her all my life. We have been companions since her mother acted as maid to mine before they both perished in an outbreak of the plague a few years ago.' Her fingers twisted tightly on a fold of her gown, and her eyes were angry as she stared out over the water.

'You have made your point,' he said tersely. 'There is no need to labour it. It was you who seemed to hate the serfs that day in Canterbury. In a day or two you will be under my brother's protection, and after that, I doubt we shall meet for a long time,' he declared bluntly. 'I shall not linger at Hugo's. There is the shearing, and all that that entails. Then, most likely, I shall go to Calais. So you do not have to fear that you will have to put up with my company much longer.' He inclined his head stiffly, and left her standing.

If Philippa had wondered what they would do after landing at Kingston-on-Hull, she would have supposed that they would hire horses and go on their way as soon as possible, and she said as much.

'Not possible! Too late in the day! Tomorrow!' said Guy roughly, taking the bundle of clothing from Rose's hand and slinging it over his shoulder.

'What do we do now?' She stood on the quay, the ground seeming to rise and fall beneath her. It was a peculiar sensation, and she felt disorientated.

'We'll have to stay at my agent's house. It's not far.' Guy began to walk swiftly ahead of them wishing they could have gone on, and praying that they would not have to spend more than one night in Kingston. Not that he did not like the place. The first Edward had planned its buildings, purchasing land and having the harbour extended. He had had streets and markets laid out, and roads built to link the town with Yorkshire's hinterland. It had a royal charter, a mint, and two weekly markets. No small honour! But he would rather be gone, to get on with his life, and to forget the would-be sister who trailed at his heels.

They stopped at a house, where the door was opened by a man of middle years, tall and gaunt, with a crop of greying hair. His surprise was swiftly masked, and they were made welcome. His wife, a woman of ample proportions, wore a wimple that concealed her hair and neck. Her gown was brown, with little material in the skirts, and her disapproval of the two women was obvious. She showed them to a bedchamber upstairs, with only a crucifix to adorn one whitewashed wall.

'We have supped, but I shall prepare something for you. But come when I call you, or it will spoil.' She sniffed, as her gaze ran swiftly over them once more, before leaving the room.

'Somehow I don't think she approves of us, Rose,' said Philippa, sitting wearily on the double bed.

'It's 'cos we're young. She likely thinks we'll make eyes at that longshanks of a husband of hers!' The maid yawned and sat beside her mistress. 'No feathers here... I was hoping, after that bunk...'

Philippa nodded. 'Help me out of this gown. I shall wear the blue one.'

With a sigh, Rose started to undo the fastenings. After Philippa had washed, she helped her on with the blue silk gown that fitted closely at breast and waist. The skirts fell in folds from the hips. She braided her hair, fastened it up in a silver net, and looked her over appraisingly and with a frowning envy. 'This isn't a feast you are going to, mistress.'

Philippa stared at her and pulled a face. 'I know, Rose.'

'Then this is for Master Guy's benefit?'

'No, Rose, it is for my own.' A nerve quivered in her cheek.

'Is it? You would tease him, perhaps?'

'You presume too much!' Philippa's brows drew together stormily.

'Mourning! We should both be in mourning!' Rose's voice shook.

Philippa's mouth trembled. All her pleasure in wearing her finery, given by Beatrice because they were too small for her now, evaporated, and she buried her face in her hands, aghast at her own thoughtlessness.

Rose looked down at her bowed head, and the bitter jealousy eased. Shared grief was not new to either of them. She put an arm about her shoulders. 'Hush, now! Tomorrow you will have to say your farewells to Master Guy, and your smiles will have to be for Sir Hugo. Tonight...'

Philippa lifted her head, attempting a watery smile. 'I wanted...to pretend...' She halted. What had she wanted? To have him look at her again with that dark desire in his face? Not to part angrily from him?

'Why not pretend?' Rose shrugged. 'It is a game I have played myself. If I was rich! If I could wear fine clothes! If a man might look at me in the way Master Guy looked at you on the ship and would speak so prettily to me.'

Philippa rubbed a wet cheek. 'I never thought about your feeling like that, Rose. How selfish I am!'

'Not really selfish—you weren't brought up to consider that serfs dreamed and hoped, could think that they had a right to more than they had.' Rose picked up a towel. 'Your eyes are red, but maybe that's for the best, if they've been told about your loss.'

'Ay!' Philippa scrubbed at her eyes with the towel, thinking of Rose's words. You don't know what it's like to be a serf, she had said on that night her father was killed. 'Let's go down, for there is little point in delaying. The sooner I go, the sooner tomorrow will come—and it might be easier, once the parting is done with.'

They went.

CHAPTER NINE

'IT WAS a waste of effort, Rose.' Philippa moved her head restlessly under the maid's hand. It was morning, and there had been no chance to talk last night. They had shared the double bed with the agent's wife, while Guy and their host slept downstairs. 'He barely looked at me the whole evening.'

'Perhaps one look was enough,' murmured Rose. 'It is not important that he didn't gawp at you.'

'You think not?' Philippa gave a low laugh.

'I didn't notice you gazing at him all evening. You kept your eyes on that agent, seeming to hang on to his every word.' Rose looped a plait about her ears.

'I wasn't listening at all.' She sighed. 'A madness has seized me that I should still think of him in that certain way, Rose. What am I to do?'

'There's nothing you can do, and you know it.' Deftly Rose began to plait again. 'There's an end to it, Mistress Philippa.'

'An end,' agreed her mistress in an unsteady voice.

'There's many a young life blighted in this age we live in,' said Rose. 'But at least we are alive.' She stepped back. 'There, you'll do! That dark green suits you, despite its plainness. And, in the circumstances, an air of sadness will be expected.'

Philippa nodded. 'You are right, of course.' She straightened her shoulders. 'If only I could have decided for myself—if only I knew really how he felt about me. Wanting perhaps is not enough. Loving? But we have made no such declaration. This time tomorrow, how will I feel about it all, Rose?'

The maid did not answer, but only squeezed her hand. Together they went downstairs to where Guy was waiting to take Philippa to his brother.

Philippa gazed down at the huddle of grey stone buildings in the valley with trepidation. She was tired. Only once had they stopped since early morning—to partake of a silent meal among the hills. So many hills, some dotted with sheep, others wooded. So much moorland, but few towns had they seen. They had passed through Knaresborough a short time ago, gazing at the castle on its perch high above the river Nidd. The Duke of Lancaster had it in his honour, so Guy informed her briefly. Now they overlooked Sir Hugo's manor.

'The house looks so forbidding,' murmured Philippa, half to herself.

'It is fortified because the Scots have been known to raid as far south as this. Lately we have been at peace, although the truce has been broken on both sides. That is why Lancaster was sent north by the king's council to mend the truce once more. England has enough trouble without the Scots invading us again,' explained Guy, his face sombre.

'I remember now.' Her fingers stifled a yawn.

'The journey was tiring?' He covered her hand with his.

'Not as tiring as some,' she said in a low voice. For a moment her hand rested beneath his and they exchanged glances, and she surmised that he, too, was remembering the flight to London. She withdrew her hand and saw a shadow darken his face.

Barely had Guy swung out of the saddle when a man appeared in the doorway of the house. Old in years, he came limping down the steps towards them, a huge smile on his crusty face.

'Master Guy, and glad it is I am to see you! The rumours we've been hearing—and the trouble it's caused in some places. Fair worried, we've been.' Briefly his glance went to the women before settling on Guy's face again.

'What trouble? And where's my brother? How is he?' Guy eased the gauntlets from his hands and stretched his aching fingers.

A crease furrowed the man's forehead. 'He's up and gone to Knaresborough. There's been such a to-do about Duke John freeing his bondsmen and going to set himself up as king. Then there have been riots in York and Beverley—attacks on monasteries, and the clerks assaulting merchants!'

'I don't believe it! Lancaster set himself up as king— never!' Guy pulled his gauntlets through his fingers with some violence.

'That's what the rumours say—it's because Richard declared him a traitor. The Duchess Constancia was refused entry at Pontefract and had to travel by torchlight through the forest to Knaresborough.'

'Sweet Jesu!' A grim smile played about his beautiful mouth. 'What fool would believe that the king would do such a thing! The peasants destroyed Lancaster's palace in the south, and Richard's not going to believe such a rumour. It is a lie set about by his enemies.'

'That's what Sir Hugo said, and the reason why he has gone to Knaresborough to discover what Duke John's going to do.' The man shook his grizzled head.

'What were you thinking of to let him go to Knaresborough? His health must have improved dramatically,' Guy said sardonically.

'You know you can't tell him,' said the man gruffly. 'And if there's a fight, he'll want to be in it.'

Guy frowned and was silent a moment, then said, 'Is my aunt still here? I have business of my own to attend to.'

'Ay, but right muddled she's getting with old age.'

'No matter. She's a woman, isn't she, and can see to our visitors. Rob, this is Mistress Cobtree and Mistress Rose. I'll see Aunt Margaret before I go.'

'Go, Master Guy? Home, you mean?'

Guy nodded.

'Sir Hugo won't be pleased! Been giving much thought to your return with the lady—and a wedding,' Rob said in a worried voice.

Guy shrugged. 'See to the horses, and find me a fresh one if that's possible. My agent is sending a lad for these in a day or two.' He turned towards the steps that ran up the side of the wall at a slant to a door on the first floor.

'Guy!' cried Philippa, swinging down from the horse without waiting for assistance. A shock had rippled through her as she listened to their conversation. Had she escaped London only to be engulfed in another rebellion? 'You would leave so soon?'

He stared down at the ground, watching her swirling skirts settle about her ankles. 'I'll see you inside, and introduce you to my aunt. I'll take a goblet of wine with you, and then leave. There's no more to be said,' he muttered. He turned and strode quickly to the steps.

Philippa was suddenly furious. 'Rob, is it? You will untie the baggage and bring it in before you see to Master Guy's horse.' She did not wait for a reply, but crossed the courtyard and climbed the steps, and came to the hall with aching legs.

Guy stood by a settle, talking to an elderly woman dressed in grey. They both looked up as she approached. Only briefly did she take in the woman's appearance, seeing a thin, sallow face framed by a goffered veil. The eyes were blue and vague. She seemed agitated.

'Aunt Margaret, this is Mistress Cobtree—my aunt Colby,' he explained impersonally, before moving over to a table on which stood a pitcher.

Mistress Margaret's hands fluttered halfway up to meet Philippa's and then dropped before touching them. 'You've come a long way, child, so Guy informs me. You must be tired. Sit down.' She smiled rather sweetly as she peered short sightedly at her.

'Thank you, but I would rather stand. I have been on horseback all day.' She could barely control her impatience. She heard footsteps behind her, and Rose was at her back. Moving out of the way, she went over to Guy.

He turned to face her, two brimming goblets in his hands. She took the one thrust rather unceremoniously at her, but did not drink even when he raised the vessel in a salute. There was a look on his face that hurt.

'Well? Aren't you going to drink to my happiness now?' he sneered. 'I do to yours—and my brother's.'

'Guy, please,' cried Philippa in a brittle voice. 'Don't! Not after...'

'After what?' His eyes were like two hard blue stones. 'If you had not been my brother's betrothed, matters would have been different. I...' The beautiful mouth twisted. 'Best forget the last two weeks and everything that happened between us.'

'Will you?' Her voice was unsteady.

For an instant, he almost smiled, and he half stretched out a hand to her, only to snatch it back before their fingers touched.

Her expression hardened, and her eyes sparkled as she tossed off the wine. 'I pray that you will be happy. As happy as it is possible for me to be—married to your brother!'

Guy rammed the vessel down on the table. 'Goodbye, Philippa!' He did not look back as he stalked out of the hall. There was such a rage in him that only by riding until he was exhausted would he be able to despatch its hold on him.

Philippa gazed stonily at a distant tapestry across the large hall, listening to his retreating footsteps. They faded. Now she could hear the drone of Mistress Margaret's and Rose's voices. Rob came in, dumped the baggage on the floor and went out again. How long she stood there, stemming the flood of short-lived memories, she did not know. Hoofbeats sounded, and then it was as if she breathed again and knew she had to see him one more time before he left.

When she reached the top of the steps, he was already riding under the gatehouse arch. Her cry came out as a croak, so tight was her throat. How stiff her muscles were! He was out of sight! As she quickened her pace, the skirts tripped her and made her over-balance. She tumbled, and her head hit the wall.

It was Rose who found her. When she saw the hunched-up figure, she thought that Philippa was dead, until she knelt and discovered that her heart still beat. Gazing frantically about the courtyard and wondering at its deserted appearance at such a time, she was relieved to see Rob come out of the stables. She called him, waving wildly. Limping, he came over and barely listened to her babbled, almost incoherent, words, but lifted Philippa in his arms and carried her slowly up the steps.

In no time at all she settled Philippa as comfortably as she knew how in a bed in a turret room, after some confused advice from Mistress Margaret. She showed no sign of coming round and lay still and quiet in the narrow bed, the covers pulled up to her chin.

Later, getting up from a stool by the bed, Rose went over to the window that let little of the evening light in. She had asked Rob to fetch a physician, but he had refused.

'Little use, mistress,' he muttered, scratching his head. 'Nothing they can do. I've seen this before when one of us grooms came off a horse. Just lay as dead for days.

He woke up in the end, but his wits had gone begging. Never the same after that.' He shook his head and left the chamber.

Guy's aunt, who had been listening, suffered a nervous spasm. 'Does he mean that she'll be mad?'

Rose had answered noncommittally, and had put aunt Colby to bed, so agitated had she become. She was far from calm herself as she looked out at the quiet countryside. What if Philippa died? Clasping her trembling hands together, she turned and walked slowly to the head of the bed. How had she come to fall? She had rushed out of the hall a short time after Master Guy—but why? She had not been able to hear all that had passed between them, trying to keep hold of the thread of the old lady's rambling conversation, but had heard enough to make her feel sorry for both of them. How would he feel if she died? How would Sir Hugo feel if she died? He would not grieve as much as Master Guy, that was for sure! Nine years since he had seen her. She pulled herself up. What was she doing, dwelling on death! Reaching out, she stroked Philippa's cheek, and it moved slightly. Rose's heart seemed to collide with her ribs, and sinking on to her knees, rested her head on the bed. All night she would keep vigil, if need be—and all the nights to come, if necessary! But she would not leave her alone.

Philippa stirred, opening her eyes on an unfamiliar room. The flickering brightness that enabled her to see Rose came from a rush-light in a metal bowl near at hand. Her tongue tried to form words, but it was too much of an effort. But the breath she drew sharply sounded loud, and caused Rose to waken.

'Praise the Virgin, you are awake at last,' cried Rose, relief lighting her face.

Philippa moved her head uneasily and winced, and her eyes closed again.

'Oh, don't go to sleep again!' Rose gripped her hand tightly.

'I'm . . . sorry.' It was just a whisper of a sound before she drifted into semi-consciousness.

The maid got up and went to stand by the window, glad of the cool air on her heated cheeks. Light-headed with relief, her spirits rose. There would be no need for greeting Sir Hugo with the news that his betrothed was dead, praise God!

The next time Philippa woke, it was daylight. Her eyelashes fluttered open, and Rose smiled, and asked if there was anything she wanted.

'A drink?' She ran the tip of her tongue over dry lips.

Rose went to fetch some water, glad that there seemed little sign of madness.

She took only a couple of sips of the water before pushing it away, and lay back with a sigh. 'I don't know this room,' she said fretfully.

'That is because you have never been in it before,' explained Rose. 'Would you like me to help you to sit up, so that you can see better? We only came here yesterday.'

A small frown puckered her brow. 'Yesterday? I can't think . . . How did I come here?' She attempted to lever herself up on her elbows.

Rose moved quickly, adjusting the pillows behind her shoulders. Anxiety dragged at her mouth once more. 'We came with Master Guy. This is Sir Hugo's manor. You fell down the steps outside. Don't you remember?'

Philippa flopped back against the pillows, her eyelids drooping. Her fingers moved restlessly on the coverlet. 'I can't remember anything about falling. Steps, you say?'

'Ay!' Rose's mouth was dry, and she sank on the stool. Had the fall scattered her wits? 'Master Guy had just left. You must remember him,' she added, leaning towards her mistress.

'Guy,' she said in a subdued voice. An image snapped into her mind—blue eyes, a beautiful mouth, dark hair. There was pain, not only in her knees and an elbow, but in her head and heart. She shut her eyes.

'Mistress Philippa! Don't go away again—please!' Rose clutched her hand tightly, but she did not answer. What was she to do if Philippa did not regain her wits? Rob's words came to her again, chilling her blood. Her glance rested on the still figure in the bed, then, crossing the room she sat down again to keep vigil.

Not long after, Philippa woke again, and her eyes met Rose's. For a moment neither of them spoke. Both were afraid to ask questions. Then Rose cleared her throat. 'Would you like something to eat? Or to drink, perhaps?'

'A drink,' replied her mistress in a low voice. 'Rose...' Rose turned quickly. 'You know me?'

'Of course I know you! Shouldn't I?' She rocked her head on the pillow as if it hurt.

'You said you couldn't remember—I thought you had forgotten everything!'

'I haven't forgotten you, Rose.' She eased herself higher against the pillows, her gaze intent. 'Did we talk earlier? You said . . . I fell?'

'Ay. Down the steps outside. It was just after Master Guy left.' She filled a cup with water. 'Do you remember now?'

Philippa pressed the tips of her fingers against her forehead. 'Vaguely I remember you speaking to me in this chamber, but I can't recall anything about falling— or coming here. You say Master Guy—has left?'

Rose nodded, handing her the water. 'You rushed out of the hall just after you had a goblet of wine together, and he had departed.'

'A goblet of wine?' She tried to concentrate—to remember, but could not. 'I have no recollection of doing what you say.' Her fingers trembled on the cup. 'If he has left—does that mean I have seen Sir Hugo?'

'No, he is not here yet. He has gone to some town or other on Lancaster's business. Something to do with him being declared a traitor, and the rebels up here. I didn't catch it all from the groom who was telling Master Guy.'

'Who's a traitor? Sir Hugo?' She was getting confused, and took a sip of water as if that could help her to work out her bewilderment.

'No! Lancaster! And it's only a rumour. I presume Sir Hugo's gone to find out what's truth and what isn't.'

'I understand. Or think I understand.' She took another drink. 'Where's ... Master Guy gone?' She did not look at Rose.

'Home. Wherever that is. You don't remember what he said to you yesterday?' asked Rose anxiously.

'I—I can't remember. I wish I could,' she said soberly.

'I heard some of what you said—and he said,' murmured Rose in a slow voice. 'It was difficult with Mistress Margaret talking.'

'Mistress Margaret?'

'Master Guy's aunt. She rambles a bit, and I had to listen, but she has a quiet voice. I couldn't help overhearing.'

'I'm glad you did—if you can tell me what he—he said.' Philippa gave a ghost of a smile.

Rose wrinkled her dainty nose. 'He said if you had not been his brother's betrothed, matters would have been different.'

'In what way?'

'He didn't say, but what he did go on to say was that you had best forget the last two weeks and everything that had happened between you.' She sighed.

'Oh!' There was a long silence while Philippa stared bright-eyed at the window slit. Then, 'What did I reply to that, Rose?'

'I didn't catch your answer with you speaking so softly. But a few moments later I heard you say something about—being happy—and about being married to his brother. Then he rammed his cup down so hard that we turned and looked at you both. And he said ''Goodbye, Philippa!'' and left the hall.'

'Did he sound angry?' Closing her eyes wearily, she felt the tears prickle her lashes.

'Sounded sort of hard—hurt, like, I would say. Looked like a thundercloud. If he'd had a tail, he would have lashed it,' Rose muttered, sensing her mistress's anguish, and hoping she would never fall in love herself. Didn't seem a very comfortable state to be in, all things considered!

'Oh, Rose, if I weren't so unhappy, you would make me laugh. Thunderclouds with tails!' She gave a watery smile. 'Do you think you could fetch me some water to wash?'

'Of course! You rest, love.' Rose touched her cheek tenderly. 'You'll get over it. We've seen through other tragedies together. We'll see through this.'

'Of course we shall! But—But if he's unhappy, too? Do you think he was?'

Rose's lips pursed. 'Ay. But men are different from us. You don't hear many tales where it's the men who languish or die for love's sake! What he says makes a lot of sense if you are to wed his brother. Forget, and look forward to the future.' She turned and walked to the door. 'I'll go and get some water, and a clean shift. If Sir Hugo returns, you don't want to greet him in that one. Perhaps an undergown would be best. Prettier, anyway.' She smiled as she opened the door. 'You rest now.'

Rest! Philippa stared at the closed door. Pretty herself for Sir Hugo! Hmmph! Forget! She did not want to forget! What had Guy said? If she had not been his brother's betrothed, matters would have been different. How different? Forget what was between them? Which meant he accepted that there had been something! What was it on his side? He had told her he wanted her. Was it more than just a carnal desire? She remembered how he had looked at her in the cabin and how her limbs had seemed to melt with the sweetness of that moment. Could Sir Hugo make her feel like that? If only there was a way out of this betrothal. But she was here in his house, and Guy was gone. It seemed that the future mapped out for her nine years ago would take place just as planned, after all, and there was nothing she could do.

Rose returned, bringing water and a clean garment. A towel also, and some soap that did not smell quite as wholesome as that which Beatrice had had from Castile. She chattered brightly as she helped Philippa to wash and change. Her talk was of the journey yesterday, of the night spent in Kingston-on-Hull, which her mistress remembered. It seemed that only yesterday was blotted out.

'Hush, Rose,' said Philippa at last. 'I'm tired, and my head is aching.'

'You wish me to leave you?' said Rose, gathering up the soiled shift. 'You do look pale.'

'You go and rest yourself, Rose,' she murmured, closing her eyes. 'Come back later, and we shall talk again—but I doubt you will jog my memory of yesterday.'

Rose nodded and left the room. Before the door closed, Philippa had drifted into sleep.

It was evening when Rose returned with a bowl of broth. 'I thought you might be hungry by now.' She set the tray over her knees.

'I am. And I tire of this bed, but when I tried to get up, my head spun so much that I quickly got in again.' Philippa picked up the spoon. 'Has Sir Hugo returned yet?'

'No. But he is expected soon, I think, for there is such a bustle of activity in the kitchen. One of the maids said that a squire had ridden ahead so that supper can be prepared, and suddenly the whole place seems alive. Perhaps it is when the master's away...'

'Most go about their own business,' said Philippa. The broth was good, and she was starting to feel more herself. 'That is the way of things, Rose. When he comes, you must go down and tell him there has been an accident.'

'Rob will most likely tell him. As long as he doesn't tell Sir Hugo what he said to me!' Rose took the empty bowl from her hand.

'And what was that?' said Philippa curiously. There had been an inflection in her voice.

The maid's face was sober. 'That the fall would scatter your wits.'

'Some would say I've always been slightly scatter-brained, Rose!' She gave a smile.

'Some would say anything to a sister, Mistress Philippa. Those brothers of yours—jealous they were because you had more learning. Surely you haven't re-membered childish insults all this time?'

'I must have, mustn't I, Rose? How often was I told that girls did not do this—that—or the other?' She crooked her knees and put her arms about them.

'But you didn't let their words stop you from learning more than they did!'

'I didn't let their words stop me from doing anything I had set my heart on,' she said softly, suddenly pensive.

'Just the same, isn't it, Mistress Philippa?' Rose turned to the window abruptly at the sound of voices from below in the courtyard. They exchanged glances.

'The lord of the house, Rose?' Her heart quickened suddenly.

The maid's head remained tilted as she listened in-tently. 'Ay, 'tis him, all right. I heard someone address him. What shall I do?'

'What I said.'

Rose nodded wordlessly and left the chamber, not rel-ishing the task. She remembered Sir Hugo being a large youth—no, he had been twenty. A large man, who—so the old master had said—did not suffer fools gladly. He had made her stammer like an idiot all those years ago when they had collided in the garden.

Rose came into the hall in a rush, halting abruptly, her eyes meeting those of the man who was sitting in a large chair, his leg outstretched on a servant's lap. She felt a peculiar sensation, a lifting, an awareness, an excitement, never experienced before.

'Who are you?' His voice was deep, and even as he sat one could see he was a very large man. He had massive shoulders and long arms. The hair was corn-coloured, and longer than fashionable. He wore a brown riding-dress, but his outstretched leg was clad in scarlet hose. Thick, fair eyebrows hooded his eyes, and he was bearded.

'You...are Sir Hugo?' She felt as though waking from a dream, and approached slowly, her pulses beating irregularly.

'Ay!' Still their eyes held, and it was as though the pair of them were suspended in time. 'Rob has been telling me.' He cleared his throat. 'Is the maid any better?'

'She—She has woken and had a drink, and some food.' She noticed now that Rob stood at his shoulder.

'Then it is not as bad as Rob says?' He pushed the servant away, getting up awkwardly.

'No, but she is a little confused. She cannot remember yesterday at all.' There was a flush on her cheeks.

'No? Not too good—but at least she's awake, you say?' He walked towards her with an uneven gait.

Rose nodded as he stopped in front of her. His closeness rendered her tongue-tied.

He smiled, and warmth melted her heart. 'You must have help. It seems that you sat with her all night, so the servants tell me.'

'Ay! But I doubt it will be necessary this night.'

'Good. But you must have something to eat and drink. It appears that you have had little—and that will not do.' He took her arm. 'Come and sit with me and tell me what has been happening in the south. Rob says Guy has gone.' He frowned. 'Can't understand it. Not like him. But come and sit down.'

'It is kind of you, Sir Hugo, but could you come upstairs first? The sight of you would surely reassure her. She cannot remember…coming to your house, you see!' Her expression pleaded. The hazel eyes were filled with concern.

'You must not fret yourself. If you think it will help, I shall come.' He hesitated. 'You've changed much from the old days, but now I recognise you. At first sight, I was not sure. Rob only said that one of the ladies had fallen. But I shall come up with you, and later you can tell me what has been happening.'

His talk puzzled Rose. Could he have remembered her after all these years? Surely not—if he had, he would not wish to sit with her, a serf! Lady! Rob had referred to them both as ladies. Well, they said that fine feathers made fine birds, and she wore one of her mistress's gowns. But he was looking at her with a warmth of expression, as if waiting for her to—to lead the way! She did so, although she was more accustomed to following in other people's footsteps. Her awareness of him just behind was almost tangible. Never had any man had such an effect on her. Surely Mistress Philippa would forget Master Guy with such a man as her husband!

They reached the foot of the narrow stone steps and she began to climb, but on reaching the top she paused, realising that he was not with her. She turned and saw that he was only five steps up, no longer climbing, but leaning against the wall. Swiftly she descended.

'What ails you, sir?' Even in the dim light she could see that his face was drawn with pain.

'Damn leg,' he muttered in a vexed voice. 'Think the wound's opened up again.'

Rose was just about to ask 'What wound?' when she remembered that he had been gored by a boar, and the conversation between Rob and Guy the day before. 'Perhaps you shouldn't have gone out so soon,' she murmured in concern. 'Here, let me help you.' She slipped an arm about his waist, forgetting everything but that he was in pain.

He gave a bark of laughter. 'You're only a slip of a lass. You'll never take my weight!'

'I'm stronger than I look,' said Rose indignantly. 'Put your arm about my shoulders, and we'll go down again.'

Sir Hugo stared down at her, and a small tight smile played about his mouth. 'You have changed. I remember how you used to stammer and stutter... when I spoke to you,' he gasped.

Rose flushed and averted her eyes. 'You—You frightened me!' She had ran pell-mell into him, hitting him in the stomach with her head. He had thought that she was her mistress and damned her to hell, and thinking he might have had her beaten, she had not owned to who she was, but stuttered an apology and vanished from his sight speedily.

'I never meant to frighten you,' he said brusquely, resting his weight on her as they carefully negotiated the steps. 'Rest,' he uttered briefly when they reached the foot. She was glad to do so, bowed as she was under that muscular arm.

'Which leg is it, sir?' They leaned against the stone wall.

'Left one. F-Feels like it's bleeding!' He closed his eyes and rested his cheek against her hair.

'Then you should not have your weight on it, or walk any further,' said Rose anxiously. 'Can you rest here without my arm? I can look and see how bad it is, and whether it is wiser to fetch some men to bring a hurdle to carry you on.'

'Dammit, you'll not have me on a hurdle again, lass,' he muttered, lifting his head. 'Let's go on! My bed's in the solar, and there's a separate door into it just up the passage. There's no need to go into...the hall.'

She glanced at him swiftly and would have argued, then decided against it. If he swooned, she would have to fetch help—if they reached the solar, she could fetch his aunt. Slowly they navigated the passage and came to the door he indicated, and she opened it. Shadows filled the chamber, making it difficult to steer his trailing leg round obstacles—a chest, a stool, the foot of the bed. They collapsed in a heap on to the coverlet.

Neither of them moved or spoke for several minutes, only their rapid breathing sounded in the room. Then Rose began to disentangle herself, to remove his arms from her waist and shoulders. For an instant her strength made no impression on their hold. Then she said, 'Sir, you must release me! I must get a light, and someone to help you. I shall fetch your aunt.'

'H—Help, of course!' he muttered, his arms slackening and dropping back on to the bed. 'Not my aunt, though. Rob! Fetch Rob! Tell...nobody else.'

'If that is what you wish.' When she raised herself from him, she realised that her legs could barely carry her because they trembled so much, and she had to hold on to the door before opening it.

His voice made her turn her head as she reached the doorway. 'Ph—Philippa! I—I deem we will deal well to—together, you and I.' Her face stiffened with shock, and her fingers clutched at the door all the tighter.

'Sir Hugo, you are mistaken!' she blurted out. 'I am not your betrothed!'

There came no answer—and when she walked unsteadily back to the bed, she realised why. Her hand came away with blood on her fingers. His face was shuttered. Strength came back to her, and she fled from the room in search of Rob.

CHAPTER TEN

ROSE FOUND Rob in the stable, and told him in a few hurried words what had happened to Sir Hugo. He dropped the bridle he had been cleaning and came with her immediately, muttering an oath under his breath. He reached for a box on a shelf, and tucked it under his arm.

'I knew this would happen!' He rubbed his chin as he stared down at the prone figure on the bed. 'I warned him. But he's that stubborn and impatient,' he grunted. 'We'll need lights!'

'I'll fetch some quickly,' said Rose, already moving towards the door.

'Don't tell anyone else what's happened,' cautioned Rob. 'If anyone asks what the lights are for...but probably they won't. It being you, mistress, they'll think them for the sick lady.'

She paused, wondering if now was the right time to say that she was her mistress, but already he had turned away and was attending his master. A groan from Sir Hugo caused her to go swiftly. No questions were asked, and an offer of some wine for the lady was accepted. Sir Hugo might be glad of it. As soon as she could, she would go upstairs and tell her mistress what had happened.

The rush lights immediately sent the darkness retreating into corners and showed that Rob had not been idle while Rose was away. The lid of a chest flung open revealed chaos within, but there were several lengths of torn linen hanging over the foot of the bed, along with bloodied red hose.

Sir Hugo sprawled against the pillows, his mouth compressed tightly as Rob worked on his leg. The light caught the gleam of his eyes as he lifted his head. 'Good,' he said quietly. 'You thought of bringing some wine.'

'Ay, sir.' She did not look at his leg, for her stomach was churning still from the sight of the blood on her hand. 'Should you not have a physician?' She put down the light and took the cup from the top of the flask.

'And have him tell me I should have let him cut it off? Damn it, lass, would you have me a cripple?' he grunted.

'No, sir,' she said faintly, sitting down abruptly on the bed. 'I—I never realised that your injury was so bad.'

'Would have been worse . . . if it weren't for Rob here,' he muttered, wincing. His fair brows bristled together as if to press down the pain.

Rose averted her eyes and caught Rob's glance. 'Learnt a trick or two in France from the monks when I was there with the old master! Nearly lost my own leg, but they saved it. And I got interested, like. I tried some of the remedies on the horses first,' explained the groom. 'All the poison's gone out of this, but I've put some yarrow on. Don't want it swelling again. Trouble with Sir Hugo is that he won't give it time to knit properly. Perhaps you'll be able to persuade him, mistress.' He gave Rose a grin which showed several missing teeth, and reached for a strip of linen.

'That's enough, Rob,' said Sir Hugo wearily. 'Pour me some wine, lass.'

Rose complied with his request. Words hovered on her tongue, seeking to find the right order—how to say that she was just a serf and that they had both made a mistake.

'That tastes good.' His smile was weak and hardly twitched his beard. 'I'm glad you came when you did, but now it's time you went.' He took another gulp of the wine.

'Sir Hugo,' she began, taking her courage in both hands. 'I must tell you...'

'Not now, lass. Whatever you wish to tell me, it will do in the morning.' His eyes were just narrow slits.

'Go, mistress,' hissed Rob. 'He's that weary and needs quiet now. Tomorrow there'll be time for talking.' His nimble fingers tied the bandage. 'Besides, the other lady will be wondering what's happened to you. There's her to think on. Bless me, if it doesn't rain but it pours! Off with you, for you've done all you can here tonight. And pleased it is he is to see you—that you can be sure.'

'But...' tried Rose desperately.

'In the morning,' whispered Rob, taking her arm with all the familiarity of an old and trusted friend. 'You're tired yourself, and it's to be expected you'd want to tell him about your father being killed and your house being burnt down, and all your mishaps, wanting him to deal with it all. But he has troubles enough to disturb that sleep which he needs badly.' He ushered a speechless Rose to the door—opened it and gently pushed her unresisting body through.

Rose stared at the door as he closed it firmly in her face. Master Guy must have told him some of what had happened in the south, and that knowledge now proved too much for her—that, and all the events of the last two days. Mistress Philippa would know what to do! She'd be able to sort it all out! With drooping shoulders she made her way along the passage and up the steps to her chamber.

Dusk already filled the room, but Philippa was out of bed and standing by the window. She turned as Rose entered, and started forward. 'Where have you been? Where's Sir Hugo?'

'Oh, Mistress Philippa!' cried Rose, and burst into tears.

'Rose, Rose! What is the matter?' She took the two hands that covered the maid's face and clasped them tightly in her own.

'You—You'll never...never believe...' A rush of emotion and a series of sobs prevented her from going on.

'I'll never believe what?' Philippa put her arm round the maid. 'Come and sit down. Hush, now!' She nursed Rose over to the bed and sat down with her, but could not extract a sensible word until the storm of tears had passed. Then the girl poured out all that had happened since she had left the room.

'Sweet Jesu!' Philippa exhaled a gusty breath. 'Are we so alike, Rose, that he could mistake you for me?'

'I've never thought about it before,' said Rose, wiping her face with the back of her hand. 'You'll explain it all in the morning, won't you, Mistress Philippa?'

'Of course! But it's so extraordinary that Guy, too, should have thought we were alike.' She bit her thumbnail, frowning in the dark. 'Is he so handsome, Rose? You sounded quite struck by him.'

'Did I?' She was glad of the darkness that hid the sudden flush that warmed her face.

'Ay, you did,' replied Philippa pensively. 'I wonder why he did not want anyone but Rob to know that his wound is still bad?'

'He has troubles enough,' said Rose in muted tones. 'Perhaps it's to do with his serfs.'

'You know so?' Her head turned quickly.

'No,' Rose muttered, 'it is only a guess. But you heard what Rob told Master Guy about Lancaster setting his bondsmen free. Perhaps Sir Hugo's want their freedom too. Remember how deserted the house and courtyard were the day we arrived? Was it only yesterday?' She sighed. 'They could have been having a meeting while he was away. Remember what it was like at home?'

'Ay! But I don't remember yesterday.' She folded her arms, hugging herself, suddenly cold. 'You really believe...'

'I don't know.'

'Guy mustn't have realised. He could face such a situation now on his own—Hugo's other manor! They could have seized power!' Philippa chewed on her nail again.

'We don't know,' soothed Rose, patting her knee. 'I shouldn't have spoken. Master Guy will have fewer serfs—if any. His grandfather was a serf—or his great-grandfather, and he's for getting rid of bondage.'

'He spoke of that to you?' Philippa's astonishment showed.

'On the ship. We talked about such matters. He said it was the cause of many a quarrel between him and Sir Hugo.' A hiccup punctuated Rose's words.

'What caused you to speak of such matters?' Philippa was conscious of a pang of jealousy, and regret that the time she had spent on the ship had not been in Guy's company.

'Oh, the revolt on your manor... My brother... Master Guy wanted to know if I wished for my freedom, just as Tom had.' She sniffed in an attempt to stop another hiccup.

'And do you, Rose?' It was a matter to which she had never given any consideration.

There was a long silence before Rose answered. 'If what the king promised is kept to—then I am free. But I don't doubt that his council will make him change his mind. Greed and pride will see to that.'

'You haven't really answered my question. Have you been unhappy while in bondage to my father?' Philippa suddenly wanted to know how Rose really felt about her position.

'Often unhappy,' Rose said unemotionally, 'but not all the time. I was content to be your maid, helping you in the house and the garden. But I'm not content to be an object of no importance. An ox is probably considered of more value than I. To be a woman and a serf isn't a position one would envy, is it, Mistress Philippa?'

'No, Rose,' whispered Philippa. 'If I gave you your freedom, what would you do with it?'

'The rolls were burnt when your house was—so there's no writing to bind me to you any longer.' She moved uneasily on the bed.

'They weren't,' Philippa told her. 'I took them out of the chest and hid them when I escaped.'

'What? So they destroyed the house...'

'But did not destroy all that they sought to. But you still came seeking me, Rose, when you could have fled. You saved my life—and even now you are with me. Why, when you thought that all that bound you was destroyed?' She sought Rose's hand and squeezed it.

'Reckon we've been through a lot,' answered Rose gruffly. 'You were kind to me in the best way you knew. And you needed me—even Master Guy said so.'

'I still need you, Rose! Dear Rose!' she exclaimed in a tear-filled voice.

There was a not unemotional silence as Philippa got up to pull back the covers of the bed, and slid beneath them. 'If you get in at the bottom end, there should be room for two—unless you have your own bed?'

'Mistress Margaret said I could share hers, but I'd just as soon not. She snores,' said Rose dispassionately.

'Then let's get some sleep.

Rose agreed, and within the hour both were fast asleep.

Philippa woke first and lay looking up at the rafters, thinking. When Rose stirred, she called her softly.

The maid yawned and stretched and sat up. 'What's that you say, Mistress Philippa?'

'I said—see if you can find a mirror when you go downstairs, or ask for one.' She piled the two pillows behind her and sat up, hunching her legs.

'A mirror?' muttered Rose, sliding out of bed. 'Now where would I find a mirror?'

'It's difficult, I know. Perhaps if you asked Mistress Margaret, is it? She could have one in her chamber.'

Rose's brow wrinkled in thought, and then her expression lightened. 'Now why would you be wanting a mirror? Although you're right. Mistress Margaret does have one on her wall.' She fastened her gown swiftly.

'To look at my reflection, of course,' she retorted sweetly.

'But why? You aren't getting up yet, surely, Mistress Philippa? That bang on your head...'

'Not yet. But see if you can find out from this Rob anything more about Sir Hugo's...troubles.' She smothered an unexpected yawn. 'And I don't know about you, Rose, but I'm starved.'

Rose smiled. 'You must be feeling better! I'm hungry, too. I'll see what I can do.' She fastened her girdle neatly, and made for the door.

'Rose!'

'Ay!' She faced Philippa, whose countenance was now wreathed in lines of concentration.

'Don't try to explain to anybody about me being you. Leave the explanations to me.'

'Gladly,' said Rose, and closed the door before she could be called on for anything else to do.

Philippa leaned back against the pillows and twiddled her thumbs. What was Guy doing now? Was he thinking of her? Or was it as Rose said, and out of sight, out of mind. He would have banished her from conscious thought and instead was seeing to his sheep. He had said that he would soon be leaving for London with the packhorses. Unless there was trouble from the serfs. Her longing to see him was an ache, and she found herself remembering her first sight of him, and that was even more painful. She shed a few more tears for her father, and wished he could have had a better burial-place. She seemed to be alone with her melancholy thoughts for a long time before Rose returned.

The maid let the circular metal mirror slide from beneath her arm on to the bed, and dumped a tray beside it, with a thankful gasp. 'Mistress Margaret said she hopes the devil don't peer over your shoulder when you look at yourself. She still has this fear that your fall might turn you mad.' Rose's cheeks were flushed with exertion.

'Mad, Rose? The devil?' Philippa paled slightly. 'What does she mean?'

'It's just nonsense! Have some bread—and there's some sheep's cheese. And small ale.' She sat on the bed and filled two cups, handing one to her mistress.

Philippa took some bread and cheese and had a sup of ale, before drinking deeper. It was a good brew. For a short time there was only eating and drinking. But at last the tray was removed, and the mirror brought forward.

Tentatively Philippa stared into it. No sign of a devil! Only a rather pale face with a dashing of freckles across the nose and upper cheeks . . . slanty green eyes, straight nose and dimpled chin. Wisps of almost white hair curled on a smooth forehead, which frowned at her. She tried to impress the reflection into her mind before looking sideways at Rose. 'We are alike,' she said slowly.

She held the mirror in front of Rose, who gazed interestedly at herself. Seldom had she seen her reflection—in a river a couple of times, and once she had caught sight of herself in passing, in Philippa's bedchamber. She had been brought up not to pay attention to her appearance, and she had never had any money to buy herself pretty ribbons or clothes. Occasionally some had come to her after her mistress had done with an old garment, or had made a new gown, or bought ribbons from a fair.

For several minutes she admired herself before turning her eyes to Philippa's. 'Ay, there is a likeness—but not a twin likeness.'

'No,' murmured her mistress, 'but we are like enough.' She put the mirror aside. 'Tell me, Rose, did you see Rob?'

She nodded. 'Seems this tale about Lancaster freeing his bondsmen is a big trick—and his setting himself up as king! He's gone to Scotland, where he has been offered sanctuary until the traitor matter is all sorted out with Richard. Lancaster has written to the king to declare his loyalty.'

'Sir Hugo told Rob all this?'

'Before I saw him last night, apparently.' She ran a finger along the edge of the mirror, the slightest of blushes on her cheeks. 'He's asked to see me—you—later. He's still abed, but awake.'

The blush was not lost on Philippa. 'Then what is this trouble Rob talked about? Did you ask him?'

'Oh, 'tis real enough, and he was willing to tell me, thinking me Sir Hugo's betrothed and the matter of concern to his lady. Those were the words he used,' she said softly.

'Rose! Tell!'

'There was an attempt on Sir Hugo's life, but nobody knows about it but those involved. He disarmed them and knocked their heads together. You haven't seen him yet, Mistress Philippa, but he could easily do it. He's a big man, and strong,' she insisted earnestly.

'You don't have to champion him for my benefit, Rose!' Philippa's glance was filled with understanding. 'What happened to them?'

'They were put in gaol in Knaresborough—and that hasn't pleased the other serfs on the manor. There was no manor court they were brought before, and nobody's told them why they're imprisoned.'

'But why doesn't Sir Hugo tell them? Surely that's the answer.'

'It was a blow to Sir Hugo's esteem—that's what Rob called it. Said he was real shaken by the attack. Never—never thought his scrfs felt like that. He treats them well. Like a father almost, he reckons.' Rose smiled grimly. '*He* doesn't see, either, that grown men don't want a father telling them how to do jobs they know back to front. Or a father who thinks the old ways are always best, and won't move with the times.'

'Is that what my father was like, Rose? Or is that what he just appeared to be to Tom and the rest?' said Philippa sadly.

Rose sighed. 'The trouble is that some lords think that we poorer folk can't think for ourselves—that any notions we have aren't worth considering. Fear, that's what it is. Fear that if more are paid wages, they'll eventually be able to buy their own land, or to leave the land altogether—and the lords to fend for themselves.'

'Not all are like that, Rose. My father...'

'Your father was a good and just man, Mistress Philippa, but even he expected too much from too few labourers. Since the pestilence struck, you know how it's been everywhere.' She stood up. 'Master Guy has the right notion for here and your manor.'

'Sheep?' Philippa also got up. 'Does Master Guy know about the attack on his brother?'

'I asked, thinking that I should. He doesn't. It seems that he's been at Sir Hugo for an age to have sheep on this land. With the money brought in and fewer workers, they could afford to free the serfs and pay them a wage.'

'You seem to have found out a lot, Rose,' murmured Philippa with a reluctant admiration.

'You asked me to—and besides, I was interested. If I were a man, and free, and had money and land, that's how I'd make my fortune,' she said vehemently.

'If you were a man, and free, and had money and land...' reiterated Philippa softly. 'Oh Rose, you are as much a dreamer as I. Do you really wish you were a man?'

Rose screwed up her nose, and grinned. 'Not if there was any other way. And besides...' She stopped abruptly.

'Besides what? There is a man you would rather stand as a woman next to?'

The maid's smile faded. 'I can never stand next to him in that way,' she muttered. 'Never.'

Philippa did not force her to say more, but instead asked if she had anything to add to what she had already told her.

Rose nodded. 'Perhaps I should have told you this first. It concerns you, perhaps, more than the rest. Rob is to visit Master Guy. Apparently he told Sir Hugo about your father being killed. This morning he asked if Guy had left any messages, so he thought it better to tell him, thinking it would be easier for Mistress Philippa Cobtree to have such a task done with. So Sir Hugo wants Master Guy to visit your manor while he is in the south and to find out how matters lie there.'

'Guy is to visit Cobtree! I knew it was possible, but then I thought that Sir Hugo might rather have gone himself, before I realised the extent of his injury—and the trouble up here!' She clasped her hands tightly in front of her. 'What's to do? What can I do?' she cried fretfully.

'There's nothing you can do, mistress, about him going,' soothed Rose. 'There, you're still not yourself. Perhaps you need to rest a little more. You've been through a lot in the last weeks.' She put an arm about her and hugged her.

Philippa nodded, and was just about to allow herself to be put to bed when there came a knock on the door. They exchanged quick glances.

'Are you there, Mistress Cobtree?'

'It's Rob,' mouthed Rose silently.

'Answer him,' whispered her mistress.

'Ay! What is it you want?'

'Sir Hugo awaits you in the garden and would have me take you to him. You not knowing your way about, yet.'

Rose gazed frantically at Philippa.

'Tell him *we'll* be out in a moment, and to wait,' she told her in a low voice. Rose quickly did as ordered. 'A surcote, Rose!' Philippa smoothed her gown, and glanced nervously in the mirror on the bed. 'A head-dress and veil also!'

The maid hurried over to the chest that stood against the wall and delved into it. Never had she prepared her mistress more swiftly! Philippa looked again in the mirror, pushed back some loose wisps of hair, caught sight of the betrothal ring on her finger, and impulsively slipped it off and placed it under the pillow, ignoring Rose's puzzled look.

Rob's face broke into a reluctant grin when he saw Philippa. 'I thought you'd be abed longer than this, mistress, but the master will be pleased to see you on your feet.'

She stared at him questioningly. 'Your name? I do not remember that we have met before.' Half-formulated ideas were taking shape in her mind.

'Is that so!' He appeared partly taken aback, but gratified in some way. 'That will be the fall—because we have met! I'm Rob, groom to Sir Hugo and to his father before him.'

'I see.' She pouted and appeared scared. 'I can't re-member falling at all, but I know that I did because she has told me so,' she held on tightly to Rose's arm. A pucker creased the maid's brow, and she flashed her mistress an uncertain glance.

'Now there's no need for you to worry, mistress. You ain't half as bad as a groom we had.' He gave her a reassuring smile. 'You be careful going down these here steps, and I'll go in front to make sure you don't fall. Perhaps you'd like to take my arm?'

'You are kind...Rob, is it?' Her smile showed her gratitude, and releasing her hold on Rose, she tucked her hand in the crook of his arm. This was the man who would be visiting Guy. It would do no harm to make a friend of him, for perhaps... She did not allow herself to indulge her fantasies any further, but carefully descended, clutching Rob's sleeve.

Sir Hugo looked up eagerly as he heard the sound of footsteps. His remembrance of meeting his betrothed the evening before were overlain by pain and discomfort. Yet still the memory of her face and figure, her determination to minister to him, had moved him to feel an emotion that he would rather not own. He was finished with love, and to imagine feeling such for a proposed wife was nonsense. He stood up with some difficulty, leaving the stick, that Rob had insisted on, resting against the bench, as she appeared suddenly from behind the hawthorn hedge. Her gown was plain russet but moulded her breasts and hips in such a way that he caught his breath. She smiled shyly at him with lips so red and prettily curved that he immediately wanted to taste their softness.

'Good day to you, sir. I—I am pleased to see you on your feet.'

'I am delighted to see you in every possible way, lass.' He bowed his head, and before Rose could retreat, he kissed her briefly, full on the mouth. Their lips clung before parting.

'S—Sir!' she stammered, her eyes wide and nervous. 'I...' Her head twisted as Philippa came on the scene, Rob hovering just behind. Her mistress touched her arm briefly and scrutinised Sir Hugo, as he sent Rose a questioning look before returning his gaze to Philippa with a slightly puzzled frown. She had seen enough on rounding the hedge to dare the next move.

'You are Sir Hugo? My cousin told me that I would be meeting you.' She heard Rose's gasp, but did not show it by the flutter of an eyelash. Instead she held out her hand to her betrothed. He had not changed much. He was broader, his beard was thicker, there were more lines on his countenance—and the sight of him did not raise a flicker of dancing excitement within her. Indeed she was strangely calm, considering what she planned.

'Ah, that explains the likeness between you,' said Sir Hugo, his deep voice hinting at a smile, as he took her hand and held it for a moment, awkwardly. 'You are feeling better now?'

'Much, sir. Although...' her brow furrowed, 'I find there are gaps in my memory, which causes me some anxiety.' She shot a glance at Rose. 'Philippa tells me that I came here with your brother, Master Guy, which I can't remember at all. Perhaps the fall she speaks of has scattered my wits.' A light laugh escaped her, and from the corner of her eye she saw Rose's mouth fall open.

'It is to be expected that such a fall would have some effect,' said Sir Hugo gruffly, uneasily setting free her hand. 'But time will probably set matters right. Rob would tell you that.'

'Of course.' Philippa sighed. 'But all is strange here, so unfamiliar! Only my cousin is known to me...and I feel lost.' She sighed gustily again. 'If I could go home to Kent, where she says I have lived all my life, maybe I would remember all.'

'It would be difficult for you to return at this moment,' said Rose swiftly, groaning inwardly, wondering just what her mistress was about. Unless the fall really had affected her in such a way? Yet there had been no sign of her not remembering her past last night when they had talked.

'Of course,' smiled Philippa sadly. 'You are here to wed Sir Hugo, and I am to attend you. Will it be soon?'

A muffled squeak sounded from Rose, who was gazing at her with astonishment over the hand clapped to her mouth.

'I would have liked it to be soon,' answered Sir Hugo gravely, 'but your cousin's father was murdered most foully by rebels in the south. You might not remember? She will need time to mourn his passing. Perhaps in a few months. September, maybe?'

'September? But what month is it now?' cried Philippa. 'A few months before I could remember again!' Her anguish sounded real. 'Months before I visit my home!' Tears filled her eyes, and turning away, she picked up her skirts and left them.

'I—I shall have to go after her,' muttered Rose apologetically. 'She's not herself. Forgive us!' She fled after her mistress, leaving Sir Hugo and Rob staring at each other. Sympathy and interest were clear on the groom's face, but his master's wore only a scowl. The meeting had finished in a fashion not at all to his liking.

Rose did not catch up with Philippa until she reached the bedchamber, and she was hurried through the doorway and the door closed fast behind her. 'Mistress Philippa!' she gasped. 'What are you thinking of to say such things to Sir Hugo? He'll be furious when he finds out! You must really be mad to pretend you aren't yourself.'

'Perhaps I am not myself,' said her mistress breathlessly, collapsing on the bed. She lay there, her eyes shut, getting her breath back. Her head ached.

'What do you mean?' There was a scared note in Rose's voice.

'The old Philippa Cobtree would never have behaved as I have in the last few weeks . . . but she had never been in love.'

'Mistress Philippa, you're frightening me! You do remember who you are? You aren't . . . mad?'

'Perhaps I am—a little.' Her eyes opened and she
looked up at Rose's worried face. 'Oh Rose, you have
dreams, and so do I. You told me that Master Guy is
going to Kent. I want to see him. I want to go *home*,
where perhaps . . . lies an answer to my dilemma. As
Philippa Cobtree I can't go, but as Rose Cobtree, maybe
I can.'

'But there isn't a Rose Cobtree! You made her up!'

Philippa gave her a searching look, but kept her
thoughts to herself. 'Who is to know? No one here.'

'Master Guy knows.'

'Ay, but he isn't here, and will not be returning for
some time. He goes south, as I wish to go. I consider
that Sir Hugo could be persuaded that it is necessary for
my sanity and happiness that I be returned to Kent—
and who better to take me there safely than his brother?'

Rose gasped. 'You *are* mad! *He*'ll know it's you.'

'Of course he will! But what if I take the pretence a
little deeper? My memory is so uncertain, and I have
had such a bad time lately, that he might be persuaded
that it is better for me to go with him. Maybe, too, there
are certain events I could remember: that there was
something between us? Something delightful!'

'What of Sir Hugo? What of him, if he finds out I
am deceiving him? You do expect me to deceive him?'
she asked, suddenly angry.

'Oh, Rose!' Philippa rolled over on her stomach and
propped her chin in her palms. 'You can't deceive *me*!
You have fallen in love with him, so make the most of
playing me. And, who knows . . .'

'You ask too much,' Rose declared mutinously.
'Playing him for a fool, that's what you are doing! And
I'll be your scapegoat when it all comes out. He'll have
me beaten, that's for certain. He'll despise and hate me
for tricking him.'

'Do not be so sure! I saw the way he looked at you.'

'That's only because he thinks I'm his betrothed,' retorted Rose, her colour deepening.

'Nonsense! You are pretty, much prettier than I. He is half in love with you already. The angels are on our side. Persuade him that it would be good for me if Rob took me to Guy—and home!'

'Angels! More like devils,' moaned Rose. 'We'll burn in hell for such wanton, deceitful behaviour.'

'Don't say that! Never say that!' Philippa's voice shook, and her face took on a terrified expression.

Rose stared at her, and pitied her. 'No, I won't,' she reassured. 'I didn't mean it.'

She drew in a deep breath. 'We aren't doing anything really wicked,' she whispered.

'No.' Rose patted her shoulder. There had been real fear in her eyes! 'It's not an unforgivable sin.'

Philippa gave a low laugh. 'You must wear my betrothal ring. He is bound to notice sooner or later that it is missing. And, Rose, I shall give you your freedom when this is all over. Or now, if you will still go through with it!' Rolling over and reaching beneath the pillow to take out the ring, she gave it to Rose.

For a moment the maid stared at it on the palm of her hand. 'There's no changing your mind?'

'No.' Philippa took an unsteady breath. 'Once you put that on, there is no going back.'

'You will give me my freedom—and set down the truth of this deception?' She moistened her mouth.

'You may ask Sir Hugo for writing implements. I trust you not to renege on our agreement.'

'What of clothes?'

Philippa put her hand under the pillow and drew out a handful of silver buttons. 'They were my father's. You remember?' Rose nodded, and her throat went tight. 'We shall divide them—and the clothes. Sir Hugo should be able to sell the buttons for you. In all honesty, you can tell him that all we had was destroyed. Our gowns have been given to us.'

'You are generous.'

'No, I have begun to see life in a different way. You will speak to Sir Hugo about my going with Rob?'

'Ay!' Rose eased her shoulders. 'I shall go now, but a prayer would not go amiss, Mistress Philippa.' She put the ring on her finger and was gone.

Philippa stared after her, and smiled tremulously. If the angels were on her side, soon she would see Guy.

CHAPTER ELEVEN

SIR HUGO WAS annoyed. Rose could tell that even from this distance. Her heart sank, and she came to an abrupt halt. What if she could not persuade him to allow her mistress to go with Rob? Would Philippa change her mind about all she had promised? Sir Hugo was leaning on his stick as he walked stiffly round the pond. Ducks sailed busily, their quacking as they delved for tasty morsels of food the only noise to be heard on the still morning air. She gnawed at her bottom lip. If she really were his betrothed, what would she do? For a moment she stood still, then bracing her shoulders and tilting her chin, she sallied forth.

He did not look up at her coming, but gazed over the pond. A deep breath, and, 'Sir Hugo, please forgive my cousin—but most of all forgive me for letting her bother you. The blame is all mine that you should be vexed with me, but she so much wanted to see you, thinking you would be like your brother and that the sight of you would jog her memory.' She gazed soulfully up at his stern profile.

'My brother?' She had startled him into speech. 'Why should she think that I would remind her of Guy? Or that it would bring her wits back?' He glanced down at her, met her eyes, experienced a drowning sensation as he was held in their greeny-gold caress, and had cause to clear his throat. 'There's nothing to forgive. Rob said it was to be expected after such a fall. Even so...'

'Even so, you had matters to discuss with me—and my—my cousin prevented such a discussion.' Rose had not lived close to Philippa all her life without knowing every inflection in her voice, and the words she would use. 'Perhaps, now we are alone for a short while... Not that I shall be able to stay out here long. My cousin *needs* my attention, even though I find her company irksome.' She allowed her hand to rest on Sir Hugo's sleeve. 'But what can I do? If there was a way of transporting her to Kent, I would that it could be done!' she added recklessly, deciding to go straight to the heart of the matter.

'You would?' Sir Hugo was slightly bewildered by her rapid speech, and overwhelmed by her closeness. There had been few women in his life since Catalina, and none remotely as pretty or compelling as this woman, whose breast pressed against his arm.

'I would,' said Rose dolefully. 'Can you not think of a way—so that we can spend some time alone to know each other again?' Now she was in it, up to her ears, she thought uneasily, but there was no other way of doing it, except wholeheartedly.

'A way?' He would that he could! The thought of spending time in getting to know his betrothed better appealed to him mightily!

'A way,' she repeated, wondering if she would have to put every word of Philippa's plan into his mouth. He seemed stunned by what she had said. Had she gone too far? There was no drawing back now. Her fingers toyed with the silver buttons in her fitchet, and she dreamed of the fabric she could buy to make into a gown to be beautiful for him.

'There is a way,' Sir Hugo said suddenly, making her start. 'Not that I'm sure that Guy will like it—but then he shouldn't have gone off so quickly without waiting to see me. Not the sort of behaviour one expects when one's considering favouring him with a reward. Despite wrongs done in the past,' he added darkly, bewildering Rose utterly, who knew only of the disputes between the brothers concerning peasants and sheep.

'You mean, by asking Master Guy to take her to Kent?' She gazed up at him with wide-eyed admiration, choosing to ignore the last part of his speech.

'You think it will serve?' He beamed down at her, delighted to bathe in her obvious adoration.

'Perfectly!' She stood on tiptoe and kissed his cheek, then started to retreat, but he caught her to him and kissed her soundly. Her eyes were filled with stars when they drew apart. 'I must tell my cousin,' she said huskily, then turned and ran as if her life depended on her getting away from him.

'You have the agreement safe?' asked Philippa, pulling on her gloves.

'Ay! In the chest in the turret room,' replied Rose, impatient for her to be on her way to Master Guy; only then would she believe that the plan could really work. What was it that made her mistress . . . no, not her mistress, since she was now a freewoman. The agreement said it was so. What was it that was in Kent that made Philippa believe there was a way out of this tangle? Questions she had asked, but had received no reply, only 'Wait and see.' 'You must hurry. Rob is waiting and Hugo might still change his mind.'

'Hugo?' Philippa laughed. 'You have become close to him!' But Rose's words were enough to send her hastily out into the courtyard where Rob waited with the little baggage she possessed, now that it had been divided.

'You will return?' hissed Rose as she handed her a napkin with some food in it. 'If all goes well, that is?'

'I shall come back, whatever happens, cousin,' she smiled wanly. 'Pray for me.'

'For all of us.' Rose blew a kiss as the horse began to move.

'Safe journey, and God grant that all goes well with you,' called Sir Hugo, his arm going around Rose's shoulders.

'Amen to that,' whispered Philippa before putting an arm about Rob's waist. They passed under the arch of the gatehouse and headed for the distant fells.

Guy eased his shoulders. He had been on his feet all day and was tired. The last of the sheep had been shorn, and the fleeces sorted and bundled. In a couple of days he would go with the wool-train. Two weeks earlier, he had left Philippa at Hugo's manor, and he would have liked to have prayed that they were pleasing each other. He scrubbed at the dust on his cheek, staring across the meadows towards the fells. When he had told her to forget, she had asked 'Will you?', and he had thought he could, once he was home again and working. Perhaps, in another woman's arms, he might. There were women aplenty in London and Calais—not that he had sought their services. Instead, he had concentrated his energies on working and saving the money from the fleeces, hoping to possess this land one day. He had no mind to give it all over for a woman! Doubtless Hugo would be angry that he had not stayed, but it was better the way he had done it, even if his brother had failed to keep his promise and hand this 'least' of all his possessions over to him.

Narrowing his eyes against the evening sun, he discerned two people on horseback approaching.

'Are you all right there, Mistress Rose?' Rob lifted his voice. 'Nearly there now.'

'I realise that, Rob.' Philippa's voice was taut with nerves now that their journey's end was in sight. Her pulse began to beat with thick heavy strokes. The success of her plan depended on the next few minutes. Would he denounce her? Send her packing back to Hugo? Or could he want her still? Would he pity her situation so much that he would take her south with him? Her heart seemed to turn right over in her breast as she met Guy's incredulous gaze with a rigidity that she hoped did not betray her fearful apprehension.

'This is Mistress Rose Cobtree, Master Guy.'

'Mistress Rose...?' It was definitely a question.

'Ay, sir. You, I presume are Master Guy Milburn?' she asked with a stiffness that could have been taken for coldness.

'I am.' He shot a glance at Rob. 'What's this about, man?'

'Your brother sent us. I have a letter that will explain just what he wishes you to do, Master Guy.' He dismounted.

'Wishes me to do?' Guy's face was suddenly still. 'Here, give me the letter!' He shot out a hand. Rob took a scroll from inside his tunic and handed it to him. Casting another glance at Philippa, who stared at him blandly, he unrolled the parchment. He read it swiftly, then read it again in disbelief, and a third time, muttering an oath under his breath. Rob and he exchanged looks.

'Interesting business,' said Rob, his face lighting up. 'You ask her yourself, Master Guy. She can't even remember your bringing her to your brother's house. I carried her upstairs. Just like one dead she was, but she came round the next day, with some gaps in her memory, like.'

'My brother wants me to take her to Kent!' His voice rose. Guy stared at Philippa, and she allowed herself a smile. 'I don't believe this,' he groaned, putting a hand to his head.

'You don't want to take me, Master Guy?' Philippa asked in a forlorn voice. 'I would be a nuisance to you, no doubt.'

'Ay! No!' He ran a hand through his hair, raising it into a crest. 'Best you come in and rest, and refresh yourself. I need some time to think.' Without pausing to help her from the horse, he turned and strode towards the stone-built house a short distance away.

Rob grinned at her and shrugged, then helped her down. 'Don't you worry about Master Guy now, Mistress Rose. He'll help you if he can, as you'd know if you could remember.'

'I'm sure you are right, Rob. But I don't believe he likes me.'

'Now you can't be saying that,' responded the groom in a soothing voice. 'The man's had a shock, that's all... Been working hard, too, no doubt about it. All the sheep shorn, if he's ready to go south within a day or so.' He lifted her baggage down and they made their way to the house, Rob leading the horse.

Guy was outside, sluicing his half-naked body in a bucket near the well. 'Go on in,' he called. 'Supper is on the table, and I won't be long! Ann will see to you.'

Philippa made to do as he directed, while Rob went to the stable, then she changed her mind and went over to him. There was a need in her to speak to him—to be near him. He glanced at her, then away again.

'It—It looks a sturdy house...strong,' she stated firmly.

'Has to be strong to stand the winters here.' He was staring at her fully this time. 'Cruel they are. When the snows come, we might as well be on the moon since we are so remote from any other human contact.'

'You—You make it sound terrible! Why do you wish to live here if it is so remote? There is no town or city for miles and miles. Not like your brother's manor.' She leaned against the wall of the well, not looking at him, afraid to, in case he saw the look in her eyes.

'My grandfather built the house,' replied Guy, beginning to dry himself with a rough towel. 'It was the first permanent home of the Milburns, but when the family became wealthy, it was considered too small and remote.' He gave a slight smile. 'But it is its remoteness that made the land cheap, and we own a fair parcel. Not as much, though, as the Cistercian abbey you'll have passed on the way here. They grow more wool than all of us smaller sheep-farmers put together.'

'Rob says that you go with your wool soon—that perhaps you will take me south with you?' Her voice was low, hesitant.

'Why do you want to go, if you cannot remember? Was it your—your cousin's suggestion?' He looped the towel round his neck, and his blue eyes were sharp.

'No, it was mine. You cannot understand what it is like to wake up in a place you do not recognise and have no remembrance of getting to! I knew it was not my home. I knew I came from Kent, for my cousin mentioned how we had fled and how you helped us. She and your brother seem...content with each other.' She flicked him a glance, caught his gaze and felt a singing in her veins. 'He wishes to wed in September,' she added in an unsteady voice.

'Wed *her* in September?' He moved towards her. 'And *you* are happy about that?' There was an impatience in his expression that almost unnerved her.

Opening her eyes wide as if in surprise, she stepped back a little. 'Why shouldn't I be? I pray that I shall be able to return for the wedding.'

'But, dammit, don't you even remember...? Oh, what's the use!' He clamped his jaws tight, and brushing past her, strode towards the house.

Philippa followed more slowly, not unhappy with the exchanges between them so far. He had not told Rob who she really was—and there had been a glint in his eyes when they had met hers that gave her hope, despite his obvious annoyance and bewilderment. But she must be careful. Not until they were beyond the boundaries of Yorkshire would she breathe easily.

A cup of mulled wine calmed, even as it warmed her. A fire burned brightly in the centre of the long low room.

The walls were washed white, but were grimed with smoke and lacked any form of decoration. The furniture was old but beautifully carved, but there were no cushions, and a veneer of dust coated the settle and the chest against the wall by the front door.

Ann, who had cooked the meal, was ancient and seemed to have difficulty in walking. The supper was hot and filling, but plainly presented. Pork, onion and barley flavoured with thyme, it lacked the spices Philippa was accustomed to, although there was a small pot of ginger on the table to sprinkle over the food. An expensive luxury, which perhaps he had obtained through James Wantsum? There was enough food for all, and she wondered if perhaps she and Rob had eaten tomorrow's dinner! The groom had been seated next to Guy, and they had had their heads together in conversation, little of which she had caught. Enough, though, to presume it was about Lancaster, and she had little enough interest in the man now that it seemed he was not declaring himself king.

Oatcakes and honey followed the first course, and although they were slightly burnt she enjoyed them, and told Ann so, and earned herself the faintest of smiles. She was far too old for the task of ministering to Guy's needs in the house. Did he not see that? Or was there not a woman on the manor who could do the work? Philippa had spotted only a scattering of roofs from the hill as they descended into this valley. If that were so, he did have need of her, and it would be one extra challenge to persuade him of the fact. But first things first! She lifted her eyes from her food, and looked at him.

Almost as if he had been waiting for this moment, he broke off his conversation with Rob and returned her gaze, his brilliant eyes keen as they scanned her features. 'Do—Do you have any notion, Mistress Cobtree, what it is like to travel south when the wool-trains are on the roads?'

'No, sir, but I should imagine it will be slow—and dusty if the weather is fine.' Her cheeks were warm with that penetrating stare.

'Ay,' he replied grimly. 'Dustier than you can imagine, I'll be bound. But if it rains, it is worse, much worse, and the journey becomes even slower and more tedious. Also the company is rough and not suitable for a lady. I cannot think what my brother was about in sending you to me to face such a journey when you have suffered already!'

'Perhaps he did not think of it? And, besides, I told you it was my idea to go south in the hope of resolving the dilemma I am in.'

'Did not think!' He blew an exasperated breath. 'No, likely he did not, for he takes little interest in the sheep— only in his share of the profits, which could be larger if he did show an interest.'

'I know nothing of that, sir, only that perhaps—from conversation, I have heard, you understand?—what with the trouble with the serfs, it might be the time soon to broach such a subject with your brother again.'

'What do you mean by that?' His eyes narrowed suspiciously.

She cast a glance at Rob, who had fallen on his food now that Guy had turned his attention to Philippa. 'I don't think your brother wishes you to know, but he was attacked by some serfs, who are now imprisoned in Knaresborough Castle.'

'His own serfs?'

'Ay! I consider that the situation is similar to...' she stopped abruptly, 'that which my cousin told me about at Cobtree manor.'

Guy stared at her, then turned to Rob. 'Is this true?'

'What's that, Master Guy?' He spluttered out some barley.

He repeated Philippa's words. Rob gave a sigh of relief. 'I told him he should have let you know, but he's that stubborn, Master Guy! You know him. Especially as you've told him that matters might be easier if you both freed the serfs and put sheep on the land. But what you can do about it, I don't know.'

'Is there still danger?'

Rob hesitated, then said cautiously. 'The others are disgruntled. No manor trial, you see—and the two that stood up to him are cottars, with not much of this world's goods. They demanded more wages for the work they did for your brother, and he refused, saying that they didn't earn what they did receive!'

Guy's lips compressed into a thin line. 'What's the answer, Rob? I take it that he does not wish for my help?'

'Doesn't want you saying "I told you so", Master Guy! And his leg's giving him trouble still. I reckon he'll have to work this through himself—and maybe he'll come to see things the way you do. Maybe the lady will help him. Fair struck with her, he seems.'

'Does he?' Guy smiled soberly. 'That's interesting. You may tell him I shall do as he requests. I shall not go with the clip but shall send John, the bailiff, in my stead. He knows what's what. Mistress Cobtree and I shall set out in the morning, before the roads get crowded.' He toyed with the knife on the table. 'If that is acceptable to you, mistress?'

'To me?' She lowered her eyes, not wanting him to see the triumph in them. 'I am perfectly satisfied, Master Milburn.'

There was a silence before he said in a gruff voice, 'Then it is settled. We ride tomorrow.' He pushed back his chair. 'You will sleep upstairs. Best go up now, for we shall start early.'

Philippa rose, for she was tired with the journey, and having got her way, did not want him to change his mind. 'I bid you a good night then, sir, and shall see you in the morning.'

He inclined his head, and Philippa went over to a ladder in the far corner. Her last sight of Guy that night was of him staring moodily into the fire. Almost her heart misgave her, for he did not look happy, but she had come too far to tell him the truth yet. So much still hung in the balance.

Guy glanced up as Philippa came down the ladder. The faint light of dawn penetrated the shutters at the window. There was apprehension written in her expression, and he knew then why he had not told her, or Rob, the truth last night. Thus had she looked when first he had seen her, and he wanted to remove such fear from her for ever. When she did remember her past, he wished to be there. Surely there was some way of settling this matter so that Hugo would free her from their betrothal agreement? But what had Rose been thinking of to take her place—or to let her travel south? Surely she realised that Philippa would find out the truth about herself when she came to her manor, and was recognised?

'Good morning to you, Master Milburn.' She smiled at him tentatively.

'Not so good a morning, Mistress Cobtree,' he said brusquely. 'It's raining. But sit down and have some bread. There is butter and honey, if you are content with them. Or I can ask Ann to cook you some eggs.'

'No, I am perfectly satisfied with butter and honey, thank you.' She sat down opposite him. 'The rain? Does that mean you must put off our journey?'

He shook his head. 'Not unless you want to?' He took a mouthful of bread and egg. 'It is different from the last time we set out on a journey, you and I?' he added softly, several minutes later.

She stopped spreading honey on her bread and butter. She had not expected him to allude so soon to the time they had spent together. 'You and I?' she reiterated, rather breathlessly.

'Surely *your* cousin told you we already know each other—quite well?' He took a gulp of ale, watching her intently. Just how much had Rose told her? The maid must have realised that he would know the truth, and could unmask her. What was her aim in allowing Philippa to come to him? There was the faintest of blushes on her cheeks. Sooo!

'My—My cousin did hint that...there was something...between us. That seeing you might help me.' Was she going too far, too soon? But surely she was only following his lead in accepting without remembering that they had had a fondness for each other. Was that not what he meant by knowing each other quite well? And the expression on his face when he said it indicated that he wished it so.

'And has it?' he said drily. 'You don't appear to remember me.'

'I don't feel that you are a stranger.' She took a large bite of bread and honey, and chewed pensively as if in deep thought, leaving the next move to him.

'What do you feel towards me?' Deliberately he put his hand over hers, and raising it to his lips caressed it with his mouth, before turning it over and kissing her wrist. She did not answer, or pull away. 'Could we have been lovers?'

She had to clear her throat. 'Lovers?' Her voice was husky. 'It is too soon for me to answer that.' Her fingers quivered beneath his, and he held them more tightly before realising that her betrothal ring was gone. It seemed that Rose was in earnest if she had taken the ring from her finger! Had she done so while she had lain as one dead as Rob had described? A spurt of anger shot through him. He would not have thought it of her, but perhaps the revolt had fired her with the same kind of desire as with others to rise in the world? But that still did not explain why she had allowed her to come to him? Did she think that he...? His face darkened.

'Ay, 'tis too soon for me to tell you the truth of the matter. You need time.' He released her hand. 'Time to remember, yourself. If taking you to your old home in the south will help you to do so, the sooner we start, the better.' Guy tossed off the remains of his drink and pushed back his chair, and without another word left her to finish her breakfast.

Philippa wondered at the sudden change in him: from would-be lover to the Guy who would be about his brother's business. Which would he be when she did 'remember'? She could only pray that he would see the same way out of the situation as she did when the time came!

It rained all through Yorkshire, but it lightened to a drizzle by late afternoon when they entered the county of Derbyshire. Much of the journey had passed in silence, which made Philippa wonder if Guy was regretting his decision to take her to Kent. As they steamed in front of a welcome fire in the almost empty inn where they were to spend the night, Guy spoke suddenly on a matter to which she had foolishly given no consideration. 'I gather you know something of the rebellion in the south?' He dipped his spoon into the bowl of pottage.

'A little,' she replied, lifting her head swiftly from her dreams of what the future might hold. 'Why do you ask?'

'You know you fled from Cobtree manor?'

She nodded. 'My cousin fled also.'

'Ay!' he said impatiently, waving his spoon as though brushing Rose aside. 'So it could be that you will not be welcome there. I should have thought to bring a couple of men.' He paused to eat another spoonful of food. 'You do know that the house was burnt to the ground?' He was hesitant, wondering if she still experienced bad dreams.

'I know.' Convulsively her fingers tightened on her spoon. 'There will be no shelter over our heads.' A shadow darkened her eyes.

'That will be the least of our problems if the rebellion still simmers in Kent! But, no matter, we shall visit London first, since we have to pass through it anyway.' He tore a hunk of bread from the loaf and wiped the bowl with it. 'Do you remember London?' He stared at her. Damp tendrils of hair clung to her forehead, and she looked tired and pale.

'I stayed there?' She moistened her mouth, remembering that there were supposed to be only some gaps in her memory. What should she choose to remember? How she wished that she knew for sure that he would wed her if it were possible! Why had she ever started this deception?

'With my cousin and her husband—Beatrice and James Wantsum, they are called. Some peasants climbed the wall while you stayed in their house, don't you remember? They filled London to overflowing; looting, destroying, burning, don't you remember?' he insisted, his hand covering hers now. His eyes seemed to bore into her, and she was suddenly frightened. What would he do if she told him the truth at this moment? Would he be furious, and take her straight back to Hugo for playing such a trick on them both?

'I—I don't think I want to remember, if it was so terrible,' she whispered. 'Sometimes I dream.' Her fingers clung to his. 'There are men...' A sudden note of urgency entered her tone. 'Master Guy, I don't think I want to remember, if the past is so fearful. I would rather only think of the future—and that my cousin and your brother could be happy together, and...' Words failed her. She looked down at their clasped hands and made to pull hers away.

But he would not let her go. 'And?'

'And that... I could... be happy too.' She could no longer think clearly.

'Isn't that what we all want? But it is an elusive state... although it has a habit of coming when least expected. I'm not happy *now*, but I could be if circumstances were different.' He caressed the back of her hand with the ball of his thumb.

Swallowing, she said, 'What circumstances?' The noise of water dripping from the thatched eaves and the murmur of men's voices in a far corner suddenly seemed loud in the silence that followed her question. Was he going to tell her the truth?

'I am no saint, sweeting, but even I cannot take advantage of this situation! I could tell you anything about us, and maybe you would choose to believe me. But I won't do that.' He gave a twisted smile. 'We could both choose to forget the past—and that there is a future to take into the reckoning, and just live for the moment. We could pretend that we had met only yesterday? That we each find the other to our liking?' He kissed the hand he now held between both of his. 'More than liking, perhaps?' he said in a barely audible voice as he nibbled one of her fingers.

An unbelievable touch of magic held her. To forget utterly all that separated them just for the moment while they were on the road appealed to her greatly. 'Master Guy,' she whispered, 'you could choose to tell me anything, and I would believe you—but perhaps it is better as you say. No past—no future—only now!'

'So be it.' His eyes gleamed. 'You have finished eating?' She nodded. 'Good. I would be alone with you.' He lifted her to her feet and sent a glance through the still unshuttered window. 'Do you have a mind to stretch your legs? The rain has just about stopped. We shall not go far.' He faced her. 'It is madness to go out again, I know, but inns are not the most private places.'

'Madness—if it is such—is a state I am beginning to feel happy in! Your aunt considered me mad because I could not remember falling.' She let him lead her to the outside door, oblivious of the indulgent looks that followed them. A man and a maid, hand in hand, could mean only one thing, and the ancients who had come to sup their ale remembered their summer madness of long ago.

It smelled sweet and fresh after the smoky atmosphere of the inn, and although the grass was wet, the air was not cold as they walked aimlessly away from the building. Philippa revelled in the touch of his hand and the sight of him so near. In truth she suddenly was Rose, a country maid out with her lover, with no thought of manors or betrothals—although weddings were on her mind! They came to the edge of a copse, and there paused amid the trees. Deliberately Guy raised her hand and put it on his shoulder, looking deep into her eyes.

'I shall say only that, in days, we have not known each other long, unless you count a short meeting when you were ten years old, but we have spent hours in each other's company, and then you were not averse to my kissing you.'

'W—Wasn't I?' Her expression was bemused as he brought her close, and she could not help but hold her face up to his. Only for a moment was she undecided whether to respond, and then her feelings were beyond rein, and they were sharing a kiss that went on for a satisfyingly long time.

'Well!' he exclaimed unsteadily when he lifted his head.

'It is well,' she responded in a hushed voice, caught up on a wave of love in response to the emotion in his face.

'I wanted to forget you,' he muttered, 'but I haven't been able to get you out of my mind.'

'Then all is well,' she said liltingly.

'Is it? I wish I could say that is true.' His face darkened and he caught her close again. 'But it isn't!' Then he was kissing her again as though he never wanted to let her go, and she was lost, drowning in a haze of desire that threatened to overwhelm her.

CHAPTER TWELVE

IT WAS GUY who came to his senses first. He pulled himself jerkily out of her arms and leaned back against a tree trunk, his chest heaving. 'I believe I could take you now, but it would be wrong!'

'Wrong?' For an instant Philippa could not think at all as she gazed up at him. His doublet was undone and she could see the dark hair on his chest. Had she done that? Then she realised that the fastenings were undone on her bodice, and her fingers sought them. The need to be close, skin to skin, had been powerful.

He gazed at her, and almost flung his scruples aside. 'Could you be content, knowing naught of your past?' he said vehemently.

'I thought we—we were to forget the past—nor to think of the future, but to live for the moment?' Her voice shook.

'I thought we could, but they cannot be separated. I know the one and can perhaps foresee the other, and one cannot live a lie always.'

'No,' she whispered, suddenly apprehensive.

'You are my brother's betrothed! You are Philippa Cobtree—not her cousin. The woman who says she is so is your maid, Rose.' He rubbed his forehead wearily. 'I'll take you back to Hugo in the morning.'

'No!' she cried, backing away from him. This moment had always been a threat to all her plotting! 'I—I don't want to believe that! We must go on to Cobtree,' desperately, 'to find out the truth!'

'I've told you the truth, and there is no need for you to make such a long journey.' He lunged and seized her arm, pulling her towards him and gazing into her stricken face. 'Perhaps I shouldn't have told you in such a way, but there was no other. You've been ill, Philippa. Earlier, you talked about dreams and men! Well, they are connected with the revolt on your father's manor, and maybe it will be too much of a shock for you to go there yet. Later... Later, perhaps, Hugo will take you there and can resolve the situation?'

She felt cold and sick as she stared up into his sombre face. Her dreams were falling about her ears. 'And what of—us?'

His throat moved. 'There was never any future for us,' he returned harshly.

'Then why did you not tell me so yesterday instead of bringing me so far? Why tell me of "this" between us?' she insisted despairingly.

A muscle moved in his cheek. 'Because of "this", as you call it! But if matters are as difficult for my brother as Rob hints, I have no cause for making them worse by trying to steal the affections of his betrothed.'

'It doesn't matter about *my* feelings? That I care nothing for your brother?' She wrenched her arm from his grasp.

He hesitated, then said harshly, 'When have such feelings mattered in marriage? You once said yourself that love has nothing to do with such a state—and, outside its bonds, love is always ill-fated.'

'And you accept that?' she demanded, stunned by the swift change in his stance on the subject. Before, he had wanted to forget Hugo, and now...

'I have to. Hugo is my brother! There is no honourable way out of this!' His voice was heated, his face dark.

''Tis a fine time to talk of honour! Fine talk from a man who said he was no saint!' She threw the words in his face. 'You talk of love,' her voice breaking, 'without talking of sacrifice—unless it is of sacrificing me on the altar of your honour and your brother's rights! What of me?' She whirled from him, and before he could prevent her, she had fled among the trees.

Guy stood rigid for a moment before he went after her. Thrusting aside soaking branches that she had dodged beneath, he slithered on the wet grass, yet still he gained. She darted a glance behind, and he saw what was going to happen before he had time to warn her. The low branch caught her cheek and she staggered backwards, clutching her face. He reached out and turned her round.

'Do—Don't touch me!' Her eyes were tear-filled as she tried to pull away from him.

'Don't be stupid,' he said roughly. 'I'm not going to hurt you!'

'I don't want to go back to your brother. Let me go! You have no right to force me.'

'I don't intend forcing you.'

She stopped struggling. Her breath caught, so that for a moment she could not speak, then she said, 'You expect me to do as you say, then? Without demur?'

A laugh escaped him. 'Philippa, I never expect you to do anything—without demur! You seem so set on going to Cobtree that maybe there's...something in your inner thoughts that says—go! So we'll go, despite the danger.'

'Oh!' It was only a thread of sound. She took her hand from her cheek, and there was a long scratch there. 'What about Hugo, and Rose?'

He shrugged. 'They will have to wait until we return.' He touched her cheek, and frowned. 'That will have to be seen to.'

'We...shall be returning?' She pulled a little away from him.

'Ay! If there is a way for us, it has to be legal and binding. My brother has to know the truth, and there are matters between us that you have no notion about.'

There was a touch of bleakness in the smile he gave her.
'But now—that scratch!'

'And—tomorrow?' She wanted to be sure.

'Tomorrow we go south.' He kissed her gently before
they turned and made their way back to the inn.

That gentleness was a foretaste of the manner in which
he treated her in the following days. The scene in the
woods had affected her much more than she liked to
admit, and though there were often times when she
wished him to make love to her in a more passionate
style, she realised his wisdom in not doing so. That she
had not told him the truth yet about how she had deliberately set out to deceive his brother teased her conscience, but she judged that it was still not the right time
to do so. Besides, they had enough to occupy their minds
as their journey took them further south.

Tales of the revolt and its aftermath buzzed in every
town and village they passed through. In Leicester they
were told how the mayor had called the citizens together
after receiving warning that the rebels were returning
from London. They had assembled outside the town and
waited, all armed, to face them. The keeper of the Duke
of Lancaster's wardrobe had also returned to the duke's
castle in the town and taken his possessions to the abbey
for safe keeping. But the abbot, terrified that the rebels
would burn down his abbey for receiving the goods of
such a hated man, had refused to take them in, and they
had been deposited in the yard of the church of Saint
Mary of the Castle. As it was, the rebels had never arrived, only news of their leader's death. This news caused
Guy to wonder whether Lancaster still waited the king's
summons in Scotland. There were many who would press
for his exile; others might insist that he was a traitor
who deserved death.

They arrived in St Albans to find the town alive with
expectancy. The king would soon be there to judge the
situation after the townsmen and villeins had risen

against the monastery. Their leader had gone to London and received one of the king's letters, the outcome of the meeting at Mile End. It had been given to the Abbot Thomas de la Mare, who had bravely faced the rebels still in the town. At first he had refused to believe the commands in it: to deliver certain charters concerning common, pasture and fishing rights into their hands. The rights had been given to the monastic house in former years, but after several involved and lengthy negotiations with the rebel leaders, some of the charters had been handed over, and the most hated burnt in the market square forthwith. Now it was expected that the king would revoke his own letter and give the rights back to the monastery. The townsmen's leader, an educated and good man, who had kinsmen in the monastery, was under arrest.

It only proved, as Guy said to Philippa, that the rebellion had gone beyond a struggle of the bound serfs in the fields to a dissatisfaction with the unequalities between those who had and those who had not. How could they better themselves, if charters took away their means of doing so? The guilds with their master craftsmen had regulated matters so that their journeymen could not afford to belong to them and therefore could not set up in business for themselves, but still had to work for the masters. The church, which should have shared what it had with its flock, instead jealously guarded old rights given in the past when the need was there and the monastery was poor.

'You feel strongly about it, Guy. I remember...' Philippa's voice tailed off.

'You remember?' His keen eyes went quickly to her face. 'I have noticed that you do seem to be remembering more and more when we talk now. I pray that your memory does not return too quickly—and that it is not a harmful awakening.' They were now only a short distance from London. 'Do you remember last time we came to London?' His hand strayed to his horse's neck, and he caressed it fondly.

'I—I remember we had to walk.' Her conscience pricked her painfully again. 'I remember how your horse broke its leg, and how, later, you rescued me from the attentions of a gaol prisoner, and...'

'And how I punished you?' he said moodily, his smile fading.

She nodded, smiling a little, not adding that it was then she had first given thought to what it could be like to be wedded to him instead of his brother. But it seemed that he still blamed himself for what, to her, now seemed fated.

The way had been busy for some time, but now it became even more crowded as they neared London. Memories crowded in as they approached West Smithfield. They passed the ruins of the priory of Saint John of Jerusalem, and the walls of the city could be plainly seen beyond the fields where the peasant army had met Richard. Was it only last month? Saint Bartholomew's was on the right, and the Aldersgate ahead. Her fingers quivered on the reins and her throat tightened, and quickly she averted her gaze from the remains of a corpse hanging on a gallows.

Guy glanced at her, and taking hold of her reins, he urged both horses on and into the city. 'I mean to delay our journey in the city by only an hour or two,' he informed her briefly as they forced their horses on through a network of crowded and smelly streets. Evidence of the last month's riots were everywhere, while rebuilding had already started in some places. Vendors had set up stalls in the spaces where once homes had stood; beggars squatted in small hollows, whining that they had lost all in the recent troubles, and thrust out their hands for alms. Clerics could be seen bustling about in their robes, and members of the different guilds in their livery talked at corners. It was a far cry from the sights of her last visit.

'Where do we go?' she asked, as they approached the river, wondering if he intended visiting his cousin and her husband—a thought that made her nervous.

'I must inform the owner of the ship that will be taking the clip to Calais that it is John whom he will have to deal with. I hope that Master Jack will be able to give us news of the situation, not only in London, but in Kent. He is a man who keeps his ear firmly to the ground.'

'You will not be seeing Master Wantsum?' she asked tentatively.

'Not if I can help it. I want no questions asked that would surely prove awkward.'

She smiled her relief, and relaxed a little.

They found Master Jack perched on a barrel, munching his dinner of bread and salted herrings, looking out over the river. He was a jovial-looking man with a ruddy face, a bald pate and eyes that seemed to gaze on the world with a cheerful cynicism. Only by the raising of bushy grey brows did he express surprise at the sight of them as they dismounted.

'You're earlier than I thought, Master Milburn. No riots in the north, then?' He took a swig from his horn cup. 'Or are they all content with their lot?' He gave Philippa the barest flicker of a stare.

'I doubt that all are! Are any of us, Jack?' Guy wiped a neighbouring barrel with his sleeve and lifted her on it, before resting his back against it. 'How is it with you?' They exchanged pleasantries, and Guy told him of his change of plan before passing on to enquire how matters were in the city and in Kent.

'Settling down now fairly well, from all accounts. The lawyers have come out of hiding, blethering about justice and crying for vengeance, while the other lot went into hiding. Some in the city have been dragged out into the light of day and recognised and quickly hanged.' He scratched his chin. 'One lad came from Essex, claiming to have murdered the Archbishop, and persisted that he had come to accept the reward for his deed. They gave it to him: you'll find his head on the bridge, in company with those of some of the leaders of the commons!'

'What of the priest, John Ball?' asked Philippa, her expression sombre.

'He escaped the city, but rumour has it that he's been taken by the men of Coventry and will be brought before Master Tresilian, who has been passing judgment on most of them. It's reckoned he'll be hanged, drawn and quartered, if the other Chief Justice's punishments are anything to go by.' He took a deep gulp of his ale, peering at her, noting that her face had paled. 'Best you not think on it, mistress. They all knew what fate would be theirs if they failed in their aims—and they would have done the same to the lords and justices if they had won.'

'What of Kent, Jack?' Guy's arm slipped about her shoulders, and she rested her head on it.

'Is that where you be bound?' He eyed them with renewed interest. 'They say that the local justices are dealing with the disputes there. It was told that the peasants were gathering again and that the king had assembled an army to go against them—but he was persuaded to change his mind by the magnates of the county that were with him, and to leave the matter to them. Different from Essex!' A rumble of laughter shook him. 'They were still demanding their liberty, saying the king had promised it not so long ago. Buckingham and Lord Thomas Percy were sent into Essex to crush them.'

'And have they?' asked Guy with great interest.

'They say a great number have been slaughtered, but there's still more who've taken shelter in the woods. I reckon there could be trouble there for some time.' He took a great bite of his bread and fish. 'Some did come forward when the king was there at Havering, bare-headed and bare-footed they were, and begging the king's mercy,' he mumbled.

'And did they receive it?' put in Philippa.

'So they say, but not until they revealed the names of their leaders.'

'So they have achieved little,' muttered Guy, frowning.

'Certainly not what they wished for,' responded Jack. 'All that was promised at Mile End has been revoked, although they say that many are being pardoned for their part in the revolt.'

The three of them fell silent. Gulls wheeled overhead and water lapped the jetty a short distant away. Then Guy stirred and lifted Philippa from the barrel. He gave Jack his hand and wished him well, before turning and going over to the horses.

On London Bridge, Philippa kept her eyes on the road ahead, having no desire to gloat over the fate of those who had sought to turn England upside-down by violent means such a short time ago. For a while she had hated and feared them, but now she felt devoid of such emotions. Love for the man by her side had changed her, just as her sufferings had. In some ways she felt stronger than the girl who had fled from Kent, and yet in others she knew herself more vulnerable. Rose's conversation had made her understand a little of what it was like to be a serf, and it was as the maid had said, an unenviable position.

They were across and out of Southwark as swiftly as possible. How different was this return journey from the one in June! That one had been an ordeal in its way, and yet a time of discovering so much about herself. The nightmares that had plagued her then had barely darkened her dreams since she had heard of Tom's death. Yet she found them recurring now she was in her own county, but Guy was always there to soothe away her fears.

At last they came to more familiar country. Branches heavy with swelling fruit appeared in orchards on either side of the road. Then, beyond apple and pear and cherry trees, there was a bridge, and beyond that a village.

A dog barked as they crossed the bridge, and some children paddling in the stream looked up. One recognised her and sat down suddenly in the water, seemingly oblivious of the scoldings of his playfellows as he stared. Then he was up, and calling to her.

'Mistress Philippa, they thinks you're dead, and they've taken my Pa to Canterbury, and they...' pointing to the other children, 'they say they'll hang him!' His bottom lip wobbled, and he brushed a wet hand across his eyes.

'What is this, Matthew?' Philippa dismounted on the other side of the bridge, years of training reasserting itself. 'Come, boy, tell me!' She held out a hand, and he approached slowly, almost cautiously. The other children watched round-eyed, their feet still in the water. Guy also watched, frowning in thoughtful concentration.

'Ma will tell you. She's still here, but me brother's gone with Pa. Not in gaol, but to make sure he gets some food—and to speak up for him.'

'Who else has gone?' She lowered herself until her eyes were level with the boy's. He shook his head, suddenly dumb, and when she would have persisted, he turned and ran away.

'Best speak to Ma,' said Guy softly at her shoulder. 'Do you know who his father is?'

'It is Adam the smith. He is a freeman, and I met him in London, and it was because of his intervention that I escaped from Tom, Rose's brother.'

He stared at her. 'I remember now. It was when you left the house alone.'

She nodded, her face absorbed. 'Let us go and speak to his mother. I must do something for Adam. I cannot let him be hanged!'

'If that is what you want.' He followed her on foot, leading the horses. It was quiet, and only women were to be seen with their children working in gardens. They lifted their heads and stared unbelievingly at Philippa as she approached the silent smithy and the house attached to it. Rapidly they left their toil, and without a word being spoken, gathered about her.

Philippa chose to ignore their silent presence, and rapped on the door. It was opened quickly. Adam's wife, her long thin face blotchy with tears, gazed at her. 'He said you had come—and I—I didn't believe him!' Her voice was as thin as her face and figure.

'You should have believed him. Adam—he is in gaol, the boy tells me?'

'Ay! He said you weren't dead, but your uncle didn't believe him.'

'My uncle?' cried Philippa in astonishment.

'He came with a group of men to seek you and your father. They were back from London, then, our menfolk. All but three, who had perished in the fire at the Savoy.' She folded her arms across her scrawny breasts. 'Adam told them the truth of the matter, and how it had been Tom who had killed your father. Told them also that he had met you in London, but they didn't believe him. He fought them, but they overpowered him.' She fell silent.

'What of the villagers, Emma? What did they do?' persisted Philippa. 'Are they in gaol also?'

'A couple still hide in the woods, but the rest who ran were hunted down. Peter the cottar was killed, and Gilbert the reeve wounded, but they still carted him off with the rest.'

'What of Walter, my bailiff?' She was suddenly conscious of a great weariness.

'He is in Canterbury, giving evidence against them. If he and your uncle have their way, you'll have no workers left on this manor, Mistress Philippa,' she said with a spurt of sudden fury. 'They ain't bad men! Not really!

They were swayed by all the talk of freedom and having goods like the masters.'

'What of my father, Emma? I know Tom killed him, but the others could have done something to prevent it.'

The woman dropped her eyes, and a low murmur went through the group behind Philippa. 'Most were agin it,' called a voice. 'My man wasn't even there!' shouted another. 'He was seeing to the pig. Gone missing, it had!'

Philippa turned, and her eyes swept the huddle of women with an icy disdain that silenced them. 'I would expect you to say such things to save your menfolk, but justice must be done.' There was an uneasy murmur. 'Yet,' she held up her hand, 'I shall do my best to save their lives.' Without another word, she brushed them aside.

'God bless you, Mistress Philippa!' Emma darted after her, and seized her hand. 'May the saints grant you success in all your endeavours.'

'May they indeed,' replied Philippa in a dry voice. 'But I would pray earnestly, if I were you, that I shall not be too late—and that they will heed a woman's pleadings.' She reached her horse.

'Are you certain about this, Philippa?' asked Guy, helping her into the saddle.

'No.' She forced a smile. 'I know it is late in the day, but I fear I am too late to save Adam, and there are some others I would rather not see hanging from a gallows.'

'You've changed,' he said roughly, vaulting into the saddle.

She made no reply, only digging her heels into the horse's flanks. There was no time to spare to look upon the remains of her old home, or to consider that perhaps justice would best be served in letting those who had acquiesced in her father's death take their punishments. No time for her to rest . . . or to seek out that which she had travelled all the way from the north to rescue. There

was no time at all for such actions, only for the realisation that most of the men who were being tried belonged to her, and that it was her right to have a say in
their punishment.

It was not until they came to Canterbury a little before
sunset that Philippa realised she had no idea where to
find her uncle, and said so to Guy.

'If your villeins are in gaol, the constable will most
likely have his direction.' He had been silent for most
of the journey, as silent as she, and as deep in thought.
'But, love, it is too late now to look for him. You are
tired and will not be at your best. Let us see if we can
find shelter at the pilgrims' inn, although I think it unlikely, and we might have to look elsewhere.'

'I had forgotten that only recently was it the Translation of Saint Thomas,' she groaned, her head drooping.

'I doubt many will have given much thought to it recently. I haven't forgotten what it was like here in June.'

'Of course! I wasn't thinking. But perhaps such a
happening will have drawn more people to pray at his
tomb.'

'And doubtless there must be more men than yours
on trial here, Philippa.' He swung down out of the saddle
as a boy ran forward to take the reins of his horse. 'Is
there any room inside, lad?' he asked, spinning him a
groat. The boy caught it deftly.

'Not much, but if you're friendly, and don't mind
sleeping on the floor head to tail like a barrel of salted
fish—and can pay more than it's worth, you'll get in!'
He grinned, and took Philippa's horse as she
dismounted.

'No doubt he exaggerates,' murmured Guy, taking her
arm as she stumbled.

'I hope so!' she said faintly, trying to smile.

It was as they neared the entrance to the inn that a
man came out. He looked at them, then halted dead in

front of them as if transfixed. 'Niece! Philippa Cobtree! Can it be you?'

'Uncle William!' Her hands went out to him, and he grasped them firmly. 'We have been looking for you.'

'So one of my former neighbours informs me.' He smiled thinly. 'Only this day I thought to see how the men were getting on with clearing away the rubble that is all that remains of my former house.'

'We sought you in London, but could not find you. Now I am here on a different matter.'

'Your serfs?' He looked at Guy interrogatively.

'This is Master Guy Milburn, Uncle William,' she introduced them swiftly.

The two men shook hands. 'I am glad to meet you at last, Master Elston.' said Guy.

'Ah, I remember you, Master Milburn. You have filled out somewhat since then! Your brother—he is well?'

'He has a leg wound that is giving him some trouble. But my being here is a long tale, sir, and we are in haste to have the matter of Mistress Philippa's serfs dealt with.'

'Ah, the serfs! You are fortunate if you wish to give evidence against them, Philippa. The trials of those who caused murder here in Canterbury were dealt with first in the presence of the Earl of Kent, and...'

'I don't wish to give evidence *against* them,' she interrupted him ruthlessly. 'What will happen to the land if there are no men to labour in the fields and orchards? And Adam the smith, who rescued me from the attentions of the man who killed my father, I believe he saved *my* life!'

'You don't wish to...' His mouth gaped open. 'By Saint Thomas himself, I believe your father's murder has turned you mad! As for this man Adam, I have a witness who...'

'If he is Walter, my bailiff, you may tell him his witness could cost him his position on my manor!' she declared hotly. 'He never came to help me after my father's death.'

She took a breath. 'It is time for all to return to normal again. The seasons don't wait, and I need workers in my fields and craftsmen in the village. I need to have a house built. Indeed I need my serfs back on my manor!' She glared at him defiantly. 'If you have any affection for me at all, Uncle William, you will help me instead of working against me.'

'Working against you,' he spluttered. 'I thought I was doing what your father would have wished.'

'My father is dead.' Her throat moved and she had need to pause, before continuing, 'But I am very much alive! I must have a working manor to bring to my husband when I wed.'

'To bring to your...? Ahhh!' He nodded in Guy's direction. 'You are here as your brother's envoy?'

'You might say that,' drawled Guy, raising one dark diabolical eyebrow, and smiling enigmatically.

'Ah, then that's a different matter. I shall do my best. The smith saved your life, you say?'

She nodded. 'And the man who murdered my father was killed in the explosion at the Savoy.'

'You know that for a fact? The smith did mention...'

'Ay! 'Tis true!'

'Ah! Divine justice!'

'You could say that in court,' murmured Guy. 'Tell the justice that God took a hand in this case, and that a lady is in distress and in need of mercy and leniency for her serfs.'

William gave him a look that spoke volumes. 'You do not need to tell me what to say, Master Milburn.' He sniffed. 'Just leave the matter in my hands. Unless you wish to speak for them?'

Philippa and Guy exchanged glances, and he answered for her, noting the weariness in her face. 'It would be better if you could do it. We have travelled far, and your niece has been through much.'

'True, true!' William tut-tutted. 'You are staying here, I presume?'

Guy nodded. 'The town is crowded, it seems.'

'That is true. I would offer you a place to lay your heads, but I am staying with an acquaintance, and have only a share of a bedchamber.'

'We understand, Uncle William,' said Philippa. 'When is the trial to be?'

'Tomorrow, niece. You came just in time. Perhaps one could see the divine hand in that!' He smiled thinly.

'We shall not wait.' She smiled slightly. 'If they are freed, then tell them to come home, where there is a place for them.'

'You think you can trust them to do so?' He frowned.

'Most have wives and children—I think they will come.'

He nodded, bid them a good night and left.

'So we go back to your manor tomorrow, Philippa,' said Guy. 'What then?' His voice was quietly serious.

'I must do what I said. Arrange for a house to be built—talk to the men. The women will not have coped with all the weeding in the fields. Much work needs to be done if there is to be food for all in the winter.' She looked up at him and caught the gleam of his eyes. It was almost dark. 'You understand I have to do this, Guy, before returning to Yorkshire?' She pushed her hair back wearily.

'Oh, I understand. You do intend returning, then?' His hand was on her shoulder.

'I have to. And there is Rose, of course. The situation there has to be dealt with.' She rubbed her cheek against his hand. 'You do understand?'

'I'm not sure.' His face was unreadable now. 'How long will all this take—all that *you* have to do?'

'I—I don't know.' She gave a yawn. 'But it has to be done. Besides, I *want* to do it.'

'Then there is no more to be said.' There was a stiffness in his tone that caused her to frown, but she was too tired to ask what was wrong.

They went inside the inn, and it was as crowded as they had been warned. But just as the boy said, for a few pennies more than the asking price they were able to obtain shelter. That night they slept wedged against each other, but there was nothing lover-like in the act, and Philippa fell asleep almost as soon as her head touched the floor.

The next day they returned to Cobtree manor, and so caught up was Philippa in planning what needed to be done there that she did not notice how silent Guy was.

'Have you thought of where you will sleep?' he asked, when they dismounted outside the smithy.

She nodded. 'I shall have Rose's old home swept out and cleaned and stay there for a short while.' She turned, as Emma emerged at a rush from inside her house.

'Mistress Philippa, what has happened?' She was paler than the day before.

'I don't know yet. My uncle is seeing to the matter. God willing, they will return home. You must prepare— and if you could also clean Rose's house for me?' She turned as Guy spoke her name.

'What is it?' Shading her eyes from the sun, she looked up at him, wondering why he had remounted.

'I just want to say farewell,' he said quietly.

A shock rippled through her. 'Farewell?' she stammered. 'What do you mean? Are you not staying?'

'To do what, Philippa? You have it all arranged. Perhaps this was what you planned all along. You are the lady of the manor, after all.' He grasped the reins firmly in his hand. 'I am my brother's steward, and must be about my business. If you are serious about returning to Yorkshire, I shall return in a few weeks and take you there. Until then, I wish you well in all your endeavours.' He blew her a kiss.

'But, Guy, you don't understand,' she cried, stepping forward as the horse did. 'Wait!'

He shook his head. 'No, I don't. But then what man ever understood a woman?' His knees touched the horse's side firmly, and he was away.

She ran a few paces and then her feet faltered. What was the use? What had come over him? Tears were near, but she fought them back so determinedly that her face ached. A hand touched her shoulder and she turned to face Emma's anxious face.

'Mistress Philippa, did you say Rose's house?'

'Ay, I have to sleep somewhere,' she said huskily.

'But where is Rose? She was seen in London, but since then... What has happened to her?'

'She is well, and in Yorkshire.'

'Where's that? What's she doing there?' Emma stared at her in bewilderment.

'I wish I knew,' murmured Philippa, longing unexpectedly for the company of her former maid. Only to her could she have poured out her sudden fears. Why had Guy left in such a hurry? Where had everything gone wrong? Were circumstances any better for Rose in that northern land? She wished she knew.

CHAPTER THIRTEEN

ROSE TUCKED a curl into the silver net about her hair, frowning at herself, then rubbed her cheeks until they glowed, and smiled at her reflection. She replaced the mirror in the corner of the bedchamber. Straightening her red linen skirts before crossing the room, she looked forward to the excitement of a day at the Knaresborough fair with Hugo.

It seemed an age ago that she had been to such an event with Mistress Philippa. How strange it still felt at times not to have her near, or to answer her call and do all that was required for a lady by her maid. Although she was becoming accustomed to playing her part, there had been some difficulties she had not anticipated. Hugo had asked her to help Mistress Margaret in the smooth running of the household, and the lady had been unexpectedly helpful. Fuddled she might be at times, but if one got her talking of the past and the days when her husband was alive and she had her own house, a lot could be learned from listening. She asked her questions and sooner or later the answer came back out of the old lady's ramblings.

As she entered the hall, she saw that Hugo was conversing with a stranger, so she sat on a settle and waited patiently. The man was dirty and sweat-stained, but he did not appear to be a serf with a grudge, and she wondered just who he was and why he was in the house. The conversation came to an end and the man departed. Hugo turned to face her, and smiling, held out a hand. She rose immediately and went to meet him as he came towards her.

There was still the slightest of limps, but his leg was healing nicely. If only he would be more sensible, it might recover altogether, but he was not a patient man. She had fussed and coaxed, scolded and kissed. And he had argued, and occasionally given in to her with bad grace, and sometimes gracefully, with a charm that had reminded her much of Master Guy, despite the differences between the two brothers.

'You are ready to go?' He leaned down and kissed her rosy mouth.

'Have I not been waiting for you?' she murmured, when at last he drew away from her. 'Who was that man?'

'A messenger.' He took her hand and tucked it in his arm. 'We must make the best of this day, my lass. Tomorrow I shall have to leave you.' His pale grey eyes scanned her oval smooth face. 'Will you miss me?'

'Of course. B—But why...? Where do you go?' Her fingers tightened on his sleeve.

'Lancaster has been summoned by the king to attend him at Reading. Richard believes that all the charges against him are false, yet the duke would face in front of the king the man who acted on the rumours, and upset his duchess.'

'The Earl of Northumberland?' She had not been listening to him without remembering how the earl had figured in his tales about Lancaster. It appeared that Northumberland had wanted to have his revenge on the duke for some time, ever since the duke had spoilt his plans for returning the surprise the Scots had dealt him when he was taken unawares at Penrith on their fair day and goods and several prisoners had been carried off. But it had been the English who broke the truce first, by capturing a Scottish ship and stealing an extremely rich cargo. He had seen to it that the duke and duchess had been subjected to humiliation.

'The duke wishes an apology from the earl, and wants to make a fair showing of his power, just in case there is trouble.'

'Trouble? You mean fighting?' She had turned pale.

'What other can I mean? But do not fret yourself. I am well able to take care of myself. Besides, in front of the king, I doubt it will be so.' He patted her hand. 'Now forget my leaving and let us make the most of the day. You have some money in your purse and there will be fairings to be had.' He pinched her cheek. 'Give me a smile.' She did so, and forced herself to chatter about the fairs she had been to in the south, but all the time she was wondering when she would see him again—and whether Philippa and Master Guy would have returned by then.

The market square in front of Knaresborough Castle was crowded with booths and stalls, not to mention people. The groom who had accompanied them saw to their horses, while they pushed their way through the crowds. The air was pungent, and Rose forged her way to the spice stall, jostling for a place in the front. Her way was made easier because of Hugo's great bulk at her side. Once the spices were purchased, they went to the fabric stall, and she enjoyed herself rummaging for a cloth she had dreamed about, and delighted in a fabric of palest blue with a hint of silver thread.

'Now we can enjoy ourselves,' she said, allowing Hugo to take her purchases from her.

'I thought you were,' he teased, holding her hand. 'Let us go now and watch the play.' He pulled her through the throng.

They stood side by side, watching as the fall of Adam and Eve unfolded, listening and smiling at the sly allusions made by the man playing the Serpent. Then they moved on to watch the antics of a bear on a chain, and tumblers and jugglers. A man cried his wares, and they bought pies topped with a cross to ward off evil spirits.

They fingered furs from far northern lands, and admired jewellery. Hugo purchased her a brooch of silver and amethysts, which he pinned to her breast, brushing off her gratitude. The gift dulled her spirits, just as his refusal to change her silver buttons had done. She hated deceiving him while accepting his gifts, so that when he suggested that they leave the fair and wander down the river, she agreed, not wishing to take more from him while practising such a trick. The sun had disappeared, and clouds were banking in the west as they strolled along the river bank. Their progress was slow because there had been a climb down to the water, and Hugo limped again.

It was as they were returning to the path that led back to the High Street that it happened. Suddenly a figure sprang from a clump of bushes, raising a dagger and would have plunged it into Sir Hugo's chest if Rose had not shouted a warning. Hugo managed to seize his assailant's wrist as the blade came up, and with a twist he forced him to drop his weapon.

'How dare you attack me!' The knight grabbed a handful of his tunic and lifted him into the air, shaking him like a rat, as he peered closely into his face. 'I know you! You're the brother of that fool who is in prison for trying to kill me. Well, you can join him!' he said grimly.

'I don't care what you do with me! Rather gaol, than be your slave!' He swung a fist at Hugo and caught him a blow on the chin. 'You don't even know that Nat's dead! Dead, you hear, because of you!' His voice broke, and he swung another fist at him, but this time his captor moved his head so that the blow glanced harmlessly past his ear.

'You just listen to me, lad,' growled Hugo. 'Your brother and your cousin tried to kill me—except that they chose a night when it was foul and dirty—and another man was with them. Three against one is hardly fair!' He lowered the man to the ground, and Rose was able to see that he was only a lad of perhaps twelve years old. His hair was matted, and his face was filthy.

'What are you going to do with him?' She experienced a pang of sympathy, remembering what it had been like to be hungry and dirty. 'He's only a boy, Hugo.'

'He's old enough to try to murder me!' he responded grimly, shaking the lad again. 'You would think he would have more sense. His family are cottars—that means that they have no land to work except a garden. His mother's a widow. I used to pay the brother wages to work on my land, but he wasn't satisfied. He wanted more money so that he could buy a bit of land. And Guy thinks that freeing them and paying them wages is the answer to all this unrest!'

'I'm sure Master Guy doesn't think it's that simple, Hugo,' answered Rose in a soft voice. 'But if his mother is a widow, and the brother is dead, who is to help her? Are there more brothers or sisters?'

He shook his head. 'Just this imp of hell.' He shook the lad again.

'Hugo, let me have charge of him. I'll have a word with his mother, and perhaps this fright will make him behave himself.'

'Let you have charge of him?' Hugo and the boy were both suddenly still. 'Are you sure you know what you're saying? He's just tried to kill me!'

'Have pity, Hugo. Perhaps if the priest had a word with him?' She placed her hand on his arm. 'You have the power to show mercy, and thus the other serfs might not be so dissatisfied.'

Hugo grunted. 'We'll take the lad home with us. But you won't have the trouble of him. Rob will.'

She smiled in relief. 'I'm perfectly content to leave him to Rob.'

He nodded, and gave the lad a push that sent him flying. 'You have the lady to thank for your life, my lad, and don't you forget it!'

The boy turned and stared at them, his lower lip jutting out mutinously. His eyes went to Rose's, and there was the slightest hint of warmth in them before he stared at his bare feet.

'Move, lad! Let's be getting home.' A blow on his back this time propelled him uphill several feet. In such a manner they made their way to the stables, where the boy was hoisted up behind the groom, and home they went.

It was with a heavy heart and a jumble of confused emotions that Rose waved farewell to Hugo the next morning. She wondered what she would do with herself now that there was only Mistress Margaret and herself in the house, but there was still much she needed to ask the older woman about running a household, and it made her feel wanted.

The days fell into a pattern that was somewhat monotonous, and if it had not been for the thought that when Philippa returned with Master Guy they could change drastically, she would have wished them away. When Hugo would return she was uncertain, but he had said he hoped to be back in September. The memory that he had once mentioned that month for a wedding shone in her mind. The weeks passed, and September came in. The corn was scythed and gathered before, one glorious autumn day, the master of the house returned with his men.

The horses clattered into the yard during the afternoon, setting the dogs barking and the chickens fluttering and squawking. The women, hearing the commotion, came hurrying from the garden. Rose, her face warm with gladness, waited for Hugo to dismount. He did so awkwardly and limped heavily over to her.

'You are pleased to see me, lass?'

'Ay, my lord.' Her voice shook with emotion.

'Then I am pleased.' He placed his great arms about her waist and swung her high before lowering her to meet his kiss.

With Hugo's return, life changed. Gone were the quiet days. He brought noise and vitality into the house, along with his men who flirted with the maids, making them waste time instead of getting on with their tasks. But there was a feeling of festivity in the air. The harvest celebrations were under way, and afterwards... afterwards. She did not want to think of afterwards too deeply.

There was trouble brewing between Northumberland and Lancaster that could be more serious than they had thought. Duke John had demanded satisfaction from Percy at the meeting with the king at Reading. Threats and recriminations had been exchanged until the king had commanded silence.

Lancaster had obeyed, but Percy had lost control of his temper and thrown down his gage of battle. Immediately he had been placed under arrest, but his release had been allowed when the Earls of Warwick and Suffolk had gone surety for his appearance at the forthcoming session of parliament in November. Hugo would have to go with Lancaster when he went to London, and he wanted to make Rose his wife before he went.

She did not know what to do! Wishing to be his wife, and yet fearing his anger when he discovered—or was told—the truth. Part of her longed to be done with deception, to show him the agreement drawn up by Philippa. Part of her thought of fleeing, but she loved too much not to want to stay in the hope that all would be well. If Master Guy came... He had a way with words, and perhaps he would be able to explain everything in a way that was acceptable to Hugo. After all, it was his brother they were cozening! But she knew that it was a forlorn hope. Still she wished he would come.

*   *   *

The journey had been long, and silent for the most part. When Guy had come back to Cobtree, Philippa had thought it would be easy to return once more to their old footing, but it was not. She still did not understand why he had left in the way he had, or his scant perusal of all she had achieved on her manor in his absence. The men had returned, but they had fines to pay of twenty shilling each. For some of them it was a large sum to raise, even for Adam, who made a fair living as the smith. So she had sold her silver buttons and paid the fines, demanding extra labour in exchange. Her new house was already taking form, her wheat had been harvested and the picking of the orchard's crop had been started. Even the beans had been saved, and some eaten. Most important of all, her father's remains had been reburied in hallowed ground, so the reason for her coming south in the midst of such ferment had been achieved. Whether it would prove to be the answer to all her hopes was yet to be seen. She had made no mention of it to Guy, for she found it difficult to broach the subject. He had made no mention of weddings or love. When they had talked, it had been of the places they stayed in—of Calais and the price of wool and sheep. Now they were almost at Hugo's manor, and what would be said and settled between the four of them was still undecided. Perhaps when she saw Rose, all would come clear, but until then she would remain silent.

For the last twenty-four hours a headache had plagued Rose. Now that all the preparations for the harvest feast had been made, she tried to relax by bathing in a tub of warm water. But she found it impossible to rid herself of the tension that had hold of her, and did not linger in the water. As she made her way down to the courtyard, she could hear drums and pipes playing in the meadow where the feast was laid out. When she passed beyond the outer walls, she saw Philippa and Guy, but there was no sign of Hugo, so swiftly she made her way over to them.

'Well, Mistress Cobtree, you *do* look the part,' murmured Guy, taking in every detail of her finery from head to foot, causing her to flush.

'And you, Master Guy, and the mistress,' she muttered. 'You are both well?'

'We are tired, but well enough,' he answered for both of them. 'Where is my brother?'

'Dressing, I think,' answered Rose nervously, her eyes going from one to the other. Something was not right! Had they quarrelled? Lovers often did, so she had heard tell.

'If there is any hot water, Rose, I would like to bathe,' said Philippa softly. 'And to talk to you.'

'Of course! I shall see to it,' she responded swiftly. 'Come with me. Will you be able to attend the feast? It is the harvest gathering.'

'So I presumed,' said her former mistress. 'Does Hugo suspect anything?' She eased her shoulders.

Rose shook her head, and bit her lower lip. 'Not in the least. I was hoping that you would both come, for I do not know what to do. He wishes to wed in a few days!'

'Wed you, Rose?' asked Guy, lifting an eyebrow. 'You have done well for yourself.'

'Master Guy, I—I don't understand. Hasn't Mistress...'

'Later, Rose,' whispered Philippa hastily, seizing her arm. 'The tub first, and then I shall tell you all that has been happening.'

'Ay, tell her, my love, and then perhaps you can explain it all to me.' Guy smiled sweetly before turning on his heel, and brushing past them, he went on into the courtyard.

'What is the matter with him?' hissed Rose as they hurried in his wake. 'Is he furious still for what we have done?'

'He doesn't know. At first, all went reasonably well, and then...' She sniffed, and rubbed a gloved hand across her face. 'Later. I'll tell you later, but now I need a rest and that tub.'

Rose did not press her, but her expression was anxious as they made their way upstairs.

Philippa gave a sigh of contentment and wallowed a little in the cooling water that Rose had vacated.

'You feel better now?' Rose took a towel and waited patiently.

Philippa nodded. 'I shall get out in a minute. Could you find me a gown to wear? I fear they will all be creased and grubby.'

'You can wear the green linen,' said Rose. 'It is here in the chest, and there are some scarves I can make into a chaplet for you. Will you wear your hair braided?'

'No, loose.' She stood up, dripping, and stepped out of the tub. Soon she was dressed, but in the time it took she told Rose some of what had happened in the south and during the journey there. Rose had told her all that had taken place while she had been absent, and of her need to know just what they were going to do.

'I'm not sure what would be best,' Philippa murmured soberly, as her hair was being combed. 'I thought that Master Guy might have given me a lead, but he has not. Even now he might be telling his brother the truth.'

'In that eventuality, we should have a plan,' said Rose in a tense voice.

'I know. But until we know for sure, we had best wait and see.' She stood up, and placed the chaplet of plaited scarves of green and yellow on her head, flicked her hair back over her shoulders, and looked at herself in the mirror once more. 'We are alike, aren't we, Rose?'

Rose nodded impatiently. 'Let us go and discover our fate, Mistress Philippa. I would have it over. Truthfully, I would!'

'So be it!' Philippa squeezed her hand, and they left the room.

The two brothers were standing side by side when they came into the meadow, and the women sought each other's hands, gripping firmly as they walked over to them.

'Welcome to Milburn manor, Mistress Rose,' said Hugo, lifting Philippa's proffered hand and taking it to his lips. 'My brother tells me you are feeling much better.'

'Ay, Sir Hugo, I am.' So Guy had not told him yet! Why not? 'My cousin tells me your wound is much better, although your recent journey has caused you a setback.'

'A trifle, lass. Only a trifle.' He sent Rose a rebuking glance. 'But come, let us not think on such matters this evening. It is a time for celebrating. Let my brother give you something to drink and eat.' He released her hand and instead took Rose's in his grasp. 'The musicians await us, lass, and the table is groaning with food and drink.'

Rose sent Philippa a frantic glance before allowing herself to be pulled away.

'Well,' murmured Guy, 'shall we go and join the festivities?' He offered her his arm, and she took it after a moment's hesitation that caused his mouth to tighten.

'Rose has grown fond of your brother.' Her voice trembled, and there was a flush on her cheeks.

'As he has of her. I even wonder if he might love her?' There was a glint in his eyes as he glanced down at her. 'Are you hungry? I confess I am famished after the journey.'

She was disconcerted by the sudden switch in the subject, but nodded and went with him to the table. For a while they did not speak. They helped themselves from a great haunch of mutton. There was also roasted goose, and bread, cheesecakes, oatcakes and buttered leeks. A serving-maid filled their cups with wine.

Some children had began a game of 'Hoodman blind', and they giggled as they hit one of their number wearing his hood back to front. Some of the adults had formed a carol, and were moving in time to the music.

'Would you like to join in?' Guy's words took Philippa by surprise, but she assented. When he pulled her to her feet, she noticed that his eyes were bright with anticipation.

A thrill raced through her body as his arm went round her waist. He had not touched her in such a way for weeks. They began to dance. The music quickened, and they twisted... glided... leapt in the movements of the carol. She began to forget Hugo frowning at them, Rose's longing expression and all the other faces at the feast. She had eyes only for Guy, and he, it seemed, had eyes only for her. They danced until she was breathless, and laughingly had to beg him to stop.

'Perhaps I have played with you too hard.' There was a note in his voice, and an expression in his eyes, that made her legs turn to water. He led her to a bench where they sat, hand in hand, and she was content. A mood, so glorious, wrapped her round, and she had no wish to end it. The sky darkened; more wine and ale was poured and drunk, more food eaten. A bonfire was lit. It burned merrily, casting shadows, lighting some faces. The young men gathered about the fire, calling to each other, daring each other to leap the flames.

'No, 'tis too high yet,' called Guy. 'You must wait.'

'Scared, brother?' shouted Hugo from along the table.

'No! But I am no fool.' His face flushed with anger.

'Master Guy's right,' said one of the men. 'Let it burn down a bit.'

'Ay! He's in the right of it in many things,' grunted one greybeard.

'I'm the master here!' Hugo thumped the table. 'I say the fire's just right.' He took his arm from Rose's shoulders and stood up, swaying slightly. 'If you won't show them how it's done, Guy, I shall!'

'You're drunk!' said Guy harshly, getting to his feet.

'Drunk, am I?' Hugo limped from behind the table, glaring at his brother. 'You dance so prettily, brother. Let's see instead if you can jump the highest?'

For an instant Guy hesitated, then he began to undo his blue doublet. He flung it at Philippa. 'I'll go first, then,' he rasped, meeting Hugo's stare.

'Guy, please don't,' pleaded Philippa, her fingers clutching the blue cloth.

He gazed down at her, a small, grim smile playing about his mouth. 'Don't fear. I've never failed yet, and if I don't go first, that foolish brother of mine might not clear the flames with his dragging leg.'

'It is you who are the fool!' Her voice quivered.

Guy shook his head. A lock of dark hair curled on his brow, and her heart seemed to expand within her. How vital he was to her happiness! Her chest was suddenly tight with fear.

Guy's shoulders tensed as he began to run, his feet pounding on the grass, and then his figure was a dark cut-out against the flames and the sky. Perspiration ran down Philippa's face as her fingers kneaded his doublet. He leapt, and she screamed. The garment dropped to the ground, and she was running, her heels barely touching the grass as she skirted the fire and ran straight into his arms.

'You should not have done it! You should not have done it!' she screamed, beating her fists against his naked chest. 'You could have been burnt! Burnt!'

'Hush, now,' he replied unsteadily, seizing her wrists. She began to sob, and he pulled her away from the fire. Cheers rang out, heeded by neither of them. Without sparing a glance at his brother, he urged her away from the fire and the festivities.

The sounds of revelry gradually faded as he led her out up the hill, dragging her behind him. Only the whisper of the breeze and the occasional lowing of a cow disturbed the peace.

'Where are you taking me?' Philippa swallowed her tears, gazing about her.

'Somewhere we can talk without being disturbed,' he said brusquely, needing all his breath to get them both to the summit.

At the top, he brought her to a halt. Her skirts whipped her legs, and her hair was blown into a tangled confusion. 'All this time—on the journey—you could have talked to me,' she said.

'On the journey I needed to think; and, besides, I wasn't sure of you.' He held her by both arms, staring into a face still damp with tears.

'What do you mean?' Her voice was breathless with the climb, and the realisation that he had a certain gleam in his eyes.

'On your manor you no longer seemed to need me, to want my opinion—still to want *me*. You talked only of what you were going to do, where you were going to sleep, of having a manor to bring to a husband, when we were in Canterbury. You let your uncle believe it was for Hugo.'

'I didn't think! I thought you knew how I felt about you—and I was concerned for those who had no other voice to speak for them but mine. Besides, I did want to have a manor to bring to my husband. But I was thinking of you.'

'I—I can't take you *and* your manor from Hugo!' His fingers pressed into her arms so hard that it hurt. 'Not when he sent me the deeds of the land my father promised me.'

'He has done that? When?'

'When he sent you to me.' He paused. 'I can always give them back,' he muttered.

'No, you can't do that! I know what it means to you to possess that land. But I don't want Hugo to have Cobtree—not all of it, anyway. It means much to me—and I thought we could put sheep to graze, and become rich.' She gave him a watery smile. 'It was a notion that Rose had.'

'Rose? Is that why she pretended to be you?'

'No!' She realised that *now* was the time for being completely honest. 'It all came about because Hugo mistook her for me.' She was not looking at him. 'And it was apparent that he liked her and she had fallen in love with him at sight. So,' she licked her lips, 'I decided that if he preferred her to me, she might as well pretend to *be* me. Because I'd decided that I had to go home to see if...'

'You are saying that you never forgot your past? That this whole lie you've lived is because...'

'I don't wish to wed your brother. But you are wrong! I did fall, and I couldn't remember—I still don't—aught of that day you left me here! Only Rose said...that you...' She could not go on. He was so still and silent that she was frightened. 'Guy!'

'What did Rose say? That she thought I would go along with the idea? That I'd be willing to deceive my brother? That I'd wed you out of hand?' His voice had risen with each question, and she could feel him shaking.

'No! She thought I was mad—that the fall had scattered my wits!' Her knees were shaking so much now that if he had not held her she would have fallen at his feet.

'Damn you! Could you not have trusted me with the truth? However we present this to my brother, he's going to believe I was part of the whole deception! That I did it deliberately for gain.'

'It was because I believed you wouldn't deliberately deceive him that I didn't tell you the truth,' she retorted, suddenly as angry as he was. Her eyes glinted in the starlight. 'I had to go to Cobtree because I had hopes of a way out of this tangle. But it seems that you care more for your brother than for me! So tell him the truth, and let's have done with it. I shall wed him and forget you, just as Rose told me you asked me to.'

'Philippa, you are enough to drive a man mad!' he snapped, releasing her so abruptly that she toppled forward.

She clutched at him in an attempt to stop herself falling, and he made no effort to stop her. Her fingers slid down his legs until she rested on her hands and knees, and from that position she glared up at him. 'Perhaps I am mad! Your aunt thought I was—and so did Rose,' she said in an uneven voice. Her knees hurt.

'Perhaps we're both mad!' He was suddenly on his knees in front of her, gazing into her face. 'I won't let him have you.' Roughly he eased a strand of hair from her mouth, and her heart began to thud. 'He might beat you. *I* might beat you yet, my sweet deceiver.'

Philippa had to swallow before speaking. 'You wouldn't?'

'Wouldn't I?' He pulled her against him and kissed her with a greed that was savage in its hunger.

He was not at all gentle as he eased her down on the grass and for a short while she fought him, not wanting him to reckon her so easily defeated. But there was a sweetness in touching him; and his kiss despite its arrogant demand was all that she had dreamed of in days without its comfort. He drew her hard against his bare chest, and she quaked with more than the natural fear of the inexperienced as he exposed her nakedness. He pressed kisses on every inch of her skin, and she wondered that she felt no guilt as he did so, she did not shrink from the reality of what he might demand of her this time. How long since she had known that he wanted her—since she had fallen in love with him? The length of his thigh was against hers, and she was apprehensive. Only for a moment did he pull away from her, and he touched her mouth lightly with his before murmuring, 'This time there is no stopping, love. I can't let you go.'

'I love you.' Her voice was barely audible.

Yet Guy heard it, and he stilled, trembling with sudden restraint, his hands clawing her back, the nails digging in as he buried his face against her throat. 'Are you certain this is what you want?' he whispered.

She made no answer, only reaching up to him and putting her arms tightly about him. So she surrendered that which she had kept so long as something almost as sacred as her worship of God. Her flesh was joined to his, and quickened to the throbbing of his passion. Ecstasy came unexpectedly—and just as surprisingly afterwards . . . peace.

At rest they lay together, limbs entwined. His body was her warmth and comfort, and she would have been content to lie with him in such a fashion all night. But such moments do not last for ever, and Guy was the first to move and to speak. 'We have to go down and find out what can be done. But it won't be easy.'

'There is one way by which we can make it easier.' It was no longer I or you, but 'we'.

He stared down at her, leaning up on an elbow. 'You mentioned a way before. Tell me!'

So she told him what she had discovered and worked out at her manor, and his expression lightened a little, but still he was under no illusion that what lay before them would be uncomplicated. He lifted her to her feet, and hand in hand they began the descent.

Hugo was brooding. Guy's sudden departure after leaping the flames had made him drink more heavily. Before his injury it had been he who had always led the way in féats of strength and bravery, but not any more. Physical prowess was important to him, but he had to admit that no longer would he be able to perform swiftly or skilfully many of the acts in which he had excelled.

Rose looked at him, and she pitied him, guessing how he felt, having seen the expression on his face when the cheers had been for Guy. He caught her glance, and his arm dropped heavily about her shoulders. 'Everyone is leaving for their beds. Some for beds in the grass, perhaps? Your cousin and my brother have not yet returned, but I don't think we should wait for them, my sweet.' He hugged her to him, and nibbled her ear.

'No, I don't think we should.' She tried to rise, but he held her tightly, bringing her close, and he kissed her roughly.

'Let's inside, certainly, sweeting,' he whispered unsteadily. Some of the anger and misery had gone from his face.

'Ay, let's to our beds.' Rose smiled, and he pulled her up, and with his arm about her waist they went inside. The hall was occupied with sleeping bodies, and they stepped over them carefully, swaying to and fro; only her arm about his waist kept him from falling.

They came to her bedchamber, and opening the door she meant to slip inside swiftly, but he put a hand to it. 'I'm not . . . tired.'

'Are you not, love?' she teased. 'Your eyes are almost shut.'

'Not tired.' He pushed the door wide and lurched into the room. 'Am I—I master in my own house, or not? Am I so without attraction?' he demanded, snatching at her skirt as she backed away from him. 'Is it because I'm a cripple that you would run away from me?'

'You aren't a cripple,' responded Rose in a trembling voice, attempting to unhook his fingers. 'And you are a very handsome, fine figure of a man.'

'Then let us couple, love?' His voice was suddenly unexpectedly husky. 'I need you badly.' He removed her hand from his and held it; with his other he ripped the front of her gown so swiftly that she gasped with shock.

'No, Hugo! Not like this—not before I tell you...'

'Don't want to listen.' His great arms came round her, and he swung her off her feet. She struggled, and he fell on the bed with her.

For a moment he did no more than lie with her in his arms, gazing at her. 'Love you, little love,' he said, slurring his words. Then he pulled her towards him, fondling her and muttering nonsense. With a strange sense of calmness, Rose let her resistance slip away. She lay still, crying out only when he entered her, and he smothered her face with kisses. Either he would have to wed her, or there could be no other husband for her.

CHAPTER FOURTEEN

ROSE WOKE first the next morning. Hugo's arm held her close, preventing her from falling out of the narrow bed. A tender smile eased her lips as she gazed into his slumbering face, then she sighed. He had to know the truth from her. She shook his shoulder, and he stirred. Again, and he groaned and slowly opened his eyes. 'What . . . is it?'

'Hugo, I have to speak to you.'

He stared at her, almost unbelievingly, and his hand reached out and touched her bare shoulder. 'Were we wed last night?'

'No!' She blushed.

'Then why. . .' He sat up abruptly and winced, putting his hand to his head. 'There's no need to explain—was I drunk?' He rubbed his forehead.

'Ay! But it is not that I wish to talk about.' She reached under the pillow and pulled out the agreement Philippa had signed. 'This will explain it to you.'

He took it from her, and unrolled it slowly.

'Last night you said you loved me, Hugo, and I pray that it is true, for what is written there will make you angry. If you truly love me, then perhaps you will find it in your heart to forgive me. I am not wholly to blame for this deception. You mistook me for her, you see, and I—I loved you on sight. And she was in love with Guy, and she asked this of me in exchange for my freedom.' She halted, breathless with talking so fast, and with nerves.

'Sweet Mother of God, stop blabbering, lass! Talk more slowly, or give me time to read this. And what has my brother to do with it all?' He rubbed a hand through his beard, reading the parchment.

Rose moistened her mouth. 'You will read there that I am Rose Carter, not Philippa Cobtree, your betrothed. I was her maid, and she gave me my freedom in exchange for pretending to be her.'

'What?' The word exploded from him.

'It's true! She and Master Guy, they fell in love on the journey here, you see. But he left her, intending to give her up because she was betrothed to you. And then she fell and lost part of her memory, and she wanted to go to Cobtree, and she was in love with him, and I loved you!'

'Good God, woman, it's true, then, what is written here?' He stared at her, his face dark. 'I have slept with you, and you are not my betrothed?'

'No! But you said you loved me—and I love you! I have not changed because I am not called Philippa Cobtree!'

He sat up abruptly. 'You are not my betrothed, but you were her maid? She gave you your freedom, which means you were a serf? She's in love with my brother... and he knows—he must know—she is my betrothed!' He pushed back the covers and sprang out of bed, only to stumble.

She slid out swiftly and grabbed his arm to help him up. He shook her off violently. 'I don't need your help, damn you!'

'Hugo! What are you going to do?' She backed away from the fury in his face.

'*Sir* Hugo to you, lass, and don't you forget it! If you think that by tricking me into your bed that I will wed you still, you're mistaken.' He shrugged on his doublet.

'I did not trick you! I tried to tell you the truth, but you would not listen! You were hot for me! Called me your little love!' Her eyes sparkled. 'If I had fought you, it would have been rape, because there was no stopping you.'

'It's easy to say that!' He flung the words at her. 'I was drunk, so can't remember any of it. As for all this love you talk about—when has love had anything to do with weddings!' His hands searched for his shoes, and found them. 'Taking me for a fool, all of you! And when I consider how I gave my brother that which he has wanted all these years.' He stood up and limped towards the door. 'He'll rue this day, he will!'

Rose ran after him, seizing his arm, dragging him almost over as she caught him off balance. 'Master Guy did not plan it—but he loves her! Do you know so little about love, Hugo?' she cried desperately.

He steadied himself on the door and thrust her from him. 'Don't talk to me of love. It is for fools!' Opening the door, he slammed it after him.

Guy was frowning as he came out of the stables. A ride was just what he needed to sharpen his wits before facing Hugo. There had been no sign of him when they had returned last night, and he had decided that the confrontation would be better left till the morning. His foot was on the stirrup when a furious voice hailed him.

'You can mount that horse soon enough, brother,' snapped Hugo, seeming to appear from nowhere, and grabbing his shoulder. 'But first, a few words.'

Guy shook his hand off. 'You can have as many words as you like, but keep your voice down. Let us keep our affairs to ourselves.'

'Don't tell me what to do on my own manor!' The lines on Hugo's face drew together fiercely. 'But keeping affairs to yourself is how you like to work, isn't it, brother?' His huge hands curled into fists.

'No,' returned Guy quietly, a sudden tautness about his mouth. 'I intended telling you today of the deception played on you.'

'Today? It must be a day for confession, because *she* has just told me some of it!' His grey eyes snapped furiously.

'She? Rose or Philippa?'

'The one who calls herself Philippa. You must have thought me a fool to play me for a dupe!' A nerve twitched in his cheek.

'I knew naught of it until you sent her to me to take her south.' Guy's hand lay still on the horse's mane. Now was the tricky part! 'I was going to return here, but she was insistent that I took her to her manor. I did so, believing that she had truly lost her memory and it was the proper action to take, thinking to tell you when we returned.'

'You could have told me last night! Instead, you jumped the flames; had them all cheering you. You even left the feast with her and had not returned even when I—I retired.' He almost choked on the words, and his fists were clenching and unclenching.

'I intend making her my wife, Hugo,' said Guy. 'We love each other!'

'Love! She talked of love! What has love to do with taking a wife, brother?' he said sarcastically. 'But you have wed for love before—and taken that which was mine in the doing.'

Guy was quiet. 'Your memory fails you, Hugo, that you forget the circumstances of that episode.'

'Just as my betrothed's was supposed to have failed her?' Hugo trembled with anger. His head ached abominably. 'Well, Mistress Philippa Cobtree is my betrothed, and I will wed her, so you can forget any thoughts you might have in that direction, brother!'

Guy went white. 'Damn it, Hugo, you don't want her. Only her land interests you, and there is a way round that. You obviously care for Rose, and...'

'That trollop!' muttered Hugo. 'If you think I would wed her just to make everything right for you and that scheming wench, you can forget that also!'

Guy took a deep breath. 'I understand how you feel, but will you not listen? We are brothers, and surely that counts for something?'

'Brothers do not seek to deprive each of what is rightfully his!' He curled his hands on his hips.

'Don't they?' flashed Guy, his blue eyes glinting. 'It has taken years for me to obtain that which is rightfully mine—and I had to work for it.'

They stared at each other, and the past was today. Hugo could suddenly see the youthful eager face of his brother prepared to shoulder the blame for his own indiscretion—and he had allowed his father to die, still believing that it had been Guy's. He could not bear the memory, and something snapped inside him.

'Get out,' he cried, losing control. 'Keep the deeds of what you claim is rightfully yours, but do not come back here until I send for you.' He lashed out, and caught Guy a blow on the cheek.

He staggered, but remained upright, and putting a rein on his temper, tried to reason with his brother. 'Hugo, if you would only listen to me!'

'No more! I don't want to hear any more. Get off my manor, and stay off!' He let out a yell, and several men came running. 'See my brother off my land, and don't let him back until I give the order.'

Guy was seized, but he elbowed one man in the stomach and stamped on the other's foot. A couple more guards made a grab at him, but he pulled his dagger and turned on them. 'Don't attempt it!' His face was tight with anger. 'I'm going, but this is not the end of it, Hugo.' The men stood back as he mounted. 'You always were a stubborn swine, brother, but this time you've gone too far.' Digging in his heels, he urged his horse towards the gatehouse and was gone.

Philippa stared up, and realised by the splash of light on the ceiling that the morning was almost spent. Had Guy already explained to Hugo the whole confusion? And, more important, had he listened and forgiven them? She pushed back the covers and swiftly dressed. She had spent the night with Guy in the chamber he had once shared with his brother. She met Rose when she rounded a bend in the stairs, and almost sent her flying. Her hand clutched at her sleeve. 'Are you all right? I'm in such haste. Have you seen Guy and Hugo?'

'He knows,' said Rose. 'I told him this morning.'

Philippa suddenly noticed the tear-stains on her face. 'Is he very angry?'

'Angry?' She gave a laugh. 'He's furious! God help Master Guy, that's all I can say!'

'Guy was going to tell him the truth this morning—explain everything.'

'It takes some explaining! It always did, and I don't know how you ever thought we could succeed—that our dreams could come true!' Rose sank on to the stone steps and pillowed her head on her arms. 'He said I was to call him Sir Hugo. That! After telling me he loved me and coupling with me.'

Philippa stood as still as stone. 'You, too, Rose?'

She peered at her over her arm. 'You and Master Guy? Oh, sweet Virgin Mother! These brothers!' Her laugh this time bore a note of hysteria.

'There must be something we can do,' muttered Philippa, and dragging her skirts tightly about her, forced her way past Rose, and down the steps.

She ran into the hall, and immediately her glance fell on Hugo sitting at the table, his hand about a cup. He lifted his head and stared at her, and for a moment neither of them spoke. She had already decided that

attack was the best weapon against him, intending to
fight for her happiness, but she had thought to have her
love by her side.

'Where is Guy?' She halted on the side of the table
opposite him.

'He has gone, and you won't be seeing him for some
time.' Hugo took a swig of ale.

'I don't believe you!' Her fingers clutched at the table
to steady herself.

'I have ordered him off my land.' He scowled at her.

'Why? Didn't you even listen to him? He was not to
blame—the fault is all mine. It was my plan.'

'That's what *she* said,' he growled. 'She is a cheat and
a deceiver, just like you.' He took another drink.

'Rose acted under my orders, although she is a freewoman and can do as she chooses. She can leave this
house if she wishes, just as I can,' she said determinedly.

'Can you?' Hugo pushed back the bench and stood
up. 'You forget that you are in my house—and forget
yet again that you are my betrothed.'

'There is no proof that we ever were betrothed,' she
said coolly. 'The agreement was destroyed when the
house burned down.'

He blinked, and took another drink, taken aback. He
had expected her to come to him pleading for forgiveness, and to ask him to release her from their betrothal, not this! 'No matter,' he grunted. 'I'll wed you
without it.'

'No!' cried Philippa, startled. 'I will not wed you. I
love Guy, and he wishes to be a husband to me.'

A spurt of jealousy shot through him. 'Guy the silver-
tongued! I wager he spoke soft words to you, and you
believed all he said! Can't you see that he is after your
land? He is greedy for it—to feed those sheep of his.'

'That's not true! He could have wed me without even
trying to explain all to you. We could have found a priest

to perform the ceremony. But he is an honourable man and would not do so behind your back.'

'You would say that! He's bewitched you! Is it because I am a cripple that you do not want me for a husband? Is that it?' Suddenly he felt pain in his head and heart.

'No!' She sat on the bench, her legs trembling. 'I loved him before I ever set eyes on you again. Why is it that you are so insistent on wanting me now? In the last nine years you did not bother to claim me, and I know why. It is because you loved another.'

'He told you that!' He went scarlet, and then white, and then scarlet again.

'No, your cousin told me. Surely, this time, you can behave honourably? You have lain with Rose—and you should wed her!'

'How dare you! You talk of honour, and you have lied and tricked—and so has she! She tricked me into her bed.'

'You are so weak?' she said scornfully. 'Why do you not admit that you prefer her to me!'

'She is a serf—and she lay with me to try to persuade me to wed her when the truth came out. She thought to wrap me round her little finger with her coaxing ways,' he sneered.

'Rose is not like that! She is good and kind, hard working and generous natured. And brave—she saved my life. You would be much better off if you wed her!'

'You think to persuade me so that you and my brother can have your way—can have it all! Well, I will not be swayed by your words—or his—or hers. I can have you both. I shall wed you—and she will be my whore.' He scrubbed at his beard with an unsteady hand. 'You may go and tell her so. Now get out of my sight, woman!' He hunched his shoulders and turned his face from her.

Philippa felt a sense of overwhelming hopelessness, and for the moment, beaten. She got up and left him without another word.

'I will not be his whore,' declared Rose, her face hard, having listened to all that Philippa had told her. 'I am a freewoman, and he shall not treat me like a serf! I shall find a way of leaving this place. I still have your silver buttons, and I can sell them. He would not let me exchange them for money before.' For an instant her expression was tragic, and her lips quivered.

'We shall both leave this place—but how? He is bound to have us watched. I would not have thought it of him, for he used to treat you so kindly.' Philippa sank on the bed. 'We need time—time to think and for him to calm down. He might regret all he has done and said, once he becomes accustomed to thinking of you differently. If only he does not plan to wed me speedily!' She looped her hands in her lap, and her brow corrugated in thought. 'It—It would not be very wise of him to do so. The servants, and those who have seen much of you, will know the difference between you and me.'

'That is true,' murmured Rose, sitting beside her. 'If the wedding could only be delayed! He had considered in two days' time?' Again her face quivered.

'Could we get word to Guy?' Philippa patted her hand.

'What can he do? Hugo has more men. Although the serfs might still be somewhat rebellious even though they now know why those men were put in prison, they are not going to rise up against him. And there are the guards.'

'I must speak to Hugo again. At least to persuade him that it would be unwise to make me his wife yet.' Philippa sighed and got up. 'Tomorrow... It can wait till tomorrow. Maybe by then he will have calmed down a little. In the meantime, we shall stay close to each other just in case he has any plans for forcing himself upon you.'

Rose nodded. It seemed a year since last night when he had said that he loved her and they had held each other. But she must forget about that. There seemed little hope that he would change his mind and ever take her for his wife.

The next morning, Philippa determined to seek Hugo out. He had not been in the hall when they broke their fast, or at morning prayers. She found him at last in the stables. He looked up as she entered, and grunted, before turning to his horse again.

'I wish to speak to you.' She put her hands behind her back and clasped her restless fingers tightly. 'Alone!'

'I have nothing else to say to you.' He did not look at her. 'Help me up, man!' Rob hurried forward and complied with his order.

'But I have something to say to you. I shall say it in front of Rob, if you wish. It is about your wedding . . . I think it should be put off. We still grieve, you see. And she is especially unhappy.'

'Rob, leave us,' he growled, staring down at her. 'So she is unhappy. I'm . . .' He paused, watching Rob leave the building. 'I'm pleased to hear it. I'm not very happy myself,' he added sarcastically.

Philippa took a breath. 'I comprehend your anger with me—with all of us. Although it is my sin that has caused the upset. But have you given thought to how it will appear if you wed me after having spent so much time in Rose's company?'

'I have. And I'll just have to bear them thinking me a fool to have been taken in. At least they won't say anything to my face.'

'B—But would it not be better if you put off the wedding and instead allowed Rose and me to return to Kent for a short while? People have short memories—

and there is a likeness between us. They might not realise the difference if only one returned. Then there
would be no need for anyone to consider you a fool.'

He frowned. 'I don't trust you, and I'm not a fool.
You are playing for time. Yet there is something in what
you say.' He stroked the horse's neck absent-mindedly. 'I
agree, but I cannot have my betrothed and her maid
roaming the country without an escort. In October I go
to London, and I shall take you both south with me. In
the meantime, you will keep to your room as much as is
feasible—only coming down for meals. If it is necessary,
I can rid myself of all those who ever set eyes on you.'
He gave a twisted smile, and bid her good day.

She went, having gained more than she had hoped for.
All that was needed now was to get a message to Guy.
Not for a moment did she really believe what Hugo had
said about his wanting her in order to gain her land. Nor
did she think it possible that he would be able to arrive
like a knight in a tale and snatch her from this house.
Real life was not like that at all. But perhaps there was
a way of getting in touch with him. She would ask Rose
if it were possible, for she knew much more about the
activities and the people on Hugo's manor than she did.

'There is a way.' Rose set a stitch in her tapestry. 'A
serf for whom I put in a word with Hugo. His name is
Robin, and his mother is a widow. As cottars, they have
little in the way of this world's goods. He would perhaps
take a message for us if he knows the way to Master
Guy's manor. He works in the stables now—he can
perhaps enquire from Rob how to get there.'

'He would have to be discreet,' murmured Philippa,
her hands clasped on her psalter.

'I shall give him one of the silver buttons—that will
ensure it.'

Philippa nodded, her eyes on the maid's sad face. 'Has
he tried to—Hugo, I mean—tried to force his attentions
upon you?'

'So far, no.' She lowered her eyes to her work. 'You saw him at the supper table last night. He would not even look at me.'

'I consider that a good sign,' said Philippa softly. 'Remember how I would not look at Master Guy when we were in Kingston. I was frightened that he might see how much I cared. Nor did I see you looking at Hugo.'

'No.' Her hands stilled on the fabric. 'I do care—but I knew that it could come to this, and shall just have to bear it. Now please may we talk of something else?'

So the subject of Hugo and what might have been for Rose was not broached again.

The days passed slowly, unbearably slowly. Only the realisation that Guy knew that they would be going to London comforted Philippa. Often she took out the note that Robin had brought her, reading the words of love and his restated belief that they would be together again in London.

It was different for Rose. She grew pale, and there were great dark circles beneath her eyes. She dreaded not seeing Hugo again once she had returned south. Yet she had set her mind on a future, considering ways of earning some money, if it was possible. Maybe Philippa would allow her to keep a couple of sheep on her manor. She still had the silver buttons. Part of her wanted to have the parting over, while the other ached for the days when she and Hugo had shared so much together.

Then one cold frosty day late in October, Hugo announced that they would be leaving for the south the next morning. At Leicester he was to join the Duke of Lancaster's forces, and they would follow on with an escort of two of the grooms. One of them was to be Robin, the other Rob, which suited the two women's purposes perfectly. He would meet them again in London and escort them to Cobtree manor. In a frenzy of activity the two women made ready for the journey.

It was to prove uneventful, but to do something instead of marking time waiting, raised their spirits. Philippa was uncertain as to how Guy would arrange it so that they could be together, and often she found herself looking behind her, hoping to see him. One night only did they spend in Leicester, and on the following morning all the duke's men, with Hugo among them, rode out of the castle. Philippa, estimating their number, began to realise that the situation between Lancaster and Northumberland was perhaps more serious than she deemed. But it was not until they neared London that she discovered just how tense the situation was between them.

Lancaster and his men were to stay outside the city, quartered at Fulham. The earl had enrolled himself as a citizen of London, and installed troops of his Borderers in the city. Barricades had been thrown up and guards set at the gates to prevent the duke and his men from entering.

Dismay was the feeling uppermost in Philippa's heart, for she was convinced that it was in the city that Guy would try to meet them.

'They might let us in—two women and their grooms,' ventured Rose, her eyelids drooping. They sat in front of a log fire, trying to thaw out frozen toes. She dreamed of how it would have been much more pleasant to have shared a bed with Hugo that freezing night. Tears squeezed their way under her lids—for there was much she had to cry about.

'We could try in the morning. Hugo is bound to be out of the way at Westminster when parliament meets. It should prove a stormy session if Lancaster and Northumberland attend with all their men.' She wriggled her toes, gazing into the heart of the fire. 'He should have his hands full, and I cannot see Robin and Rob giving us much trouble if we do meet Guy. Perhaps he will be at the bridge—or maybe we shall find him at

Beatrice's.' She yawned. 'I'm for bed.' She was impatient for the night to be over.

Everything went as they had hoped, and they had no difficulty getting into London, but the streets were crowded and it was difficult forcing their way through. Philippa was starting to feel quite desperate, when a hand snatched at her reins and her horse was forced to a standstill.

Her fingers trembled as the rider's hand covered hers, holding it firmly. She had waited, and longed, and expected, and was not disappointed as she foundered in the depths of Guy's blue eyes.

'I think you are expecting me?' There was a singing in every nuance of his voice.

'Ay,' she whispered, 'but I did not know the hour. I only prayed it would be this day.' Her fingers laced through his, and he lifted their joined hands and rubbed hers against his cheek.

'Will you come with me?' He kissed her gloved hand.

'To the ends of the earth,' she said, flushing slightly.

He chuckled. 'I don't ask that of you.' He turned to Rob and Robin. 'I shall take care of the ladies now.'

Robin nodded, but the older man looked uneasy. 'Don't know about that, Master Guy. Your brother said...'

'You may tell my brother that he will find the three of us at Cobtree manor. We shall await him there. You aren't going to argue with me, Rob, are you?'

'Don't like to.' He rubbed his unshaven chin. 'He's been unhappy these last weeks, considering how happy he was before that. I don't understand what's going on, but if by your telling me that he's to meet you at this manor that means everything's going to be resolved between you, then I'll do it.'

'I pray so, Rob.' Guy clapped him on the shoulder. 'God go with you.' He gave Rob's horse a smack on the rump, and the grooms departed.

'You mean for Hugo to come after us?' said Philippa, leaning towards him.

'I do. Has he been unhappy?'

'We all have. Only the hope of seeing you again has kept me from falling apart.' She smiled into his eyes. 'Do you think he will come?'

'I pray so.' He turned to Rose. 'Would you welcome him if he came?'

'I might. But I doubt he wants my welcome, or me.' Her face was pinched and sallow-looking.

'You never know, Rose. I think he might have need of you. But he's stubborn, and will need reassuring.' He patted her arm. 'Let us be on our way. You look cold, and it is a long journey ahead.'

He drew his horse alongside Philippa and together they turned their faces towards London Bridge and Cobtree manor.

It was a tiring journey, yet there was a lightness in Philippa's heart as they travelled, although her nose was cold and the tips of her fingers often seemed to have frozen altogether. At last, after three days of travelling, they came to familiar country. Orchards, their branches stark, gnarled and black against the grey sky, appeared beautiful to her. Smoke rose lazily from a roof, and she realised after several astonished moments that it was her new house.

'They have finished it! I never thought it would be ready in time for Christmas! I thought that once I left, they might stop working.'

'I came here several weeks ago after receiving your message, and made sure it would be finished.'

'Oh, Guy!' Tears sparkled in her eyes, and she flung her arms about him, pressing her cold lips against his. He returned her kiss, and then insisted that they went on, adding that there would be a fire to welcome them and, with luck, a meal fit for a wedding feast. She made no answer to that, only wondered with a rising excitement.

The house inside was somewhat sparse. The walls were bare but the windows were glazed, shutting out the cold wind. A fire burned brightly on the hearth to welcome them. There was a single settle, two benches and a trestle. The two women settled themselves in front of the fire, with no thought of who had lit it, or whence came the smell of cooking chicken. Rose's eyes drooped, and Philippa rested her head against the back of the settle.

'My lady, we have business to attend to,' said Guy, picking up Philippa's gloves and handing them to her.

'We have?'

'Ay! I've had the banns read,' he said quietly. 'The vicar knows only that you are betrothed to a man called Milburn. He is new since you were last here, and has some revolutionary ideas.'

Instantly she was wide awake. 'The banns? Then let us go! Is he a Lollard? The last priest never returned after the revolt in June, and I remember his preaching once what some would call heresies.' She twinkled up at him. 'He believed that one could pray direct to God without the intervention of priests or saints.'

'So do I, but priests do have their uses.' He took her hand and pulled her to her feet. 'Are you willing to marry this heretic?'

'Willingly—but what of the betrothal agreement? I told Hugo that it was destroyed. I really would like it to be so before we wed.'

'Then let us do it now, if that is what you wish.' He pulled her hand through his arm. 'You do remember where you put it?'

'Of course! I'll just tell Rose where we are going.'

Rose hardly heeded her words, for, weary to the bone, she was nodding in front of the blaze.

They walked hand in hand until they came to the forest. Then it was a matter of scrambling over tangled woody brambles and browning undergrowth, and stepping across moist yellow carpets of leaves. Philippa led Guy straight to the shattered tree, hesitating before plunging her hand into the hole. She turned over bits of bark and dead leaves, and the occasional stiffened insect, until she dragged it out. Some woodland creature had nibbled at the leather, and it was damp and coming apart at the seams. She handed it to Guy.

'You open it, and confirm what I told you about Rose.'

Impatiently Guy dragged off his gloves with his teeth, and with cold fingers undid the pouch. Together they read the Latin on the betrothal agreement. Then they unrolled the lists of names and dues.

It took some time to go through them, but she knew what they looked for. Some of the names went back over generations, sons and daughters, mothers and fathers. 'Here! This is it!' Her finger stabbed at a name. 'She was also called Rose. Daughter of a Thomas and mother of a Thomas, but note, there is no father named. Of course this is not proof and wouldn't perhaps stand in a court of law, but I think it proof that at some time one of my forebears lay with one of Rose's.'

'It can be the only answer to that similarity between you.' Guy rolled up the scroll and placed it inside his doublet. 'Shall we go to church now?' His voice was carefully casual.

'Do you need to ask?' They kissed.

'Do we tell Rose first?' asked Philippa.

'Ay!' He rubbed noses with her slowly. 'But somehow I doubt that she will be surprised.'

Rose showed little emotion when they told her. 'It is only what I have thought myself on occasions, but what use could my telling Hugo have made?' She shrugged slender shoulders.

'It could make a great difference, Rose. But brighten yourself up, and come to church with us.'

So they went to church, and the villeins led by Adam filled it for the Mass afterwards, and all wished their mistress and her master every happiness.

It was a quiet company who sat down to the food set before them. Guy declared that it was one of his favourite meals. There was roast chicken in Vyaund de Ciprys se Ryalle sauce, which made Philippa's eyes widen, since she had not yet set foot in the new kitchen.

'The cook was sent down from London. He was trained by Beatrice.'

'Beatrice!' She gazed at Guy. 'Did you explain to her?'

He nodded. 'She did not seem surprised that we were getting wed. Sent her best wishes, so she did—and they both sent us a gift. It is upstairs, and you shall see it later.' His fingers tightened about hers, and there was a look in his eyes that caused her pulses to quicken, before she turned to the cheese tarts spiced with ginger, and her wine.

The sound of hooves came unexpectedly as they were eating nuts. At the shout of a voice raised in anger, they rose as one and faced the door. It was thrust open with a violence that caused Guy's hand to go to his dagger. Hugo stood in the doorway, his cloak billowing. He was alone. Guy got up and went to meet his brother.

'Welcome, Hugo, to our wedding feast. There is wine and food enough, if you come in peace. Although I did not expect you quite so soon.'

'Lancaster and Northumberland settled their differences sooner than we thought.' Hugo was breathing heavily as he dragged off his gauntlets. 'You did expect me, then?'

'Ay.' Guy stood, his feet slightly apart, tense, waiting for his brother to make the next move.

Philippa rose and put her hand through his arm. 'I'm sorry, Hugo, for deceiving you and making you unhappy.'

His heavy brows drew together in a fierce frown. 'He and you are alike. Tricky devils, the pair of you! I believe you'd get rid of any obstacle in your way to gain your ends.'

'No, Hugo, we simply wanted each other enough to go to such ends,' said Philippa. 'I duped Guy as much as you.'

He nodded. 'I believe you. May I have a drink?' His eyes went to Rose sitting at the table, dressed in a green woollen surcote. He limped towards her, as she rose and handed him her own goblet. 'I've ridden hard to find you.' His fingers clung to hers.

'Why?' There was strain in her face. 'I will not be your whore.'

His throat moved. 'Because you are all that she said you were. Kind, brave, generous! Did you mean it when you said that you—you loved me on sight? That you don't care that I am a cripple?'

'I meant it.' She held her head high.

'Then perhaps you would do me the favour of becoming my wife,' he said, his voice rough. 'I see no other way out of this tangle without appearing a fool.'

'You are not a fool! But you could have worded your proposal better.' Tears shone in her eyes.

'I'm no good with words,' he muttered. 'Not like Guy.'

'I would not say that.' A smile broke on her face.

'You would not? I've missed you.'

'I'm glad,' she said simply.

'If you are to wed Rose, Hugo, then I think you should know that she will bring you a third of this manor—on condition that you agree to put sheep on the land. There is a shortage of labour here, and it will be the only way to make the most of such a gift,' said Guy, grinning.

Hugo stared at him, and slowly a smile creased his face. 'Trust you to get your own way! But why do you give me this third?'

'Because Rose is kin to me,' interpolated Philippa. 'A long time ago, we think that my ancestor and one of hers came together.'

Rose turned, and her tears spilled over. 'You told me of that, but not that you would give me part of Cobtree.'

'We wanted you to have something to bring a husband, and that he is to be my brother makes me very happy, Rose,' said Guy. His hand went out to Hugo. 'Shall we put the past behind us?'

Slowly Hugo took the hand offered, squeezing it tightly, and lifted the goblet. 'To the future.'

'A future that will, I hope, be blessed with a son,' whispered Rose, staring into his face. 'I do not only bring you land, but I carry your child: an heir to that land.'

'Lass,' he murmured, coming round the table, 'that is the best gift of all!' He put down the goblet and embraced her for an extremely long time.

Later that night, Philippa lay beneath Guy in the gift from Beatrice and James. It was a large bed with an embroidered coverlet, and a canopy and curtains. Never in her darkest dreams... Never in the best of her dreams had she dared to imagine that in such a bed...

Guy kissed her, and her happiness soared. She had wondered when it actually came to being a wife whether it would be different—the joining—the entwining—the whispering kiss of flesh upon flesh. Husband and wife! Lovers!

'Guy!' she murmured, when their lips parted.

'Hmmm!'

'Now that we are wed, tell me—do you not agree that all I did was right?'

'Right?' His arms tightened about her. 'Only a woman would reason that out. You lied and deceived me just to get me where you wanted.'

'Sadly, that is true.' She nuzzled his ear. 'But was I not right?'

'You were mad—quite mad, my precious lady deceiver. But now is not the time to talk,' he muttered, his passion rising as she wriggled beneath him.

'But all is well?' She gave a whisper of pleasure as they became one flesh.

'It is perfect.' He closed her mouth with a kiss, and they were in complete accord.

A WORLD WHERE PASSION AND DESIRE ARE FUSED

CRYSTAL FLAME — *Jayne Ann Krentz* _____ £2.95
He was fire — she was ice — together their passion was a crystal flame. An exceptional story entwining romance with the excitement of fantasy.

PINECONES AND ORCHIDS — *Suzanne Ellison* _____ £2.50
Tension and emotion lie just below the surface in this outstanding novel of love and loyalty.

BY ANY OTHER NAME — *Jeanne Triner* _____ £2.50
Money, charm, sophistication, Whitney had it all, so why return to her past? The mystery that surrounds her is revealed in this moving romance.

These three new titles will be out in bookshops from October 1988.

W☀RLDWIDE

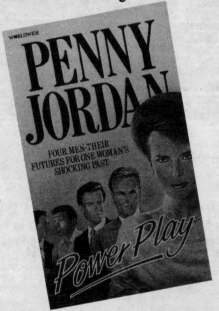